Always a Cold Deck

A Harry Reese Mystery

The Harry Reese Mysteries

Always a Cold Deck

Humbug on the Hudson (short story)

Crossings

Kalorama Shakedown

Emmie Reese Mystery Short Stories

The Birth of M.E. Meegs

Hidden Booty

Psi no more...

For a glossary of period terms, biographies of the characters, and a complete chronology, please visit:

streetcarmysteries.com

Always a Cold Deck

Robert Bruce Stewart

Street Car Mysteries

Florence, Mass.

Second Print Edition, January 2014

Includes the short story *Humbug on the Hudson*

ISBN 978-1-938710-10-0

Street Car Mysteries

streetcarmysteries.com

To Susie

For a crib sheet with maps, characters and a short glossary, please visit:

streetcarmysteries.com/always

1

One thing very often leads to another. But until my little adventure that summer of 1900, my life had never been ruled by the cliché so thoroughly. I left Brooklyn as an underemployed insurance investigator in desperate need of ready cash and returned ten days later in much the same condition—though not without some additional baggage. In between, events unfolded with a determined unpredictability. And while the various forms of fraud held no novelty for me, the three murders did. Nevertheless, they had little to do with the unsettled feeling that would be with me ever afterward.

I was bound for Buffalo on the one o'clock limited out of Grand Central. I had a contract with a group of New York insurance companies to investigate a fire that had destroyed a grain elevator the week before. There was nothing surprising about a fire destroying a grain elevator. But the Eastern Elevator Company had enjoyed a colorful history. There had been accusations of shortchanging by grain shippers, a securities manipulation scandal had brought down a member of the New York Stock Exchange, one former officer was on the run from the law, the corporate secretary had disappeared just a month earlier, and to top it off, the firm had recently defaulted on the mortgage and had had the elevator sold out from under it.

The structure was insured for more than $200,000, and each of the New York companies had taken on a portion of the risk through reinsurance policies. The new owner of the elevator had inherited the insurance coverage, but if the reinsurers could prove it was issued based on a fraudulent application, they stood a good chance of not having to pay some part of the claim, maybe just five or ten percent, maybe a lot more. To completely nullify the policy would require an act of extreme fraud, or arson. But even five percent of $200,000 is $10,000.

When there's enough money at stake, the insurers hire outside lawyers and investigators, like myself. I had started with a firm just out of college, but after a few years on the payroll I had been good enough, or at least lucky enough, to set up on my own.

Unfortunately, my luck had run out sometime that May. I had worked steadily for two years. But then, drought. I asked to go back on the payroll with my old employer. He was considering it when this job came up. I believe there were two reasons I was offered it. First, just about everyone else was working on claims arising from the huge fire at the Hoboken docks which had occurred that same July. Second, the vagueness of the situation made a profitable outcome less than likely. Not wanting to put their own money at risk, the insurers offered me ten percent of any sum I saved them, and a per diem of just four dollars a day, to include expenses. I wangled a four-day advance, neglected to drop off August's rent, and arrived at Grand Central with something just under forty-eight dollars in my pocket. As soon as I bought my ticket I was down nine dollars.

After my meager dinner of sandwiches I'd brought from home, I entered a game of quarter-ante poker with three salesmen from New York. These fellows had been passing flasks around all afternoon and I was hoping to augment my funds by exploiting their compromised condition. One of them could barely keep his eyes open and I took that as auspicious. But working against me was the fact these men were drummers, and while there is surely something positive to be said about men who are willing and able to peddle anything from carnival acts to fine jewelry, it has to be admitted they tend to take a broad view of the norms of society. That's not to say they are common cheats. They aren't. More often than not, they're damn good at it. A first-rate drummer can get the better of you and then make you feel guilty for having noticed.

I had decided on a stratagem of deliberate stagnation. I would bore my opponents into submission. Never has a game of poker moved as slowly as this one did. If it was my deal, I would shuffle, then reshuffle, then shuffle a little more. When it was my bet, I'd stare at the cards, set them down, reach for a coin, stop, pick up my cards again, maybe scratch my head, etc. By the time the deal had gone around once, the lingerie man was out cold. He gave us a loud snort about every thirty seconds, just to let us know he was still breathing. A half hour later, the hat man went down. He took on the melody with a kind of half-snore, half-grunt. By now I was up two dollars and two bits, but the leather goods man seemed to get his second wind and I was soon barely even. I redoubled my lethargy and finally, through tiresome effort, the field was mine. The leather goods man added an almost soprano wheeze to the chorus. I withdrew four dollars from the pot—enough to appreciably strengthen my capital account, but, I hoped, not so much as to be missed. Then I moved to the other end of the car. The racket by then was pronounced.

It was close to midnight when we reached Buffalo's Exchange Street Station. I took my bag across the street

3

to McLeod's Hotel and found a note waiting for me at the desk. It was from Ed Ketchum, a crack fire investigator I'd been told to check in with. He informed me that the out-of-town insurance men were keeping court in the Broezel's taproom. The Broezel was the hotel of choice for commercial travelers. It was close to the station, but not so close the trains would keep you awake all night. Unfortunately, it was also two dollars more per night than McLeod's—just fifty cents, on the European plan.

"Hey, Harry! You're late!" a fellow yelled from the bar. Half a dozen New York men were there and I exchanged small talk with each of them. Whenever there's a big fire, train wreck, or natural disaster, you'll find the fraternity of adjusters and claims investigators holed up in some saloon they've designated as a temporary clubhouse. I spotted Ed Ketchum sitting alone at a table, engrossed in his paperwork. He beckoned me over.

"I think they're stuck paying here, Harry. I don't know why they called you in. It looks like a classic case of spontaneous combustion." Ed was now glancing at his notes. "The Eastern elevator was a wooden structure with metal cladding and had a capacity of 1.5 million bushels in 211 separate bins. The grain had been held for up to nine weeks in some of the bins. There had been a period of sustained rain and moist air. And, as is typical of this time of year, temperatures were rising. By the 24th of July all the ingredients were in place."

This is why Ed was sitting alone. He'd much rather spend time with a good treatise on spontaneous combustion than with a crowd of boisterous dipsomaniacs.

"So no chance it was arson?" I asked.

"There's certainly no evidence of it. No, I'm sure it was caused by natural conditions. There are another

4

dozen elevators out along the waterfront and I wouldn't be surprised if another explodes before summer's out."

"The powers that be seem to be hoping that there was some misrepresentation by the Elevator Company in the policy," I said. "But they didn't offer any clues as to just what they had in mind."

"Well, I did find something that struck me as odd—an elaborate brick storeroom, but no one seems to know what it stored. It's not on the builder's plans. And there's no addendum to the original policy. We can look over the site tomorrow morning and I'll show you."

Ed's news gave me hope. Meaningfully altering a building after a policy has been issued required notification of the insurer. How meaningfully it was altered would determine how much the insurers might be able to withhold, ten percent of which would be mine.

We joined the others at the bar and found things had deteriorated markedly. They were at the stage where each of them half-recollects some blurry memory of what happened sometime or other, to someone or other. The saving grace was that no one could remember who bought the last round. I got out without dropping a dime.

2

Ed picked me up the next morning and we walked the few blocks down to the river.

"We can hire a ferry to take us over to the island," he said.

There was a large excursion boat taking on passengers just down the river from us, but nothing that looked like a ferry. He led me down some steps to a little dock where there were half a dozen flat-bottomed skiffs. In each of the first two was a dozing old man. Further on several boys were tossing coins in another.

Ed asked who was next and one of the boys directed us to his boat. After some physical discussion with another boy over division of the spoils, he got in and pushed us off the dock. He stood near the rear of the boat and had a single long oar that sat in a crotch at the center of the stern which he used to both steer and propel the boat. It wasn't at all like the dinghies you typically see on the waterfront, but sort of a Yankee version of a Venetian gondola.

River traffic was busy and our gondolier spent most of his effort just staying out of the way. Tow tugs were backing a grain ship downriver and another was pushing a small float of canal boats upriver. Somehow we ended up between the two processions and were buffeted a good deal by their competing wakes. We had only gone 150 yards, but the trip had had an epic quality.

We climbed out at what remained of the Eastern Elevator's wharf. It seemed incredible that, just a week before, a giant 160-foot elevator had stood on the spot. Now, all that was left of it was a series of piles being sorted by a small army of laborers. To the right, there were piles of charred wood. Just in front, there were piles of uncharred wood. And to the left, where there was a rail spur, there were piles of metal sheets on flatcars.

"That's what I was referring to last night, Harry."

Ed pointed back toward a brick vault about ten feet from the far end of the wharf. The masonry was completely blackened and a lot of the bricks had cracked from the heat. It had rounded sides and a rounded top. It was about six feet high, more at the peak, and maybe twelve feet long by six feet wide.

If this was all there was to it, it wasn't going to be much help to me. It would have amounted to maybe one-tenth of one percent of the original structure. Ed went over and yanked the steel door open. Inside was a little derrick on wheels.

"This is just how it was after the fire, except I had a lock cut off," said Ed.

We wheeled out the derrick and it just fit through the door. It had a long arm that could be folded up. When extended it was about twenty feet long. And at its base was a hand winch.

"I don't think this could lift more than a couple hundred pounds," Ed said.

We went back into the vault and by lighting a number of matches verified that it was otherwise empty. There seemed to be a concrete floor, but it was impossible to tell because the whole vault was lined with tin sheet, neatly brazed at the seams.

"This was below one of the grain bins," Ed explained. "There was a timber superstructure supporting the bins, and those timbers surrounded the vault. But it wasn't on the builder's plans submitted for the policy. I've interviewed the foremen and most of the rest of the Eastern's crew and they said it was a storeroom, but no one could say what it was used to store."

"What in the world would they be storing that needed a lined brick vault?" I asked.

"It might have been to keep out rodents," Ed suggested. "These elevators are crawling with rats. You see those holes everywhere? Rat holes."

He was right. The ground was dotted with holes in between the pilings of the foundation.

"You'd need masonry to keep them out," Ed continued. "And with the lining you wouldn't have to worry about any cracks or gaps in the mortar."

"Have you ever seen anything like this in another elevator?" I asked.

"No, and the fact no one down here has any idea what purpose it served leads me to assume it's unique. And perhaps was used for some illicit purpose."

I was going to have to rethink my strategy. The vault wasn't large enough to make a plausible argument that the structure had been materially altered. But if it was used for some illicit purpose, then we might be able to argue that information was withheld from the insurers that compromised the policies. Since we were on a waterfront that was frequently visited by ships from Canada, smuggling seemed the most likely possibility.

Ed and I spent ten minutes wheeling the derrick around and seeing how far out the arm would extend if we brought it to the edge of the wharf.

"Do you think that would be far enough out to reach the open hold of a steamer?" I asked.

"I can't say."

I called over the boy who had brought us and asked him the same question.

"Sure it would," he said.

I'd learned long ago you can't put much faith in what a boy who lives by tips tells you. But he knew more about the subject than either of us.

"What do you think they kept in there?" I asked him.

"I don't know. But you could ask Old Mike. He might know. He might not tell you. But he might know. He was sleepin' when we went out."

I walked over and found a foreman with the salvage company and asked him to leave the vault and what was in it alone for now. He said he would. Then we headed back across the river, with only a tug and a sand barge to dodge this time. When we docked Ed pulled out his watch.

"I have to go, Harry. I need to have my report typed for the meeting tomorrow, and then I'm catching the afternoon express. Whatever this is about, it has nothing to do with the fire per se, so it's not really relevant to my report. But I will mention it."

As Ed went off, I gave the boy two bits and he pointed out Old Mike, still asleep in his boat. I went over and tried to get his attention, but he just opened one eye. He listened, then rolled over and faced away. The boys all laughed. But my guide came over, leaned down, and whispered something to him. Old Mike righted himself and eyed me warily. Then he slowly got up and said, "Get in."

I got in and the boy pushed us off. Old Mike steered us out to a relatively quiet stretch on the far side of the river.

"You want to know about the Eastern?"

"We found a little brick room, and a derrick inside. I figured maybe it was to unload something off the steamers that docked there. But no one seems to know what it was used for. So I thought maybe it was used for something that needed to be kept secret," I said.

"Secret?" said Old Mike.

"Well, why else would no one know what it was for? So I thought maybe they were smuggling something off the steamers."

"I did see some goings-on at night." With that, Old Mike stopped and stared at me. I gave him a half-dollar. He just stared at it in his hand. I gave him another.

"There used to be a whaleback, from Fort William. It'd unload at the Eastern real regular, I can't remember the name. After it'd unload, it'd be tied up there all night, and you could see somethin' goin' on. It was dark, but they'd have a light in the hold. One time I saw them liftin' crates out of the hold. And sometimes I saw it goin' on when a canal boat was there. I figured they were smugglin' somethin' they could put in the bottom of a grain hold, where no customs man could see it."

"Like what?" I asked.

"Furs, maybe."

"How big were the crates?"

"Like so." Old Mike drew a cube in the air about thirty inches on a side.

"What's a whaleback?"

"It's a lake steamer with a curved deck. Sits real low in the water. Looks like the back of a whale just breakin' the water, but with a bridge and a stack stuck on."

"When was it you saw these goings-on at night?"

"Oh, not for years."

"How often did you see it?"

"Well, it seemed whenever that whaleback was in port."

"But why were you out at night?"

"I wasn't ferryin'. I used to sleep on a tug tied up across the river, where the engine works is now. I'd keep an eye on the tugs and get my breakfast for it. When it was warm, I slept on deck."

"Is there anyone who would know for sure what went on? Maybe one of the men you saw at night?"

Old Mike stared at me again. This time I just gave him the dollar.

"Danny Sullivan. He was a foreman at the Eastern 'til last year. He'd know. He's a saloon now. But didn't buy it."

"How'd he get it then?"

"Can't say. It was one of Fingy Conners' places."

"Who's Fingy Conners?"

"A big boss, used to be a grain shoveler hisself."

"Where's Danny Sullivan's saloon?"

"He's on Elk Street. I'll show you."

We went up the river, past the dock we set out from, and then past the Frontier Engine Works. We docked a few blocks further on. Old Mike gave me directions from there and then exacted another two bits for the trip.

It certainly sounded like a plausible way to smuggle something—like furs, for instance—from Canada. They put the furs in some sealed chests and place them in the bottom of the hold of a grain carrier, then fill it up with grain at a Canadian elevator. The ship comes down through the lakes and docks at the Eastern. The grain is unloaded, or most of it, and that night the chests are lifted out and stored in the vault.

Later, a canal boat docks at the Eastern to load grain for New York. The chests are placed in the hold and the grain loaded on top. In New York, customs men don't look at canal boats and the cargo can be delivered to the buyer. That's the type of activity that nullifies an insurance policy.

Danny Sullivan's saloon was just a few blocks from where Old Mike had left me. Inside, there were a couple men at the bar and another one behind it. I asked for Sullivan and was directed to a fellow at a table in the rear. He was younger than I expected, not even forty, and oddly well-dressed for the owner of a waterfront saloon. I introduced myself and apologized for interrupting his breakfast. But he didn't really let me interrupt. He was friendly enough and spoke freely about his time at the Eastern. He'd been there from the time it was built, in 1893, until a year ago, just as Old Mike said. As to the vault, he insisted it was just a storeroom where spare machine parts were kept. It made little sense, but he wasn't going to elaborate. When I mentioned the possibility of smuggling, he just laughed and said smuggling went on all along the waterfront, but nothing you'd need a room to store it in. I didn't see any point in asking him how he came to own the saloon. If it was as Old Mike implied, that he'd been bought off, he certainly wasn't going to give me the details. Finally, we shook hands and I left.

The only chance of getting any information out of Danny Sullivan was to pay for it, and from the way he dressed, I felt sure my current cash reserves were inadequate to the task.

3

I took a car up to Main Street and located the Customs Service in the Post Office building. I was taken to the inspectors' office, a large room with a dozen desks, three of them occupied. I walked up to the most friendly-looking of the bunch and introduced myself as a New York newspaperman. I didn't want to initiate an official investigation, just get some facts.

"We've heard rumors about a smuggling ring using canal boats to bring goods down into New York. I'm trying to find out what they're smuggling and how."

"You think the canal boats originate here?"

"Well, it's close to the border. But I wasn't sure what they'd be smuggling from Canada."

"Most of what we deal with here is misidentification—someone importing finished steel but calling it pig iron. Or trying to get $3,000 worth of goods in, but only paying duty on $2,000 worth. What sort of thing might they be smuggling?"

"Someone suggested furs," I said.

"Furs come over all the time, usually on some woman's back. Then it's a matter of: Did she have it when she crossed north, or just on the way back? But we find them sometimes."

"When you do see them smuggled, how are they brought in?" I asked.

"In crates, mixed with a lot of other crates."

"In a steamer's hold?"

"No, no, in freight cars. Finished furs usually come

from Montreal or somewhere in the East. Most of the steamers come from out West."

"What about unfinished furs?"

"Well, there's no tariff on raw furs, so why smuggle them?"

"What would be the most valuable contraband?" I asked.

"Chinamen!" a second inspector chimed in. We all laughed.

"He's serious, though," the first fellow said. "We just had a case a few months ago. They brought them across the river in a rowboat."

"Well, how about things that don't need to breathe?"

"The most money we ever got at an auction was for a chest of opium. Remember that, Gus? Back in '95, I think."

"Yeah, Chinamen came from all over the East to bid on that."

"You auctioned it?" I asked.

"Well, sure. Goods that are seized for nonpayment of duty are always auctioned."

"What's a chest of opium weigh?"

"Well, this one was only about three feet by two feet, maybe another two feet deep. It was damned heavy. It took two men to move it."

"How much did the winner pay?"

"It was over a thousand dollars. This was the pre-pared stuff, for smoking."

"And it gets smuggled in often?"

"I suspect small amounts get smuggled in by men on the lake. There's no way to stop that. And out West, it's always coming across the border. But we don't see it here much."

"What's the tariff on opium?"

"Let's see...." He reached over for a book on another desk and quickly located what he was looking for. "Six dollars a pound since 1895, twelve dollars before that."

I thanked the boys and then found a telegraph office. I sent a long wire to a fellow I knew who worked as a Treasury Department agent back in New York. He was the only person I could think of who'd be likely to know about opium smuggling. I marked it urgent.

After availing myself of the free lunch at a saloon, I walked up to Lafayette Square, where the Eastern Elevator Company had its offices in the Mooney-Brisbane Building. Why an elevator company that had lost its elevator to foreclosure two months earlier still needed an office I couldn't say, but Ed had assured me he'd visited it the day before.

The girl inside seemed annoyed at my bothering her. She'd only been with the company since January, she told me, and was now its sole employee. Her name was Emily McGinnis. She was young, reasonably good-looking, and dressed casually for an office girl. I asked her for a list of the current officers of the corporation. Rather than look for a document, she simply told me from memory.

The president was General Chester Osgood, a lawyer with an office in the Erie County Bank Building. The vice president and superintendent was Harold Trumble, the only one of the officers who had worked there daily, but who'd recently taken a position with a firm in Philadelphia. The secretary was Charles Elwell, another lawyer, and the man who had gone missing a month earlier. The treasurer was a local banker named James Clayton.

"Do you know how long Mr. Trumble was with the company?"

"I believe he started when Mr. Mason left, about three or four years ago."

Robert Mason was the original superintendent, the one who'd been on the run since the share manipulation in '97. I already knew that he'd helped found the firm in 1892 and would have been involved in the construction of the elevator. Also that his name was tied to a dozen different schemes and lawsuits both during and before his time in Buffalo. So he had had both the opportunity and the disposition to run a smuggling operation at the Eastern. But where he was now, no one knew.

"I don't suppose you spent much time at the elevator?"

"Actually, I only ever saw it from across the river."

I asked to see a copy of the original fire policy. She insisted she couldn't provide it without General Osgood's permission. She gave me the General's telephone number and led me into an inner office where the only telephone was located and left me there. When I reached the General I introduced myself and gave a vague explanation of my mission. He said he would need to think about giving me access to any files. As he'd be busy the rest of the afternoon, he suggested I stop by his house that evening and we could discuss the matter then. He gave me directions and we agreed on a time.

While I was alone, I spent some time snooping about the office. There wasn't much to be found here, just a desk—which had been pretty thoroughly emptied—and a couple shelves of books. The books were mostly treatises on subjects like the storing of grain, the shipping of grain, and the drying of grain—and, of course, controlling rodents. But there were also several novels of the large and substantial type that could do double duty as doorstops. There was Trollope's *Barchester Towers* and *The Way We Live Now*, Thackeray's *The Virginians*, and Dickens' *Martin Chuzzlewit*. The first three were inscribed by Robert Mason, and the last was ex libris David Mason, perhaps his father. The only other thing of a personal nature in the room was a framed diploma on the wall. It would seem Robert Mason was a Princeton man. It was hard to imagine a graduate of Princeton being content as the superintendent of a grain elevator. Maybe he took the job with the smuggling operation already in mind. And I suppose Trumble left the diploma up to impress people who didn't look too closely at the details.

I went out and thanked the girl and said good-bye. The news that I was leaving seemed just the thing to cheer her up. She even looked up from her book and smiled.

Then I found my way to police headquarters, where I asked to speak to a detective who covered the river and might know about smuggling. I was sent from office to office but eventually wound up with Detective James Donahy.

"We don't look much for smugglers—that's for the customs boys," he told me.

I described what I had seen at the Eastern, and what Old Mike had said.

"An old ferryman? Why would he be on the river at night? They've all gone home by dark."

I related Old Mike's story about sleeping on a tug.

"Sleeping on a tug? That just happened to dock across from the Eastern?" Detective Donahy made his skepticism clear with a wide smile. "Who mentioned smuggling first, you or him?"

"Well, I did...."

"Did you give him money?"

"Not much...."

"Give one of those fellas two bits and he'd confess to the smuggling himself."

Detective Donahy's view on the matter—that I was a foolish ass—offered what many would see as a more plausible explanation than that the operators of a grain elevator were smuggling opium by way of a ship shaped like a whale. But I persevered. I told him about Danny Sullivan.

"You think Danny Sullivan was bought off with a saloon?" Donahy found this downright comical. "You want to know why he got the saloon?"

I nodded, but I could tell I wasn't going to like it.

"Up until a year ago the saloonkeepers on the waterfront had a racket where they controlled the grain scoopers. They contracted with the elevator operators to supply the scoopers, then paid the men doing the work some small part of what the contract paid them. But only after they deducted whatever they had advanced the men in beer and food, which never left much. Finally, the scoopers had had enough, so they went on strike. The saloon bosses called in the thugs, but this time the little guys won. The bishop backed the scoopers, the dockworkers backed them, the temperance union and every politician's wife backed them, and even the elevator owners backed them."

"That's an inspiring story, but—"

"Hold on. That saloon Danny Sullivan has was one of Fingy Conners' places. Under the racket, it made a nice profit. Without it, it's just another waterfront hole."

"How'd he get the name Fingy?"

"William Conners, properly. They call him Fingy because he's missing a finger. He's a local boss. He started on the waterfront, but now he has his fingers in all sorts of things—steamships, newspapers, politics."

"Well, all his fingers but one," I pointed out. "Is there a patrolman we could talk to? Maybe a man on the beat saw what the ferryman says he saw at night?"

"Let me think." He tapped his chin. "That would be Officer O'Reilly. Too bad he died just last week in a horrible fire. You see, he heard a child crying in a burning building and ran to its rescue. But the roof caved in on him. Turns out it wasn't a child, but a cat. The cat made it out and paid for the wake in gratitude."

I supposed the sad tale was Donahy's way of telling me that the subject was now closed, so I moved on to the absentee officers of the Eastern.

"Don't know anything about Trumble," Donahy said. "Never even heard the name. Mason was the clever type, always looking for a new sure-fire proposition. But a lot better at losing other people's money than making it for himself."

"When did he leave town?"

"Just after his stock scheme a few years ago. I don't really know much about it. But by the time the people in New York asked us to hold him, he was gone."

"And no one knows where he is now?"

He shrugged. "We aren't looking for him."

"But if you *were* looking for him, who would you ask?"

"I might know someone who could help you."

Then he just waited, staring at me and bobbing back and forth in his chair. I handed him five dollars and it disappeared in an instant.

"Mason used to pal around with a gal named Sadie. She goes by Parker now, but when she worked a panel house in the Hooks, her name was Collins. Sadie's a girl who's always advancing herself. She started in that panel house, then got a place in a parlor house, then hitched up with Mason. When he left, she latched on to Elwell."

"Charles Elwell? The fellow who disappeared recently?"

"That's right. That was a big step up for Sadie. Elwell was a lawyer. Of course, now she'll need to find someone new. Maybe that General." Donahy found that idea very amusing.

"How is it you know so much about her?"

"I'm from the Hooks, too. It's the far side of the canal. Mostly Sicilians now."

"What about Elwell's disappearance?"

"He was a big sailor, used to race a small yacht. It looks like he went out on it alone. Then a storm came up. A couple days later it was found adrift, with the mast broken in two. Elwell must have tried to swim for it, but never made it to shore."

"What can you tell me about General Osgood?"

"The sort of name that people like Mason and Elwell need to have on the letterhead. He's a show general, in the state guard, never seen a battle. But he knows all the right people, and if you wanted to borrow money to build a grain elevator, he could get it. And, if there were things going on, like a stock scheme, he probably wouldn't suspect a thing."

"How about Elwell—do you think he would have been in on the scheme with Mason?"

"I'd say so, but it'd only be a guess. He'd get his

share if it went over, but he wouldn't be the one needing to leave town if it fell apart."

"Do you know where I can find Sadie Parker now?"

"Last I knew, Elwell had her in the Tifft House, up on Main Street."

I thanked him and he told me to let him know if I actually found any evidence of smuggling.

It was a short walk back to McLeod's. At the desk, I was handed a wire inviting me to the Iroquois Hotel for dinner that evening with two New York men who would be coming in that afternoon. A preliminary meeting of all the various insurers was to be held the next morning where they would be ascertaining how much each company was potentially on the hook for. How much they actually paid out was a different matter.

I sat down in the taproom and waited for a reply from my friend at the Treasury Department in New York. A boy from the telegraph office brought it just before six. I took it up to my cell.

I had definitely asked the right person. I only wish he hadn't sent the reply collect. First, opium was often smuggled into the U.S. from Canada. There were opium factories in Victoria, British Columbia, and they sold it for as little as five or six dollars a pound, whereas a domestic factory would need to sell it for at least fifteen dollars a pound because of the ten-dollar-a-pound excise tax. Second, opium was usually shipped in a chest two to three feet on a side and two feet deep, which weighed 100-150 pounds. Third, opium was in high demand in New York and sold for fifteen to eighteen dollars per pound wholesale. Fourth, smuggling into New York in a canal boat was plausible, but he hadn't ever heard of it before.

If the opium had been manufactured in Victoria, it could have been easily, and legally, brought to Fort William by rail. It would only have needed a couple of men in Fort William to take delivery and get it on a boat, then a couple in Buffalo to get it off. The captain of the steamer would probably have needed to be in on it, and definitely the canal boatman. But each chest would cost just $800 or so in Canada and sell for up to $1,800 in New York. If each man in the chain were paid $100 per chest, there would still be about a $400 profit per chest for Mason, or whoever was running the show. And they probably did several chests at a time. This all fit together nicely. I was beginning to have faith in my own theory again.

4

I arrived at the Iroquois Hotel early for my dinner appointment and was just killing time watching the crowds when a boy approached me with a handbill for a Dr. Linn's Museum of Anatomy. There weren't many of these places still around and a pang of nostalgia drew me down to the entrance, where I gave up my fifteen cents.

Like the rest, Dr. Linn's museum presented itself as a scientific exploration of humanity. It began with a room of jars holding specimens of animals and organs. In amongst them were wax versions of the same type of things, but in more lifelike poses. In the next room were the typical grotesques—jars of malformed fetuses, images of facial and skin afflictions, and more serious maladies shown in wax. The latter included the torso and head of a young woman whose carefree expression gave no hint of concern that her breasts had been removed to reveal a large internal tumor.

Pride of place was given to depictions of the advanced stages of syphilis, and other diseases of that nature. Scattered about these displays were tactful hints that the proprietor, a doctor of medicine, specialized in the treatment of such cases. Only when I made it to the third floor did I get to the part I remembered so fondly from my youth: Female Beauty. There they were, the shapely wax figures lying fetchingly on their pillowed couches, and all as naked as Eve. Just about exactly what any sixteen-year-old is looking for in the way of enlightenment. Some exhibited horrific growths, and others had large chunks of their flesh removed to reveal internal organs. But neither was enough to cool the ardor of adolescence.

The Iroquois was Buffalo's premier hotel and this was likely to be the best meal I'd had in weeks. I was meeting Samuel Keegan, the owner of the Gotham Insurance Bureau. He had created a massive file of the names of insurance applicants and claimants. Its purpose was to allow insurers to find out if an applicant already carried a large amount of insurance through other companies, or had made an unusual number of claims. In other words, to prevent fraud. Its existence was not something made public and the insurance press never mentioned it. The member insurers paid a nominal fee and they provided the Bureau with the relevant names from their own files.

But Keegan made the real money by identifying fraudulent claims, and receiving a percentage of whatever he saved the insurers. He had clerks who looked for unusual patterns of applications and claims, and he hired his own investigators to gather the information necessary to prove fraud had been committed. He had no real competition and maintained friendly relationships with all the big men in insurance. It was Keegan who had given me my first job as an investigator, and had also provided me most of the cases that had come my way after I went out on my own, including this one. Joining us at dinner would be Jeb Cowell, of the claims department at American Concordia Insurance Company. I'd done some work for him in the past as well.

I met them in the lobby and soon after we entered the dining room. Keegan was a big man, a very big man, and as anyone who had eaten with him could attest, he was a well-practiced glutton. I know gluttony is one of the seven deadly sins and all that, but in a man who's buying you dinner in the city's finest restaurant, it can only be seen as a virtue.

We began with lake sturgeon caviar, a local delicacy. When the waiter mentioned the possibility of smoked eel, Keegan became so excited he knocked over his wine. When he returned with the sad news that some other party had just gotten the last of it, Keegan consoled himself by finishing off the caviar.

"So, Reese, what have you found?" Cowell asked.

I ran through the story of the vault, including my various conversations, and then offered my conclusion: the structure had been modified for the sole purpose of smuggling goods, most likely opium.

"How recently was this going on?" Cowell asked.

"I believe it was run by Robert Mason, the former vice president, from the time of the elevator's construction in 1893 until sometime around 1897, when he disappeared."

Keegan helped himself to most of the English lamb chops, and the veal cutlets larded with chicory. But I held my own when the broiled game sausage with purée of chestnuts arrived.

"I know all about Mason," Cowell said. "Just last year, we linked him to an arson scheme in Memphis. He was using an alias and was long gone when it came undone. But it was him all right."

"My file on Mason goes back to the eighties," Keegan said. "Do you have any leads on his whereabouts?"

"I've two people who might know, one of his co-conspirators and his former mistress. But what about the policies on the elevator? How much of the claim could be denied?"

"My estimate would be none," Cowell said. "Remember, the current owner is the linseed oil trust. We'd have to argue that they should have brought to our attention what we hadn't noticed in seven years of coverage and multiple renewals."

"And the lawyers wouldn't be able to roll over them like they might've the Eastern Elevator Company. They might even sue for breach of contract," Keegan added.

This wasn't good news. I had already spent my four-day advance, so even if I left tonight I'd be in the hole for the trip. And it sounded as if Keegan had never expected anything to come of it. I couldn't put a positive construction on the situation, so I didn't bother trying and instead concentrated on the next course, a superb duckling. But as we waited for dessert, I tried to figure out what he was up to. Then he provided the likely answer.

"It might be worthwhile for you to find out where Mason is hiding, Harry," Keegan said.

"How worthwhile?" I asked. "I mean, is there any possible percentage?"

"I imagine a number of firms have had losses due to Mason's activities, but it would be difficult to recover what's been paid unless it came from Mason," Cowell said. "And my understanding is there's a long list of creditors and victims, so I doubt it'd be at all worthwhile."

"Of course, it would be of benefit to us collectively if he were brought to the bar, just as an example, if nothing else." Keegan directed this to Cowell.

"That's true," he agreed. "And perhaps prevent some future losses as well."

"I'll tell you what, Harry. Why don't you go ahead and work on finding Mason? I think we could come up with a few hundred dollars, providing Mr. Cowell's and one or two other firms join me."

"I suppose that's possible," Cowell said.

"What would be the terms?"

"Let's say three hundred when Mason is apprehended." Cowell, the skinflint, spoke first.

"What about expenses? It's liable to involve some traveling."

"Okay, we'll say any intercity travel can be submitted as well," Keegan offered.

"All right, agreed." I raised my glass and we drank to it. I was able to enjoy my Charlotte Russe with only the usual denial of reality. There was little chance my reassignment to the Mason case was as spontaneous as the two of them had made it seem. They had performed like a couple of steerers for a circus skin game. I was beginning to suspect I had been sent to Buffalo simply to make me a little more desperate.

It was almost nine o'clock now, so I begged off brandy and cigars and made my way to the car stop. General Osgood's directions were simple enough: take the Main Street car just over a mile to Bryant Street, then walk west three blocks. Though I had made the appointment with Osgood to ask him about seeing the insurance policy, he might also be able to help me find Mason. I was at his door by half past nine. It was answered by a young girl who still had her brogue. She led me to a small study, and not long after, the General came in.

He carried himself as if he were on the parade grounds, and no doubt he was sure he cut an impressive figure. We exchanged greetings and I told him I was now charged with finding Robert Mason. I then brought up the smuggling question because I thought it might offer some clues to Mason's whereabouts. That was a misstep. The General was offended at the suggestion. He didn't remember the vault, but agreed it may have been a storeroom for parts.

"But isn't there a chance Mason could have been running something without you or the other officers being aware?"

"Of course it's possible, but both Elwell and I visited the elevator fairly regularly. And there were at least two dozen men working there. Were they all in on it?"

"What if it went on at night? I've looked into it, and it seems all he'd need is a couple fellows helping him, and I think I've located one of them."

"Who might that be?"

"A fellow named Danny Sullivan, who was a fore-man up until last year."

"He wasn't any foreman, just a dockhand."

"Well, nonetheless, I feel fairly sure he was in-volved."

"If there was something with which he could have been involved."

The General's indignation appeared to be sincere. So I tried to direct it at Robert Mason.

"Mason seems to have dragged the firm into a cou-ple of schemes: the shortchanging of shippers and the share manipulation."

"The miscalculating of goods was something that occurred at several of the elevators and it was never proven to be anything beyond honest error."

Miscalculating of goods? Only a lawyer would come up with that.

"But certainly Mason crossed the line with the share price manipulation?"

"Yes. By then it was obvious Mason was a most unsavory character. I had the board dismiss him immediately. That was three years ago. And as far as I know, no one has seen or heard from him since."

"Who was closest to him in the firm?"

"Elwell probably worked with him most regularly, but I don't think they were in any way close."

"What about Sadie Parker, née Collins?"

"Who's she? Was her husband with the company?"

"There is no Mr. Parker. Apparently Miss Collins decided she needed a new name. She has a somewhat tainted past. I've been told she was Mason's mistress."

"Told by whom?"

"A police detective."

"That's not the type of thing I would know anything about. Are you trying to find Mason to tie him to a smuggling operation?"

I saw what he was getting at, so I thought I'd reassure him.

"No, there's no way any of that could be proven now. I was just using that as a means to find him. There are plenty of other reasons to find him."

"Well, if that's the case, I wish you the best of luck."

"Would that extend to allowing me to look through the company's files?"

"What would you be looking for?"

"Maybe a suspicious correspondence of Mason's, or just an address he communicated with frequently."

"Can you assure me that you will use whatever information you come across for no other purpose beyond finding Robert Mason? And that nothing will be taken from the office?"

"Absolutely."

"Very well. I'll stop by and talk to Miss McGinnis in the morning. I may have some files I can send over as well."

We shook hands on it and he showed me to the door.

I took a car back downtown and walked over to the Broezel to see if any of the gang were still there. I didn't see anyone I knew, but took a place at the bar just the same. I needed to chew over the facts in the Mason case and this was as good a place as any to do it.

"Say, didn't we meet on the train the other day?"

It was one of the drummers I had fleeced on the way into town.

"Yes, we did. How's your trip going?"

"Fine, fine. But I'll tell you, it's been gnawing at me the way we all passed out on you. That's no way to end a card game."

"Well, no matter." I bought him a round to show there were no hard feelings. Just as I had hoped, no one had been able to check the accounting after the game.

5

The next morning, I was woken up by Detective Donahy banging on the door.

"How quick can you get dressed?"

"What's happened?"

"Your boy Danny Sullivan is being fished out of the Commercial Slip. I thought you might want to say good-bye."

"Was he shot?" I asked while splashing myself at the sink.

"Couldn't tell. But definitely dead."

I dressed and we headed out.

"The man on the beat spotted him about an hour ago," Donahy said.

"Officer O'Reilly?"

"No. I told you, he died saving a cat," Donahy chuckled. "It's George Henafelt's case. I told him you'd been asking about Sullivan, so of course he thought it a good idea for me to come and fetch you."

A few minutes later we arrived at the slip. They were lifting Sullivan out on a hook from a steam derrick. We passed through a line of cops holding back a few dozen spectators to where a smaller group of detectives and newspapermen crowded over him. He didn't look good. Donahy introduced me to Detective Henafelt, a short, tough-looking cop, who had squatted down to examine the body. He took off Sullivan's sodden jacket and reached under his shirt.

"Knife. Knife. Knife...." Apparently Henafelt was

counting wounds. There were a total of seven.

Then he stood up and announced, "Looks like the Valle d'Olmo citizens committee came to a decision as to the disposition of Mr. Sullivan."

"How's that?" I asked.

"Danny was a bit of a Don Juan," Donahy said. "And when you cross the slip into the Hooks, you've arrived in Little Sicily."

"Yeah. Danny-boy must have been eyeing one of the girls while the men were away working in the fields. A crew of them came home yesterday. Danny must not have heard the news," Henafelt added.

The boys of the press ran off to file their stories. They wouldn't even need to invent anything to get front-page news out of this.

"Couldn't it have been something else?" I asked.

"Jimmy said you had Sullivan hooked up with some smuggling ring—that what you're thinking?" Henafelt asked.

"Well, it does seem kind of a coincidence. I spoke to him yesterday morning about a subject he didn't want to talk about. Today you're pulling him out of the slip here."

"So someone finds out you were digging around and figures Danny was the weak link?" Henafelt asked. "Who do you think was running this ring?"

I recounted most of the story I had given Donahy the day before.

"Well, if you've got Boss Conners in on it, here's your number one suspect." Henafelt nodded toward a fellow approaching through the police line. He too was short and tough-looking, but not so young as Henafelt, and his blond hair was nearly white.

"Come to turn yourself in, Whitey?" Donahy asked.

32

"Yeah, that's right. I never liked the way Danny dressed."

Donahy introduced him as Mike Schuler, William Conners' jack-of-all-trades. The two detectives spoke with Schuler as if he were a colleague, but with no deference. They gave him the Sicilian revenge theory and left my story untold. After another round of jokes at Danny's expense, Schuler headed off.

"I can't see your version, Reese. Knifing a guy in the back was never Conners' game. He doesn't need to resort to rough stuff now anyways," Donahy said. "We'll let George follow his nose here. We got a guy knifed seven times, next to a neighborhood of Sicilians, a guy who couldn't keep his pants up and made a habit of pestering people's daughters."

I agreed he was probably right and told him my main focus now was finding Robert Mason. I left them to their work and had a leisurely breakfast at a counter on Washington Street. Then I went back to the hotel to dress properly and headed to the Iroquois. There was a meeting of the representatives of all the insurers and reinsurers at ten and I wanted to catch Keegan before it began.

I met him in his room. He told me he had checked with New York, as had Cowell, and our deal was on. He was having the files on Mason sent to my hotel, but offered a brief summary of the earlier attempts to locate him. He'd been out of contact with his family for years, and he didn't seem to have had any associates who wouldn't be more than happy to turn him in. Keegan had no intention of bringing up the vault, or the smuggling theory, at the meeting. So there wouldn't be any point in my attending. Then he mentioned that he'd be in town for the next several days—his wife was coming in that evening—and asked me to let him know if I found out anything about Mason.

I left Keegan and went up to the Elevator Company's office. The General had spoken to Miss McGinnis and she was decidedly more pleasant. She led me first to the office that had been used by Mason and later by Trumble. I had already searched this pretty thoroughly when I used the telephone, but I couldn't very well say so. I combed carefully through the desk and found nothing, other than letterhead, pens, pencils, blotting paper, a slide rule, and the company seal. Trumble must have taken everything else when he left. I flipped through all the books on the shelves. Alas, they held no secret messages between their pages. This left Mason's Princeton diploma on the wall. I took it down and tore the paper backing off, but there was nothing to be found there either.

There was also a large inner office which had been the clerks' room. Here there were several desks and all the accounting, inventory, and payroll records for the eight or so years the company had been in business. There were boxes and boxes of records on the floor, on shelves, and on top of desks. I calculated the odds of finding anything in here as being very remote.

The outer office held a couple of desks and several cabinets of correspondence. I was sure these files offered the best chance of finding anything worthwhile. I'd noticed that every time I entered the room, the girl made a point of looking busy, but there was a large book on her desk and it was obvious she returned to it whenever she was alone.

"Go ahead and read. You don't need to put on a show for me."

"It *is* rather silly, but there's little for me to do other than type an occasional letter and send out bills for overdue accounts. I think the only reason the General has kept me on is out of sympathy."

"It would be that hard to find another position?"

"No, I meant sympathy over my uncle."

"Your uncle? Did he pass away?"

"Oh, I thought I'd mentioned it. Charles Elwell was my uncle. The assumption is he died in a sailing accident."

"Yes, I heard. I'm sorry." I mumbled some words of consolation, but she didn't really seem in need of it. "Did the General tell you I'm trying to locate Robert Mason?"

"Yes. What is it you hope to find?"

"Well, I'm fairly certain he was running a smuggling ring, using the elevator as a transfer point. That was before the share manipulation."

"Are you serious?"

"Oh, yes. In fact, he has a long history. What I'm hoping to find is something that might provide a clue as to where he is now, maybe a somewhat personal exchange of letters. Or maybe something involving the smuggling."

Miss McGinnis offered to help and so I described in more detail the smuggling operation as I imagined it. She was most intrigued. Since the files were arranged by correspondent, there was no way of going about it other than by looking through each file for anything previous to Mason's departure. We each started at one end. After two hours, we had a list of four names and addresses in Fort William, where the opium was likely to have been shipped from, one in Los Angeles, and two in London.

The Fort William letters were strictly business, but

at least one of these contacts probably was involved in some way with the smuggling, even if it was unknowingly. The Los Angeles letter stood out because of the locale and the fact it had nothing to do with the grain elevator. It was from a Raymond Hushlaw and involved some previous business dealing of Mason's that had taken place in New Brunswick, New Jersey. It was dated July 19th, 1894, three years before his disappearance. The letter itself was typical business correspondence. Hushlaw was just asking if Mason could locate some legal documents for him. The two London letters did involve grain shipments, and sounded simply businesslike. They only stood out because of the address of the sender.

While I had been reading, Miss McGinnis had accepted delivery of a parcel from a messenger.

"The General sent these over for you." She handed me a thick pile of files. They were all related to the stock episode. There were copies of reports from the New York Stock Exchange and, more interestingly, a file of correspondence with the Ratigan Detective Agency in New York. Apparently, the General had taken it upon himself to find out which of his fellow officers at the Eastern Elevator were involved.

I knew Dan Ratigan. He specialized in securities fraud. To him, this was probably a routine case. The scheme involved floating rumors that a railroad was interested in buying the Eastern Elevator at a premium. This sent the stock up for several weeks running. But that wasn't where the money was made. Mason and his confederates waited until the rumors had done their work and then found a couple of wily brokers who would allow them to short the stock and then buy it back in the same day. The day that it became obvious there was nothing to the rumors. By doing it that way, they never risked a dime of their own money.

Ratigan had compiled a list of the names of those who participated and noted that they all appeared to be aliases. Two of them, Mr. G. Osborne and Mr. Felix Carbury, he had traced to Mason. There were two other names, Matilda Crawley and Frederick Pferd, he hadn't been able to trace positively but assumed were used by Mason as well. Ratigan reported he could find no evidence that anyone else from Buffalo was involved. I folded this document and slipped it into my pocket.

By now it was getting on one o'clock, so I offered to take Miss McGinnis to lunch. I realized immediately that I had put myself in a dangerous position. I would now be obligated to graciously accept whatever recommendation she made. If it was the dining room of the Iroquois Hotel, I could easily be out another three dollars. As we were about to leave, she reached for her book.

"Miss McGinnis, there may be those who find my company somewhat dull, but I pride myself on never having forced a luncheon companion to resort to reading a novel."

"Oh, I'm sorry. Force of habit."

She said she had just the place in mind and then headed down toward the Iroquois. When we passed it, I think my sigh was audible. A little further on we arrived at Ellicott Square, which every citizen of Buffalo feels compelled to tell visitors is the largest office building in the world. She led me down a flight of stairs, where we came upon a line of people entering a restaurant through a turnstile. I was charged two bits apiece and we found a table to ourselves in the corner.

The conversation began with me describing the

work I did and her telling me how she had come out to Buffalo from a small town in Massachusetts. But she soon turned the topic back to the smuggling ring, and wanted to know every detail. I obliged.

"How fantastic. It sounds just like a dime novel. All you need now is the kidnapping of a young white girl by these opium dealers in Chinatown."

"I haven't told you the most fantastic part. Danny Sullivan was found floating in the Commercial Slip this morning. He'd been knifed seven times."

"Oh, yes. I *should* smile." Miss McGinnis was disbelieving.

"It's quite true. The police think it was a Sicilian honor killing, but it was some coincidence."

"A Sicilian honor killing? Mr. Reese, you aren't making this up merely to impress me, are you?"

"Miss McGinnis, your cynicism is getting the best of you. I assure you, it's all perfectly true. Now let me ask you a question. Back at the office you said the assumption was your uncle died in a sailing accident. Is there any reason you worded it that way?"

"Well, I don't know if I should tell you this, but my uncle was an expert yachtsman, and I don't see how someone like that could have drowned when his boat was found afloat. And, of course, his body never *has* been found."

"Why shouldn't you tell me that?"

"Because you might get it into your head to investigate the life insurance policy my aunt is depending on. My uncle didn't leave her much else."

"Was it a large policy?" She certainly had a point.

"Well, that's a private matter, of course."

"Has he been declared dead?"

"Not yet, but it may happen soon. Tell me, Mr. Reese. You seem to think this Mr. Sullivan was killed because of his involvement with these smugglers, is that right?"

"Yes, I suspect so. He was killed just hours after I spoke to him, and by then a number of people would have known I was looking into the matter."

"Do you think it's possible whoever killed this Sullivan also killed my uncle?"

"And faked the accident? That's certainly possible. Do you think your uncle would be involved with a smuggling ring?"

"I wouldn't want to say that. But, while he was a thoughtful uncle, he did have a rather unsavory side. I shouldn't be telling you this, but I know he kept a mistress just up the street from the office."

"Actually, I knew about her. But what about his business dealings?"

"Not long after I arrived, my cousin, Charles Junior, alluded to that stock scandal. He was given a stern look and the subject was changed immediately, but he implied my uncle may have profited by it."

"It's certainly possible he was involved with the same people. But why would they want to have him killed?"

"Well, I think he may have needed money. The Elevator Company was failing, and money had been tight for some time. Maybe he was blackmailing the others involved?"

"I suppose that's a possibility." It seemed a little odd that barely a minute after she spoke disbelievingly of my story she was giving it an even more elaborate turn. And at her own uncle's expense.

"There's something else you should know. The Elevator Company has a life insurance policy on my uncle, which they are trying to collect on."

"Who's they? Is anyone left besides the General?"

"The creditors. The General has nothing to gain, but he has been trying to cover as many of the debts as possible. That's the main reason for keeping me on there. I'm supposed to hound the businesses that still owe the Elevator Company to pay their debts so it can pay its debts. Unfortunately, I'm not terribly good at hounding debtors."

"How much is that policy for?"

"Twenty thousand dollars."

"That's certainly a figure that motivates. Do you know who the policy is with?"

"I believe it's the Provident Insurance Company."

"Do you know who the Elevator Company's biggest debtors are? I mean, who would benefit most?"

"There was a second mortgage. I can't remember who it was with, but I can look it up back at the office."

"But wouldn't that mortgage be transferred to the new owner of the elevator?"

"I wouldn't know about that. The General says it's still outstanding." Then she asked, "If my uncle was killed because of something illegal involving the Elevator Company, would the insurance company have to pay?"

"Probably not. And certainly not if an officer of the company was participating in it. Why?"

"That's the sort of thing you investigate, isn't it?"

"Sure. But I'd need a little more to go on."

On the way back to the office, she bought the early edition of the afternoon paper so she could read about Danny. I walked her upstairs and said good-bye, but she stopped me before I could leave.

"Mr. Reese, why don't you have dinner with us this evening? It would give you a chance to meet my aunt and my cousin Charlie. He might be able to tell you about his father's law practice."

I accepted, but I thought it unlikely young Charlie would be willing to shed any light on the dark corners of the family's doings. I had the feeling Miss McGinnis was trying to misdirect me in some way. She said she needed to do some shopping that evening and asked me to meet her at seven o'clock at Lafayette Square. Before leaving, I reminded her about finding out who held that second mortgage. She seemed irritated by the suggestion that she needed reminding.

I wired Dan Ratigan from a Western Union office downstairs and then went by the Iroquois. I found Keegan in the billiard room passing the time until his wife's arrival. I related Miss McGinnis's information about her uncle and her theory about his disappearance.

"That seems a little theatrical. Isn't it more likely he faked his own death? Probably to share in the collection on the life policy his wife has?"

"Yes, that's what I was thinking. But he also had a mistress. What I need to find out is who else held life policies on Charles Elwell, who underwrote them, their value, and when they were written."

"So you're hoping the writers of these policies will pay you to prove he's alive?"

"Yes."

"But what about the Mason case we're paying you for?" He smiled.

Here I had to be careful. I wanted to keep both irons in the fire.

"I'm fairly certain the two are connected. If I find

41

one, either the second will be nearby, or the first will know where to find him."

That sounded plausible enough, so Keegan gave it his blessing and said he'd find out about the policies by six o'clock and leave an envelope at the desk for me. I felt a little bad about using what Miss McGinnis had provided me to the detriment of her family, but business is business, and there was little likelihood the experience could make her any more cynical than she was already.

6

The Tifft House was on Main Street just a block above Lafayette Square, so it seemed like a good time to visit Sadie Parker. The lobby was worn and dated, but you could tell it had once been a fine place. Probably during Grant's first term. I asked the clerk if Miss Parker was in.

He leaned behind a partition and shouted, "Hey, Timmy, did Becky have her breakfast yet?"

"Actually, it was Sadie Parker I was asking for."

"Yes, sorry, that's her. She's in. Room 323."

When Sadie let me in she was all breakfasted and dressed. Of course, it was 2:30 in the afternoon. She was quite shapely, with blond hair done up in an elaborate knot. While still fairly young, she was certainly no girl. The little suite was nothing grand, but had been made comfortable with many personal touches and it was obvious she had been there a while. We got through the pleasantries pretty quickly. I gave her my real name, but told her I was a former classmate of Robert Mason.

"I've been wanting to look Robert up and I happened to be passing through Buffalo, so I thought I'd see if I could find someone with a forwarding address."

"How did you come to call on me?"

"Well, Robert mentioned you in a letter several years ago. I hoped you might still be in touch with him." I could tell I wasn't very convincing.

"Were you on the Princeton crew with Robert? He was very proud of it."

"No, I was just part of the cheering section."

"I hope you could cheer better than you can lie—Mr. Reese, was it?"

"Yes, Reese, and no, I'm even worse at cheering. I suppose old Robert wasn't an oarsman?"

"No, but he told me he was nearly expelled for trying to fix a race once. And none of his friends ever called him Robert."

"But other than that, I had you going, right?"

"Oh, yes," she smiled. "Are you a policeman?"

"No, just an insurance investigator."

"Why are you looking for Mr. Mason now?"

"Well, actually, I'm looking for Mr. Elwell. I was just hoping that if I found Mr. Mason, he might be able to tell me where I could find Elwell." I wasn't sure if this made sense. But I was hoping she was angry with Elwell for not taking her with him, assuming, of course, he was alive.

"Mr. Elwell died in a yachting accident," she said emphatically. She enunciated the word yachting as if she wanted me to think she was born on one.

"How can you be sure?"

"Well, the police seem sure."

"Detective Donahy?"

"You know Jimmy Donahy?"

"Yes, I saw him just this morning when they were pulling Danny Sullivan's body out of the Commercial Slip."

"Who is, or was, Danny Sullivan?"

"A saloon owner, and a former associate of Mr. Mason's. I thought you might know him."

"I knew nothing about Mr. Mason's business associates. I'm sorry I can't help you, Mr. Reese, but I haven't seen Robert Mason since he left here three years ago."

"Or heard from him?"

"Or heard from him, either."

We went through another round of even less sincere pleasantries and I left her to whatever it is a widowed mistress does. Down at the desk I called over the clerk who had referred to Sadie as Becky and asked what it was about. He began to tell me, but a look from another, older clerk caused him to beg off. Apparently, gossiping about the inmates with outsiders was frowned upon at the Tifft House.

I then went to check in with Detective Donahy. Partly to see if they had found out who killed Sullivan, and partly to ask him why he had told Sadie that Elwell was definitely dead. He was in his office when I arrived.

"No, nothing on Sullivan yet. George has half a dozen men working with him now, but he needs to find someone other than a Sicilian who saw it. Those people close ranks something fierce."

"I saw Sadie Parker just now."

"How's she bearing up?" He chuckled.

"Oh, quite stoically. She told me you said Elwell definitely had drowned. But all you told me was that his boat had been found."

"Yeah, I thought you'd be back about that. I forgot you worked for an insurance company. You're thinking Elwell skipped and faked the accident so he could share in his own life insurance?"

"Well, I hate to think the worst of people, but the thought had crossed my mind."

"I had the same idea. Of course his wife had a policy, so I thought she might be in on something. Then I dug a little more and found out there was a policy naming Sadie. And not for peanuts: she gets twenty thousand dollars. So, naturally, I figured Sadie would happen to leave town in a few weeks, and if we could track her, we'd have Elwell."

"However, since Sadie is still here, you figured he must be dead?"

"No, it wasn't that Sadie hadn't left. You see, we found out Elwell *had* planned to skip. He arranged with this fellow who works at a lime kiln over in Canada to get him from the beach to the train station, and this fellow was also supposed to sink the boat. But Elwell never showed up, and a few days later, his boat was found adrift on the river."

"I was speaking with Elwell's niece about his accident and she didn't mention that."

"Well, we figured there wasn't much point in making him look like a crook in front of his family, or his friends. All it proved was that it really was an accident and he must've drowned."

"But you told Sadie?"

"Sure, why shouldn't she know the score? Only the ending was a surprise to her."

"What friends didn't you want to upset?"

"Well, he lived here a long time. He had a lot of friends."

He gave me the name of the man who Elwell had made the arrangements with and of the Buffalo firm that operated the lime kilns in Canada. Also, the name of the tug captain who found Elwell's boat.

"Is there any chance I can persuade you to come see the vault at the elevator site?"

"Sure, I was going to mention that myself. Let me make a call and I'll meet you downstairs in a few minutes."

Ten minutes later, Donahy joined me and we made our way down to the riverfront. We hailed a ferry and I had another adventurous ride to the island. But the vault was no more. I brought Donahy over and showed him the vault's concrete foundation, but he wasn't too impressed. Nor did he seem surprised the vault had vanished. I did find the little derrick over by the rail spur where it had been put into service. I also found a foreman still on the site, but not the one I had spoken with the previous morning. He knew nothing about anyone asking to preserve the vault and said they were told to clear everything down to the ground. He gave me the name of the salvage firm he worked for and then Donahy said he knew a saloon owner who might know something. We crossed over a railroad bridge to a bigger island and a block later arrived at an unnamed barroom.

As soon as we entered Donahy was greeted by the man behind the bar, as well as a dozen customers. The bartender filled a pitcher, grabbed three mugs, and led us to a small room in the back. Donahy introduced him as the owner, Michael O'Something, who had worked previously at one of the elevators. Then he told him about the smuggling idea.

"Well, I never heard of anything going on at the Eastern, but that doesn't mean it didn't happen."

"Did you know Danny Sullivan?" I asked.

"Sure, I knew him. I'll tell you this, if those wops hadn't gotten him, the micks would have. He annoyed a lot of women."

"An' even more husbands," Donahy added.

I outlined the scenario I had imagined, with the opium coming from Fort William in a steamer and being put on a canal boat to be taken down to New York.

47

"Damn, that sure sounds big time. I can't say I ever heard about anything like that. You can be sure there's plenty of opium that comes through here, but most of these guys ain't clever enough to come in with more than a few pounds. Then they sell it to one of the local China-men for half what it's worth. If that."

"But does it sound plausible?"

"Sure, I suppose. As long as no one talked about it. I guess the one thing that seems a little off is that they would need the same ship from Canada coming to the Eastern, and the same canal boat. That's not how it works. The ship that came to one elevator in one trip might go to a different port entirely on the next trip. Same with canal boats."

"But what if the captains of the boats and the super-intendent of the elevator were in on it?"

"Well, then it would be a lot easier, but still not a sure thing."

We left there and took the Michigan Street bridge back across the river. This brought us to Elk Street, just a block or two from Danny Sullivan's place.

"Let's go see if the boys've found out anything from Danny's friends," Donahy said.

At Danny's saloon there were two plain-clothes men interviewing people brought in by other cops. When we came in, one of them stood up and walked over and drew Donahy aside.

"It's okay, Mr. Reese can hear it too," Donahy said.

"We found a girl who followed Sullivan over to the Hooks. Her name's Rose Doyle. She says she saw the Sicilians run him through. Henafelt has her back at headquarters."

"Do you know the girl?" Donahy asked.

"The man on the beat does. He went to find her father."

"Let's go see what she has to say," Donahy said to me.

We arrived at headquarters just as Henafelt had finished taking a detailed statement from the girl. She was being escorted out as we entered the office. She was about sixteen and looked terrified. Donahy turned to the stenographer and asked him to read it all back.

He read: "I was waiting to see Danny, but I couldn't go near his saloon. So I waited down Elk Street. Sometime after midnight, Danny came out and walked toward me. I stopped him and asked him to take me with him. He said not tonight, and went on. When he was about a block away, I saw a man begin to follow him. So then I followed too, to warn Danny, but he was too far ahead of me now. Danny cut through the market, but the man following him didn't, so I thought maybe I was wrong. But then this man turned up Michigan Street, so I followed him. We turned down Perry Street, and I could see Danny up ahead of us. But now there were two men following him, on both sides of the street. When we came to Lake Street, one of the men following Danny whistled, two times, maybe three. By then Danny was at the little bridge into the Hooks, over the slip. Danny went up the bridge, slow, like he suddenly realized something was wrong. Then, three men were at the other side of the bridge. Maybe Danny saw them first. The first two men were just behind Danny now. I ran toward him, but one of these men turned on me and yelled something in Sicilian. He looked mean and angry and pointed back to where we'd come from. Then all the men were on top of Danny. They were hitting him. I just stood there. Danny fell into the water and the men all went off to the Hooks. I ran over to the side of the slip, but I couldn't see Danny. I didn't hear anything either. Then I went home. Everyone was asleep. I should have told, but I didn't. That's all."

"That girl's going to get a beating tonight," Donahy said.

"Yeah, no reason for her to make that up," Henafelt said. "Now all I have to do is find the five Sicilians. I'm hoping Danny bragged about the girl down on Elk Street and maybe someone knows her name. It ain't even worth asking any of the Sicilians about it. At least we know it wasn't Whitey Schuler, after all."

The last was directed at me, with a wink and a smile. I smiled back. No reason not to be civil, even if the mirth was at my expense. I thanked them and walked out.

In less than two hours all my leads on the smuggling case had been laid to rest. It seemed a little too pat. Yesterday, Donahy belittled the smuggling story. Today, he readily agrees to visit the site, where the vault has vanished. He makes a phone call before we leave his office, and the fellow at the saloon seems to be expecting him. And now Danny's killing is unquestionably tied to the Sicilians by a frightened girl. A girl who might just have been brought in for solicitation and told what to say in order to get back out on the street. A three-act burlesque, written and performed for my benefit.

It was now after five, so I walked up to the Iroquois to see what Keegan had found out about the policies on Elwell. The envelope was waiting for me and I sat down and read its contents in the lobby.

There were four policies on Elwell, each issued by a different company. The oldest was for fifteen thousand dollars and named his wife as beneficiary. The second was the policy Miss McGinnis mentioned, for twenty thousand dollars and naming the Elevator Company, taken out in 1895. These first two were typical of what you'd expect for a man like Elwell. The third was about a year and a half old, for twenty thousand dollars and naming Sadie Collins. I guess the Parker moniker wasn't legitimate enough. And finally, there was another naming his wife for fifteen thousand dollars taken out just this past April, a few months before he disappeared. Seventy thousand dollars altogether.

The thirty thousand for Mrs. Elwell wasn't unreasonable for the widow of an established lawyer. The last policy stood out a little because it was taken out not long before he disappeared, but there was nothing suspicious about the amount.

The policy naming Sadie was the big flag. Not many men provide a death benefit for a mistress. And the fact it was taken out over a year before he disappeared could just mean that they had planned the thing, and planned it well. Someone like Elwell would know a policy taken out a few months before his disappearance would only invite suspicion—and be easily contestable. But then why take out the second policy naming his wife just before he slipped away? Even more puzzling was why no one else was working on this. Keegan had added a contact at each of the four companies. I made out telegrams to all of them, saying I had reason to believe Elwell was alive and offering my services on the usual terms. I sent them off from a desk in the Iroquois.

By now it was half past five and I realized I'd need to rush back to McLeod's to bathe and change for dinner. I stopped by the desk on my way in to check for messages.

There was one, but it made no sense. It was a wire from Arthur Jenkins of the Provident Life Insurance Company. All it said was that they agreed to my terms. It wasn't possible he was responding to the telegram I'd sent just twenty minutes earlier. The only explanation I could think of was that Keegan had made an arrangement with them. But why wouldn't he have mentioned it in his note?

I arrived a little early for my rendezvous with Miss McGinnis, so I went back to the Tifft to see if the desk clerk I had spoken with earlier was still there. He was, and his boss was nowhere in sight.

"Back to see Miss Parker? I think she's out now."

"Actually, I came to see you. I wanted to ask about that Becky business. My curiosity's been killing me." I slipped him a silver dollar and it disappeared in a flash.

"She gets postcards from her brother and that's what he calls her, a pet name from when they were kids, I guess. So, we just picked it up from him."

"Her brother Charlie?"

"You thinking of Elwell? He doesn't need to write. I think the brother's name is James or Jonathan, something like that, but he just abbreviates it."

"Where are they from?"

"Oh, all over. The first ones were from out West, but the last couple were from Montreal, I think. He goes down south some, too. He's a drummer for Larkin, the soap company."

I thanked him and headed out to meet Miss McGinnis. As I waited, it occurred to me that the clerk's comment about Elwell was a little odd. If he thought Elwell was dead, why would he say he didn't *need* to write? It was as if he thought Elwell was alive and still nearby.

7

Miss McGinnis and I caught the same car line I had taken up to General Osgood's the night before. When we sat down I asked her if she had been able to locate anything about the holder of the second mortgage on the elevator.

"I did, but it's very odd. As far as I could tell, the mortgage came from the Magnus Beck Brewing Company. Doesn't that seem peculiar?"

"Yes, it does. But I guess a mortgage is just a loan, and it isn't so odd for one company to lend another money, especially if they have business with each other. Maybe the brewery stored barley or whatever they use at the elevator. Of course, it also may have been part of some scheme of Robert Mason's."

"Yes, that's what came to my mind. I called Magnus Beck and spoke with someone in their treasurer's office. He said the mortgage had been renegotiated as a loan secured by the company's accounts payable. That happened just before the default on the first mortgage."

We got off the car and headed in the same direction as the General's. But now I was seeing the neighborhood in the evening sunlight. Her uncle's place was just a few blocks down on Summer Street, yet we must have passed a dozen houses going up. Just as we approached the house, she stopped me.

"Mr. Reese, have you been in communication with the Provident Life Insurance Company?"

"Well, I sent them a telegram. Why?"

"But you haven't heard back?"

"No, I just sent it this evening." It suddenly occurred to me that Miss McGinnis was up to something and I had no intention of showing my cards. "Why do you ask?"

"Well, you see, I thought that if I could arrange for a reward, perhaps you could be persuaded to help prove Uncle Charles is dead. So I contacted the Provident Life Insurance people and said you had information that Uncle Charles had been murdered because of some scheme involving the Elevator Company, which would mean they wouldn't have to pay the policy. Perhaps you'll hear from them tomorrow."

Needless to say, I was a little put out. She was obviously using me, and I didn't like that one bit. But since I was using her in a similar way, I thought it was best to be charitable. "What sort of arrangement did you offer them?"

"You told me you had an arrangement to find Robert Mason for three hundred dollars. So, I thought that would be the correct amount."

"How about time and expenses?"

"You hadn't mentioned time and expenses." Then, with something having only a passing resemblance to sincerity, she added, "I hope I haven't created an awkward situation for you."

I couldn't really tell her how awkward without letting her know that I had just made an offer to prove her uncle was alive, thus impoverishing her aunt.

"Well, I generally like to have some awareness of the contracts I enter into, but it should be okay."

"What's the matter, afraid to have him meet the family?" A young, handsome, and smartly dressed fellow had come up to us.

"Oh, Charlie, this is Mr. Reese. Mr. Reese, my cousin, Charlie Elwell."

"Mother said you'd be bringing someone to dinner. Why are you keeping him out here?"

Charlie shooed us into the house. Inside, I was introduced to Aunt Nell, who didn't look much over forty, and Jack Whitner, a friend of the family. Whitner was in his thirties, and also a natty dresser. He was a tall man and had a neatly trimmed mustache. Then an older woman came into the parlor whom I took to be a servant, but who turned out to be Miss McGinnis's mother, visiting from Massachusetts. She was Aunt Nell's sister, but you would never have guessed it.

We were summoned in to dinner, and Mrs. McGinnis opened the conversation by telling us about a visit she had made to the botanic gardens. Then Aunt Nell asked how we had met. By now it was clear the family saw me as a prospect. I decided to allow Miss McGinnis to make up a story, and she did quite a job of it. She told them my cousin had been at college with her and that they had been very close. But it turned out she had lived at home during college and her mother was curious as to how she had never met this Miss Reese. So the story took a turn for the worse. Apparently, my cousin was forced to leave college before the first year was out, due to some trouble, the nature of which was left unstated. But the implication was clear enough. I didn't much like the fact my cousin had been besmirched in this way, but it did very effectively end that line of questioning, so I just mumbled something about poor cousin Carlotta. The table was silent for a bit, but young Charlie gallantly changed the subject to the upcoming horse races. The Grand Circuit trotters would be running in Fort Erie, just across the river in Canada. He and Jack, as Mr. Whitner asked me to call him, both had plans to attend. Then Mrs. McGinnis reminded her daughter that she had promised to go with her on an excursion that Sunday.

"You'd be most welcome to come along, Mr. Reese," Mrs. McGinnis said. She didn't seem at all put off by my family's reputation.

"Thank you, but I'm not sure I'll still be in town. Where does this excursion go?"

"To Chautauqua. We have a sort of Chautauqua back home, but I'm told this is the original."

"Yes, the real McCoy," I said. "I was there one summer as a boy. I was taken there by an aunt who was worried about my religious education. Carlotta's mother." The irony of this remark sat a little heavy in the air, so I tried to lighten things up a little by noting that being out on the lake at Chautauqua is quite pleasant this time of year. No luck.

Charlie jumped in again and asked me about life in New York. I told of the theaters, the restaurants, and, of course, the crime-ridden slums. For me personally, crime-ridden slums held little attraction. This was especially so since a recent visit had ended with my head connecting rather forcefully with a paving stone. But nothing enlivened a dinner conversation like a story or two about New York's underside. Anyone from outside the city was fascinated by the subject, and a certain segment of the upper and middle classes in New York took an almost civic pride in their slums. And when recounting a lurid tale of the slums, there was no need to hew to the truth. The greater the fiction, the more riveted the audience. If someone else familiar with the story offered a contradictory narrative, you merely needed to add, "Well, yes, that's what we were meant to believe."

When not thrilling the company with my colorful hokum, I spent my time trying to size up Aunt Nell. She appeared to be bearing the pain of widowhood pretty well. The only time her mood darkened a little was when Governor Roosevelt's name was mentioned. Aunt Nell was a fervent anti-imperialist.

The only one to even mention Uncle Charles's demise was Mrs. McGinnis, who was in town to console her sister. I guess she wasted the train fare, because Aunt Nell was quite gay the whole evening, as was Charlie. I couldn't make out what Jack Whitner's connection was exactly, but he seemed very friendly with both Charlie and Aunt Nell.

Miss McGinnis—Emmie to her family—was in a bit of a blue funk. She perked up a little during my account of the case that involved my head meeting up with the paving stone, but it was brief. Perhaps the resurfacing of Carlotta's woeful tale saddened her. Or, more likely, the dinner wasn't turning out as she had planned. I assumed she had intended to make me sympathetic to her aunt's plight. She had to have been a little disappointed by Aunt Nell's apparent good cheer.

After dinner Charlie, Jack, and I had a glass of port while coffee was prepared in the parlor. I took the opportunity to ask Charlie if I could stop by his office the next morning and he was agreeable, if a little puzzled. All he knew was that I had some connection to the insurance business. He probably feared I'd be trying to peddle a policy or two.

When we were all together in the parlor, someone suggested we have some music. Now, I can generally take things as they come. But when I find myself in a parlor after a somewhat awkward dinner and someone suggests Aunt So-and-so, or cousin Who's-it, entertain the company with a few songs, I get a sort of pain in my stomach. It doesn't matter how impressive the menu, or how superb the cooking, once those songbooks come out my digestion is just off. So I piped up.

"Or perhaps some cards?" I had the prerogative as a guest, so cards it was. Emmie said she would sit out and took her book to an armchair in the corner. Her mother said she would work on her knitting. We decided on whist, with Jack and me playing mother and son. As the game went on, I noticed there was something odd in how the other three spoke to each other—not that any of them was ever anything but charming. They just didn't act at all comfortable with one another, at least not like old friends would.

"Here it is, Mr. Reese." Mrs. McGinnis had set down her knitting and brought over the evening newspaper. She was showing me the entertainment page. Sure enough, a day trip to Chautauqua was advertised. Above it was an ad for a vaudeville house and a familiar name caught my eye.

"Why look, Miss McGinnis, cousin Carlotta is in town." Emmie looked up from her book with the same look of pained annoyance I'd seen the day we first met. I carried the newspaper over and showed her the ad. "You see? Or perhaps you weren't aware she had taken the stage name Cissie Lightner. Why don't we take in the show tomorrow evening?"

"Oh, yes, Emmie, you must go," her mother said. "It would be cruel not to see her."

"Why, yes, that would be lovely," she agreed. But the expression on her face hadn't softened much.

We soon finished our game of seven and I made some perfunctory excuses about needing to get back to the hotel. Then Jack stood up and said he would be running along as well. We said our good-byes and what-nots and headed over to the car line.

"Are you going downtown, Jack?"

"Yes, I'm staying at the Iroquois."

"Oh, I thought you lived in town here."

"No, I have some business that's kept me here for several weeks."

"How is it you know the Elwells?"

"I was an old friend of Charlie Senior. He disappeared just before I arrived. Since then I've gotten to know his wife and son. They've been most hospitable."

"Yes, delightful people."

He also lived in New York and traveled frequently, so we chatted about that on the ride down. When we got off the car together I told him I was stopping by the Iroquois to meet a business associate. As we entered the hotel, we ran into Keegan and his wife. There was a brief moment when Whitner and Keegan seemed to recognize each other. I made introductions and then both Whitner and Mrs. Keegan left us to go to their rooms. Once we were alone, I told Keegan about Miss McGinnis's communication with the Provident Life Insurance Company.

"Well, Harry, I'm reluctant to say it, but I think you've been outmaneuvered."

"Yes, it does look that way, but I'm not sure what her real motive is. By the way, did you recognize Whitner?"

"I, well, yes, I think I did. But I'm not sure why. What was his name?"

"Jack Whitner. I just met him this evening."

"Maybe I've come across his photograph. Is he from New York?"

"Yes, he is. I suppose it's unlikely you met him socially?"

"No, I don't think so."

He said good night and then went up to his room. If Keegan recognized a man from a photograph, it was fair to assume the gentleman had some flaws in his character. Keegan made it a point to know his opponents—the grafters and bunco men who made a habit of defrauding insurance companies. And if Whitner actually recognized Keegan, he was something more than the usual defrauder of insurance companies. I went over to the desk and asked for Jack Whitner's room, just to see if he was really registered. He was, Room 512. Whitner didn't seem the type to turn in for the night at ten minutes past ten, so I decided to see if he might go out again. I went out to the street and found a place where I could watch the two main entrances to the hotel. It had begun to rain, but luckily I didn't need to wait long. Whitner came out and went up Main Street and then into the Tifft House, Sadie's abode.

He didn't stop at the desk, but went right over to the elevator. I went up the stairs, charging up the last flight, and waited behind a corner on the third floor. Whitner came out of the elevator and went right to Sadie's door. He didn't need to look at the room numbers to find his way, and was admitted without introduction.

I started downstairs, but before I was halfway down, Whitner passed me in a big hurry. He must not have recognized me from behind. He ran out the front door and I followed at a discreet trot. When I got to the street he was already on the other side.

"Why, hello there." Charlie Elwell was just beside me. "Are you staying at the Tifft?"

"No, just checking on a friend."

"Yes? Me too."

"Say, it's nice seeing you, but I really need to get going. I'll be stopping by your office in the morning."

"Oh, right. Well, good night."

Charlie went into the Tifft House and I scanned the street for a sign of Whitner. I spotted him a block ahead, going back down Main Street. He was walking now, so I was able to follow him easily. After a few blocks we turned west, then south again. Whitner was still about a block ahead, but I realized there was someone between us making the same turns. When we turned east and then north, I realized we had gone in a circle. Whitner had spotted one or both of us. He returned to the Iroquois and I decided to follow the other man. He led me over to Washington Street and then down several blocks. Just opposite Carroll Street, he rapped on a glass door and waited. It had stopped raining and he took off his hat to shake water from it. His blond head looked strikingly like Whitey Schuler's. Someone let him in and I walked by to find out where he was visiting. It was the rear entrance of the Courier Building. Then I remembered Donahy saying Fingy Conners owned a newspaper.

I felt as if I had spent the last half hour in one of Emmie's dime novels. A drink seemed to be in order, so I availed myself of the McLeod's inexpensive, if somewhat seamy, taproom. I can't say it helped much. After the third beer I was as puzzled as when I started. If Whitner was working the insurance game with Sadie, the first explanation that came to mind was that they had collaborated in killing Charles Elwell. Because if Elwell was alive and Sadie planned to meet up with him, why bring Whitner into it? On the other hand, if Sadie and Whitner had killed Elwell, it would have been wisest for him to leave town and stay away until she received her death benefit. What would be the point of taking a room in an expensive hotel and making friends with Aunt Nell and Charlie? He must have another game going, with or without Sadie's awareness. I could think of only one solution that could account for all of that: Whitner knew Elwell was still alive and assumed either his wife or Sadie was conspiring with him. He was waiting to blackmail whomever it turned out to be. In the meantime, he was spending his time keeping track of the two. It made sense, but the one thing it didn't explain was why Whitey Schuler was following Whitner.

When I went out to the lobby, the clerk handed me a package an express company had just delivered. Up in my cell, I found it contained Keegan's files on Robert Mason. Nothing was more current than the year before, and most of it was just copies of policies that had paid out and official reports. No recent photographs, addresses, or associates, or anything else that might be useful—outside of the fact he had family in several small towns across the state.

8

On the way to Charlie's office the next morning, I managed to solve another little puzzle. It was Sadie he had gone to visit at the Tifft House the night before. He must have taken up where his father had left off. That would explain the desk clerk telling me that Charlie Elwell wouldn't need to write. I'd been referring to Charles Senior, but he was talking about young Charlie. It also would explain why Jack Whitner rushed out of Sadie's room just after arriving: she must have told him she was expecting Charlie at any moment.

Charlie had a position with a law firm in the Largest Office Building in the World. After a brief wait I was led down one corridor and then another. He had a small office on the air shaft, but it beat any office I'd ever had. He welcomed me with a friendly handshake and we sat down.

"First of all, I wanted to let you know why I'm in town." I had settled on a story that didn't rely too heavily on deceit and at the same time didn't reveal too much. "You see, I'm working with some insurers trying to locate Robert Mason."

"Robert Mason? He's been gone quite a while now."

"Yes, but last week's fire at the Eastern has brought to light some new information that might aid us in locating him."

"Really? What sort of information?"

"It looks like Mason had been running a smuggling ring using the elevator as a base."

"Well, that wouldn't surprise anyone. From what I've heard, Mason was a man who was always up to something. My father was often telling me stories."

"Given your father's position at the company, didn't he object?"

"No, he found it quite amusing. My father wasn't one to be overly concerned with ethics himself. "

"Do you think your father would have been mixed up in a smuggling operation?"

"No, no. At least not directly. But he wouldn't be terribly troubled at the idea."

"Is that why you didn't join your father's firm?"

"My father wasn't a partner with a firm. He had his own practice, on the same floor as the Elevator Company. Frankly, some of his work was a little sordid. He came from Buffalo's rough and tumble era and he couldn't expect me to relive that."

"Do you think his equivocal attitude applied to the stock scheme as well?"

"He insisted that he lost money when the stock collapsed."

"Did you believe that?"

"I know he owned common shares that did lose value. But I also know there were suspicions he was involved. All I know for certain is that no profits from it ever came into our household."

"Did you like your father?"

"Except for how he treated my mother, sure. You couldn't help but like him. Everyone liked him. But Mother, of course."

"I did notice that your mother didn't seem very upset over his disappearance. One might almost call it indifference."

"Oh, no, Mother's not indifferent. She's much happier now. I don't mean happy he died, just relieved the charade is over. Home life was a bit of a strain for both of them the last few years." He paused. "But why do you use the word disappearance? The authorities are sure he died in the storm."

"Sorry. To an insurance company someone isn't dead until a medical examiner or a court says so. But given your depiction of his character, don't you think there's some chance your father merely staged the accident?"

"Oh, I definitely thought so at first. But what would he have gained? He wasn't on the run from anything. He had debts, but nothing monumental."

"Well, what if he had an accomplice carrying a life insurance policy on him?"

"My mother, you mean. But if he succeeded in faking the death and she received the benefit, why would she share the payment with him? You see, I did think of that."

"Are you aware of any other policies on his life?"

"No, just the two naming my mother as beneficiary. Is there another?"

"The Elevator Company has a policy on him."

"Yes, I did know that. But that's not unusual. And you can be sure General Osgood wouldn't commit fraud to help out my father."

"Have you petitioned yet to have your father declared dead?"

"No, it was suggested to me that we should wait several months."

I didn't like that. That might mean no claims on the insurance had been made. "Getting back to the Elevator

Company, would you know anything about a mortgage they had with a brewer, Magnus Beck?"

"A mortgage with Magnus Beck? No, but I imagine it was one of my father's dealings. Magnus Beck is owned by William Conners."

"Is that Fingy Conners?"

"Yes, but never use that sobriquet anywhere near him." Charlie smiled. "You see, Conners came up the hard way, and he can be pretty crass. Most of the old guard in town snubbed him, but not my father. He had his faults, but he wasn't the type to think less of a man because he didn't know the purpose of all eight pieces of silver at his place setting."

Eight? I'd have to puzzle over that later. "And Mr. Conners also owns the *Courier*?"

"Yes, the *Courier*, the *Express*, the brewery, a steamship line, and, of course, the street paving business. Conners does very well on contracts with the city."

"So he was a good friend for your father to have?"

"Oh, yes. I imagine most of father's business came from Conners. But they had a bit of a falling out last year. The grain scoopers went on strike against the racket Conners had set up, then the other dock workers backed them. It completely tied up the elevators and the owners wanted a settlement. You see, they were already paying the wages the scoopers were demanding, it's just that Conners and the others were taking a large part of it before it got to the men who earned it. The Eastern Elevator Company missed a couple of mortgage payments during the strike and they were never able to make it up."

"But wasn't the Elevator Company just a side-line for your father?"

"Yes, but he had always told me he was counting on selling his share to provide for his retirement. I think he was angry with Conners for ruining his business, and Conners was angry with him for helping to undermine his racket. But I don't know how deep that anger went."

"I see. Tell me, how well do you know Jack Whitner?"

"Jack Whitner? Not well at all, really. He's an old friend of Father's who stopped by to see him. This was a few weeks ago, after Father's accident, but he hadn't heard. Since then we've seen him several times. Mother seems to enjoy his company. Why do you ask about Jack?"

"Oh, just curiosity. So you knew him previously?"

"No, I'd never heard of him. But I think Mother may have met him earlier."

I ran out of questions, so I thanked him for his time and he said it was quite all right.

"But I do have one question of my own. Do you really have a cousin named Carlotta? I can never tell with Emmie."

"Oh, yes, and we'll be seeing her this evening."

I headed back to McLeod's to see if there were any responses to the wires I'd sent the day before. All four companies had responded. The first three, regarding the two policies naming Aunt Nell and the other naming Sadie, were identical: no claim had been made on the policy. The Provident Life Insurance Company seemed somewhat annoyed. My wire to them and their response to Emmie's must have crossed paths. It appeared to them I'd made two contradictory proposals in the space of an afternoon. Their response read: "Have accepted your previous offer. $300 for evidence sufficient for denial of claim, no per diem or expenses. A deal is a deal."

I found this all a little unsettling. Here I was, confident I could solve the disappearance of a man with seventy thousand dollars in life insurance. But I had no way to profit from it beyond three hundred dollars—not even one half of one percent. I couldn't afford to wait around Buffalo until Aunt Nell and Sadie made their claims. And if I solved it before then, there wouldn't be any claims. But then, three hundred dollars was three hundred dollars.

The only lead Charlie had offered me was that his father's office was near the Elevator Company's. I decided to pay Emmie a visit and see if she could access it. I surprised her by entering without knocking. And she likewise surprised me—she was actually typing a letter.

"It's my weekly dunning. I try to make each letter sound more ominous than the last, but I'm afraid I've exhausted my rhetorical skills as a bill collector. Now they just sound rather silly."

"Have you tried threatening bodily harm?"

"The old paving stone to the head?"

"It's crude, but very effective."

"I'll save that for the next round."

"By the way, I had a nice chat with Charlie this morning."

"Really, what about?"

"Oh, this and that. Mostly about his father. He mentioned your uncle's law office was near this one."

"Yes, it's right next door."

I was going to need to humor her. "Well, it occurred to me there might be something in there to connect your uncle to the smuggling. And if we establish a connection, it may provide a clue as to who had him murdered."

"Then you do agree that it's likely someone had him killed?"

"Well, I'd say it's a strong possibility."

"I've been giving it a great deal of thought and I believe I have the outline of their plan. First, they kill my uncle. Perhaps he tried to blackmail them. But if the body is found, the method of the killing would point to the murderers somehow. So they hide the body and take out my uncle's boat and make it look as if he'd been caught in the storm and drowned. But without a body, it might not be believed. So they've cunningly stored the body somewhere in the lake, or a canal. After a few months, they retrieve it and have it wash up on shore. Now the death is confirmed, but the cause is obscured by the months of deterioration."

"I see." I didn't really see at all, but I thought it best to play along. "So all we need to do is find out where they're storing the body?"

"I hadn't thought of that."

"Or, perhaps our first step is to find out who the murderers are."

"Yes, that would make the rest much easier. So you want to search my uncle's office?"

"That would seem a logical next step." At least I didn't need to argue the case.

She pulled a small key ring out of a drawer and in getting up knocked her book on the floor. I bent down and picked it up for her. It was Thackeray's *Vanity Fair*, complete with Robert Mason's autograph. I flipped through it quickly and handed it to her. She made sure her place was still marked and set the book on her desk. Then she led me down the hall and to a door with "Charles Elwell, Esq." painted on it. A door I'd walked by five times previously and hadn't noticed. I was never a man for details.

There was an outer office and two inner offices, the same layout as the Elevator Company's. Elwell's office held his desk and shelves of law books, but not much else. It also had its own door to the corridor. I was hoping Emmie would leave me to go through things myself, but this was obviously going to be a shared endeavor. The problem was that she was looking for some connection to the local underworld, and I was looking for something quite different. We went through the desk together and found nothing that interested either of us so we went on to the next office. This looked to be a clerk's room, with a large desk and shelves of law books from floor to ceiling. We made another joint search and again found nothing of note, beyond the fact that the former occupant had used a particularly fragrant cologne.

Then we rifled the two desks in the outer office—nothing. This left just the files. I suggested she start on the correspondence while I looked through the legal and financial records. Both tasks were formidable, as Elwell had been in practice for thirty-odd years.

Elwell's practice was mainly commercial—articles of incorporation, contracts, claims, etc. But before she was even out of the A's, Emmie had a long list of clients involved in criminal cases. There was a concert saloon owner accused of procurement, a number of fraud cases, several assaults, and one murder. The last occupied her for some time, and I began to realize that she had a weakness for the sensational. But she finally agreed there was little chance that Uncle Charles was involved in a man's strangling of his mother-in-law.

Meanwhile, I dug through the financial records. I

was hoping to find some trace of assets he had kept hidden from his family. It was slow going, but from the bit I saw everything here was business-related. Uncle Charles didn't have a lot of assets. I imagined keeping Sadie in the Tifft House was his principal investment outside of the elevator.

Then Emmie cried, "Eureka"—figuratively, anyway. She had come across a saloonkeeper in the C's who was accused of smuggling Chinamen into the United States. It was fairly recent, and probably the case the boys at the customs office had told me about. The name was Henry Croteau. He owned a saloon on Canal Street and had been arrested in March on a charge of aiding and abetting the illegal entry of Chinamen.

"Croteau is a French Canadian name," she said knowingly.

"Is it?"

"Yes, there were Croteaus in Massachusetts. And you said the opium came from Canada."

"And the saloon is on the canal, providing convenient storage for bodies," I smiled.

"I don't think it's at all silly to think someone involved with smuggling Chinamen would also be a smuggler of opium. And your tale of a secret smugglers' den in the grain elevator, and of Sicilians knifing to death the only one knowing about it, is no less fantastic than mine."

There was something to her argument, but I didn't say so.

"We should go down there tonight," she said.

"Tonight? Where exactly is Canal Street? You've got so many canals here."

"There's a map in the city directory."

She went back to the Elevator office for the directory. While she was gone, I took the opportunity to slip into Elwell's private office and unlatch the door to the corridor.

When she returned, she spread the map on the desk. Croteau's was listed as a concert saloon on Canal Street, which the map showed was just beyond the Erie.

"Isn't that area what they call the Hooks?" I asked.

"The Hooks?"

"Yes, don't you keep track of your own crime-ridden slums?"

"Well, I knew the area below the canal was considered a rough sort of neighborhood. The Hooks, is it?"

I could see that supplying her with the colorful name of the place made her want to visit it all the more. I tried to dampen her enthusiasm. "Yes, and they play with knives there."

"We must pay a visit to Croteau's saloon tonight."

"You seem to forget, we're going to the theater to see cousin Carlotta."

"Mr. Reese, I apologize for giving you a fallen woman as a cousin. But what's the point of pretending this invention of mine is on the stage?"

"Oh, Carlotta's real enough. And Cissie Lightner is her stage name. I didn't know she was in town, but you're the one who brought her up."

"How could I bring up someone I had never heard of?"

"I meant to ask you about that. I'll tell you what, we'll go see dear Carlotta's show tonight, but we can dine beforehand at Croteau's. With a name like that, I imagine they have an extensive wine cellar. That way we can be out of the Hooks before dark."

Then the door opened behind us.

"Oh, it's you, Emmie. And Mr. Reese."

Aunt Nell had caught us in the act of searching her husband's office. There were a number of plausible explanations we could have provided. Unfortunately, none of these presented themselves to Emmie.

"Mr. Reese was in need of a dentist, and I thought perhaps I could find the name of the one who attended Uncle Charles. But I couldn't."

"Oh, I'm sorry, Mr. Reese. It's Dr. Freed, on Washington Street. Just a few blocks from here. Are you in pain?"

"No, it's nothing really. Just a little crack or something in the back there." I pointed toward the back of my jaw. Aunt Nell seemed to accept this as justification for our rifling through her husband's records. Or at least she pretended to. Emmie locked up the office and we all went into the Elevator Company's.

"I came to ask you to lunch, Emmie. You're welcome to come too, Mr. Reese."

"I can't, Aunt Nell, I have an engagement with a classmate of mine. In fact, I should be running along."

"How about you, Mr. Reese? Can you stand to eat?"

"Oh, I'm always up for a meal."

"I meant, will your tooth allow it?"

"Oh, that. Well it comes and goes, and it seems to have gone for the present."

9

I was glad that I'd be able to speak with Aunt Nell alone. But once again I found myself in that precarious situation of accompanying a lady to luncheon at a place of her choosing, at the end of which I would have to graciously insist on paying. Once again, we walked toward the Iroquois. But this time there was no reprieve. The Iroquois it was. There was nothing to be done now but enjoy the meal and hope Aunt Nell wasn't feeling ravenous.

After we were seated, she asked me about my work and I told her that I was in town trying to track down Robert Mason, the same partial truth I'd told Charlie earlier.

"So it was just a coincidence that you ran into Emmie?"

"Yes, we were both surprised."

"How do you hope to find Mr. Mason after all this time?"

"I have several leads, but frankly it's more difficult than I expected."

"Do you know where he went when he left Buffalo?"

"No, no one seems to. I don't suppose your husband ever conjectured about it?"

"If he did, he wouldn't have told me. Of course, you know about Miss Parker."

"Yes, but she wasn't particularly forthcoming."

"Well, for a woman like that, discretion is essential." Aunt Nell spoke of her husband's mistress as if she were someone in a novel. "Tell me about your cousin. Is she really in the theater?"

"Oh, yes. Well, vaudeville. She and a partner do the standard song-and-dance routine."

"Is she talented?"

"Not really. She can dance reasonably well, but her voice is really rather annoying. Fortunately, a squeaky voice can be an asset if you're trying to keep the crowd laughing."

Aunt Nell smiled. "I was on the stage once."

"Really? Here in Buffalo?"

"No, not in Buffalo. Little towns. I'm kidding you, really. It wasn't the stage. It was one of those traveling shows where they amuse the farmers and then sell them patent medicine." She paused to see how I would react. "I had a pony act."

It was my turn to smile. "Are you part Kickapoo?"

"No, this was before the Kickapoos. We sold Doctor Glossheim's Authentic German Cure. I had this elaborate costume, which I thought was the height of fashion. I didn't really have to do much of anything. The pony did a number of tricks and then I took the bows. It was certainly a great deal more fun than living on the farm."

"You grew up on a farm?"

"Yes, a New England hill farm. I loved it—until I was about thirteen or so. Then you start to wonder about the places you've learned about in school. Or you go to the fair and see how other people dress, and the things they can buy. At sixteen, a girl can see her future. You either are going down to the mills, like Emmie's mother, or you're going to marry into another hill farm."

"Or you join a medicine show?"

"Yes," she laughed. "Or you join a medicine show.

This one had come into town and of course we all went to the free shows. I befriended the pony and the medicine man asked me if I wanted to join the act that evening. I was a pretty girl, and I knew how to take care of the pony. That's all the job required. So when they left town, I did too."

"How long were you with them?"

"Just over a year. By then I had had enough of being a young girl with a crew of misfits and grafters. We were on the outskirts of Buffalo. One morning I took the pony and just started walking. I don't know what I had in mind. I was arrested for stealing the pony and Charles Elwell was the prosecutor. It's really a fantastic tale. Charles became my savior—he even bought me the pony. We were married soon after."

"Very romantic."

"Oh, yes. Emmie loves the story."

"Do you miss your husband, Mrs. Elwell?"

"What an odd question, Mr. Reese. I suppose I do, but not as I would have ten years ago. Why do you ask that?"

I wasn't sure myself. I had wanted to change the subject, but I wished I had done it more adroitly. "I'm sorry, I guess I was caught up in the sentiment."

"Charles and I were no longer very close, for whatever reason. He was always a selfish man, but became ever more so."

"Do you have any doubts as to what happened to him?"

"You mean, do I think he staged his disappearance?"

"Yes, I guess that's what I mean."

"No. Not that he wouldn't have if he could have derived some advantage from it. I just don't see how he could have. He often went out on the boat by himself. And there's nothing surprising about storms coming up quickly on the lake. Are you thinking that he might be wherever Robert Mason is?"

"Yes, or that he might know where Mason is."

"That I doubt. They were not friends and I don't think they would have confided in each other."

"How well do you know Jack Whitner?"

"We just met a few weeks ago. He knew Charles some years ago."

"But do you recall if your husband ever mentioned the name?"

"Not that I remember. Do you doubt his story?"

"No, just curious."

"Well, he knows things about Charles that would be difficult for anyone but a friend to find out. And I think Charlie had met him when he was away at school."

"I have one last question. What happened to the pony?"

"Oh, we had Freddie for years. Charlie rode him as a boy."

We had finished lunch and dear Aunt Nell had eaten like the proverbial bird. Not even two dollars, with the tip. I waited with her for a street car and she told me to be sure to visit them again before I left town. I said I would.

I realized I hadn't agreed on a meeting place with Emmie so I walked up to her office to leave her a note. The door was unlocked, and there she was with her nose in Thackeray's fat book. She was surprised to see me, but showed no shame for having deceived us.

"Well, I guess you do prefer that book to my company."

"Oh, I thought you understood. I just wanted to give you the opportunity to question Aunt Nell. She couldn't be as frank if I were there."

Emmie was never at a loss for an explanation.

"About her pony act?"

"About Uncle Charles."

"You know, Miss McGinnis, I am acquainted with that book, and you're beginning to remind me of the heroine."

"You seem to forget, Mr. Reese, this is a novel without a hero. But I hope you aren't referring to poor Emmy Sedley, the soft."

"I was thinking of the not-at-all-soft Becky Sharp."

"I'm surprised, Mr. Reese. Have you read much of Thackeray?"

"Oh, I never said I read the book. You may have heard, last year Mrs. Fiske produced the play *Becky Sharp*."

"Yes, I read about that. So you gained your knowledge of the book from the play?"

"Well, not directly. It was impossible to get tickets to Mrs. Fiske's show on the night we chose for our foray. But there was another show running nearby which we'd heard good things about. I believe it was called *Around New York in Eighty Minutes*."

"So you saw this timeless classic of literary drama instead?"

"Yes. But, you see, this timeless classic included a burlesque of Mrs. Fiske's show. So, I have the nub of Thackeray's effort."

"My, Mr. Reese, you are a true gentleman of culture," she smiled.

Our literary romp brought something else to mind:

Ratigan's list of profiteers. One or two of the names had sounded familiar, and now I felt I knew why. I had left the list back at my room, but I did remember one name.

"There's an Osborne in the book, isn't there?" I asked.

"Yes, George Osborne, the cad poor Emmy marries."

"One of the aliases used by those profiting from the stock scheme was G. Osborne."

"Couldn't that just be a coincidence?"

"Yes, but there's someone who has nicknamed Sadie Parker Becky, and I think it's Mason."

This left her a little puzzled, so I told her all about visiting Sadie, and that Sadie had been Mason's mistress before being her uncle's. And that the last postcards addressed to Becky were from Montreal.

"And since the book is Mr. Mason's, you assume these postcards are coming from him. That's excellent, Mr. Reese."

Frankly, I found it somewhat less convincing coming from Emmie, but she had guessed my train of thought.

"I don't suppose we'll find him by looking for Robert Mason, late of Buffalo, in the Montreal city directory," she said. "He must be using another alias, and it seems more than likely that it's a name from the same book."

"The desk clerk thought they were signed with some abbreviation, maybe for James or Jonathan."

"Or perhaps Jos? Jos Sedley."

I'm not sure why, but the more enthusiastic she became, the more I found myself doubting my own theory.

"How would we find a Jos, or Joseph, Sedley in Montreal?" she asked.

"Well, apparently he's constantly traveling, so the best bet would be to check the hotels."

"How do we do that?"

"We don't. But I know someone who could, and he's staying here in town," I said. "By the way, Miss McGinnis. Are you planning to go home and dress for the evening?"

"I hadn't decided. Why?"

"Well, it's only that the ladies I've seen in concert saloons tend to dress more... I'm not sure how to phrase it... showy, perhaps."

"Do you mean gaudy?"

"Let's say showy tending toward gaudy."

"Very well. I'll go home and find something appropriate. Perhaps Aunt Nell's outfit from her medicine show days would do."

"Oh, yes," I agreed. "I'll look into renting a pony."

We settled on a time and place to meet that evening and I assured her I would see to it that the hotels of Montreal were combed thoroughly. I went back to the Iroquois to hunt down Keegan. He was out, so I left a message saying I'd been informed that Mason had recently been in Montreal traveling as Jos or Joseph Sedley, and asking if he could have the hotels there checked.

In the meantime, I could look further into Elwell's disappearance. Detective Donahy had given me the names of the tug captain who found the boat and the man whom Elwell had paid to help stage his accident.

The tug company had an office on one of the slips off the Erie Basin, which was on the lakefront. The captain I was looking for was out towing barges but would be docking later that afternoon in Black Rock, a small port at the northern end of the city. So I went in search of Elwell's co-conspirator. He worked for a business located along the Erie Canal just a short ways from the tug office.

The W. E. Carroll Company seemed to consist primarily of piles of sand and lime. There were also a couple of small buildings, one of which held the office where I found William Carroll. He was barely distinguishable from the men working in the yard, being likewise covered in dust. I told him I was checking on Elwell's story and wanted to speak with Steuben, the man Elwell had made his arrangements with.

"He's long gone. I let him go when he came in with that story. I can't have my people running schemes like that on my time, and on my property."

"What exactly had they planned?"

"According to Steuben, this fellow Elwell approached him at our site on the Canadian shore. We have some lime kilns there, and we also load sand from the dunes. There's a fairly long pier and I imagine that's what attracted Elwell. Steuben said Elwell offered him three hundred dollars if he would get Elwell from the pier to the railroad station at Sherkston. Then Steuben was supposed to take Elwell's yacht out onto the lake and sink it. According to Steuben, Elwell was skipping town, but wanted people to think he had drowned in the lake."

"Does the story seem plausible to you?"

"Well, it was plausible that Steuben would become involved in something like that. He did his work, but was always a little too clever. I never liked him. But the rest of it never made a lot of sense to me. First off, why would Elwell involve someone he barely knew? Why not just sink the boat himself, row a dinghy to shore, and walk to the train station? There's a lot of empty shoreline over there where no one would see a thing. And the train station's just a couple miles inland. And another thing—

what made Elwell think Steuben could sail his yacht out onto the lake?"

"But if the story wasn't true, why tell it? He must have known you'd be likely to fire him."

"Yeah, that's a good question. My guess is he thought he could come across some reward from someone. But I can't say I spent much time thinking about it."

"The police seem to have believed Steuben's story."

"Did they? Well, maybe there was something more to it I didn't know about."

I thanked Carroll and before leaving asked for directions to the yacht club. The Buffalo Yacht Club was located at the foot of an old fort which was called The Front. I found a fellow mending a sail and asked about Elwell. He pointed out a Mr. Benson and said he was a friend of Elwell's. Benson was lackadaisically polishing parts of his boat and sipping beer. I introduced myself and jumped right into it.

"Was Charles Elwell a good sailor?"

"Oh, yes. Almost as good a sailor as I am," he said with a wink.

"Then was it a mistake for him to go out on an evening like the one he did? With a chance of a storm?"

"If you never went out when there was a chance of a storm, you wouldn't get out much. Maybe it was the one day he had free. I'll bet several boats were out that evening."

"But no others were lost."

"No, but that doesn't mean much. Maybe he was out farther on the lake, or maybe there was a local swell. There's no way of knowing."

"But weren't you surprised a good sailor was lost like that? While his boat was still afloat?"

"The boat was probably heeling and a wave caught him while he was hiked out. Or maybe he had to stand up to untangle a line or something. Or maybe the mast hit him on the head when it cracked in half. And if you get knocked off a boat in a storm, it's damned hard to get back on without someone to throw you a line."

"Couldn't he have swum to shore?"

"If you're two miles out in a storm, swimming to shore would be a minor miracle. Was I surprised it happened to Charles Elwell? Sure. But it just proves it could happen to anyone."

"Is that where the tug found the boat, two miles out?"

"No, it was out on the river, the Niagara. But that's just where the current took it. You see, all of Lake Erie empties into the Niagara, then goes over the falls."

"So it isn't odd there's no sign of the body?"

"The body probably went over the falls and has been washing up on the shores of Lake Ontario in bits and pieces."

Mr. Benson wasn't particularly sentimental about his old friend. I thanked him and left him to his work. I didn't see any point in looking up the tug captain now, so I decided to walk the towpath back. If Benson was correct, it was possible Elwell *was* just lost in a storm. But it didn't explain why Steuben had come forward with his obviously tall tale. Or why the police had put any faith in it.

The only explanation I could think of was that Elwell had paid Steuben—not to help him make his escape, but just to tell the story. Then Elwell did just what Carroll suggested: rowed to shore in a dinghy and walked to the train himself. He knew everyone would suspect he had faked the accident. Steuben's story was meant to satisfy their suspicions. He wanted it to look like he had indeed planned to sneak off, but by pure chance got caught in a storm and drowned. The story wouldn't hold up if someone looked too closely, but no one in Buffalo wanted to look closely. If he were dead Aunt Nell and Sadie would get their insurance money, Boss Conners would get his loan repaid, and the police could ensure everyone's happiness just by doing nothing.

I wound my way back to the Iroquois. Keegan had left me a note saying he had initiated inquiries but wouldn't be hearing back before the next afternoon. Then it occurred to me to check back at the Tifft to see if Sadie had received any more missives. My friend the clerk was there, but he couldn't place me until I handed over another silver dollar. That dollar was the price of finding out that no, there hadn't been any cards that day. But I got him to agree to make a copy of any that did come addressed to Becky.

It was after five o'clock now and I was meeting Emmie at seven. I went up to the office to make sure she had left. Then I slipped into Elwell's private office through the door I'd unlocked earlier.

I began looking through the financial records beginning where I had left off that morning. It took an hour to plow through them and I found nothing. There were also copies of the invoices his office had sent out, and the receipt books, but I didn't see any point in looking there. Finally, I found the check registers, which dated back twenty-odd years. I began with the most recent and worked backwards. Most of these were for payment on the invoices I'd already looked through. But there were also a number made out to cash, and sometimes for significant amounts. While I was in the book for 1897, I realized there was one amount that kept appearing: $123.56. These entries were spaced about a month apart and all were made out to cash. I continued the search back, and then looked again at the more recent years to see if I had overlooked any entries for the same amount. They began in early 1893 and ended in August 1897.

Based on the odd amount and regularity, I guessed these might be mortgage payments. Almost five years worth. If they were on his own home, they most likely would have come from a personal account. And there wouldn't be any reason to make them payable to cash. The only reason to make them out to cash was to hide the payee from others in the office. If it was a loan at, say, 6 percent, the principal would have been close to $25,000—the cost of a small commercial building, or a very sizable home. A lot larger than his place in Buffalo. The loan appeared to have been paid off not long after the profits from the stock scheme would have been realized. This cinched it for me. Elwell had set himself up in some other city, almost definitely under another name. Some of the other checks to cash were probably deposits to a bank in that city. But what city?

10

I didn't have time to go back to the hotel and change, but I figured a soiled collar and a well-dusted suit would fit right in at Croteau's saloon. Emmie was waiting for me at the Liberty Pole on the corner of Main and Exchange. She had certainly found something showy to wear. And it wasn't merely tending toward gaudy, it was most of the way there.

It was a short walk to the Hooks and Croteau's, but there was a marked change in the neighborhood. Most of the buildings were old two- or three-story tenements, along with a few small stores and a very healthy number of saloons. The tenements appeared to be mostly occupied by Italians, or Sicilians, as I'd been told. The men loitered about and their children were playing in the side streets. The saloons along Canal Street were peopled by itinerant men who worked on the canal and the steamboats.

The only way we found Croteau's was by the street address Emmie had jotted down. Nothing identified it from the outside. The concert saloons still around New York were of the seedier variety, but few were as seedy as Croteau's. As we entered all eyes turned to Emmie. I knew she had to have been a little unnerved, but she wasn't going to let it be noticed. I sat us at a table and then ordered wine. It came out of a large, unlabeled bottle but tasted no worse than the average patent medicine, and had a similar proportion of alcohol—not less than 30 percent. There was a small stage and a piano, neither of which was currently occupied, but no room for a band.

"Shouldn't you speak to Mr. Croteau?" she asked.

"Me? This was your idea, remember."

"Don't be childish, Mr. Reese."

I got up and made inquiries at the bar—and ten seconds later returned to make my report.

"I was told Mr. Croteau is unfortunately unavailable, but if I care to make myself comfortable, there is some expectation that he will make an appearance later this evening. I also inquired about this evening's fare and was told that while they are regretfully out of the quail and filet of sole, they can offer us a delightful stew of mystery sausage and beans, and fish that was fried up sometime in the not too distant past."

"What did he honestly say?"

"Oh, that was the gist of it, but he conveyed it in a series of subtle intonations. Or grunts, more precisely."

"How awful do you think the food is?"

"Awful enough that you'd be thankful you live in plumbing's modern era. Come on, let's go get a real meal somewhere."

"I agreed to see your cousin's show, Mr. Reese. You might at least humor me by remaining here until then. Croteau could show up at any moment."

"What about dinner?"

"There'll be food at the theater."

Just about then a piano player got going. He sang along with himself. Not well, perhaps, but one could understand the lyrics of each song and that struck me as rather novel for a concert saloon. These were the usual tunes one would hear in any parlor, but the artiste had taken certain liberties with the lyrics. In his version of the old standard, *She Loved Not Wisely, But Too Well*, "she" also did it quite often. Understandably, Emmie found the performance diverting. It took all my skills at persuasion to induce her to leave at the appointed time. In fact, I had to threaten to leave her there alone.

We arrived at Shea's Garden Theater just in time to catch the end of the opening act: The Randalles, a family of contortionists. Carlotta and her partner, Tim Madden, were next. It wasn't a choice place on the bill, but Carlotta held that it was better to be the second spot at a first-class theater than to be a headliner in the small time. And she would know, having done plenty of both. Their sketch, "A Wife's Stratagem," was appreciably better than when I had seen it a month earlier in Brooklyn. I'll leave it at that. Carlotta sang just two songs, but that was enough. Her voice is difficult to describe. It's as if she doesn't want to be pinned down to particular pitch. And while that works well enough for a comic song, anything more is a trial. Friends and acquaintances soon learn to avoid topics that might necessitate a prolonged conversation.

Next up was Julian Rose, who was in a sort of Shylock outfit, with a long beard and forelocks. He told very funny stories in an exaggerated Yiddish accent. He had a great bit about a Jewish wedding and an Irishman who unsettles the affair with fisticuffs. It included the memorable line, "Ah, he was no fighter—me and my two brothers and a cousin nearly licked him."

The first half ended with Belle Davis and Her Pickaninnies. She was a negress singer who surrounded herself with a troupe of little boys and girls who danced and sang as well. One little girl had a particularly fine voice and nearly brought down the house. Belle ended the act with a song informing her unseen paramour that he needn't visit if he didn't have money to spend on her.

During the intermission, we managed to procure a dinner of peanuts, popcorn, and warm lemonade. The second half opened with Sager Midgley and Gertie Carlisle. They were dressed up as children and did a sketch of a young boy trying to impress a young girl, while she continually cut him down to size. I had no trouble seeing Emmie at age ten in the part. They were quite good and so were the lines.

Then came Percy Fullerton, a magician who was introduced as a local boy. This prompted a great cry of civic pride. He did the requisite rabbit out of a hat and a number of rope and card tricks. I doubt if Percy was ever called to New York, but he might have made a few dollars playing the Odd Fellows' Hall.

The Morton Family was next, Sam and Kitty and daughter Clara. They were the headliners and did very well in New York. It was a variety act of skits with lots of singing and dancing. Clara had a bit where she danced while playing the piano. The key to their success seemed to be the frenetic pace of the whole thing. I felt exhausted just from watching.

The show ended with the Musical Johnstons, two brothers playing the xylophone. But by the time they went on, I was leading Emmie backstage to find Carlotta. We eventually found her in the alley smoking with some of the others. I made introductions and Emmie was almost effusive in her praise. It seemed a little out of character.

Carlotta invited us to an after-show get-together being held at the Vendome Hotel, where many of the performers were staying. I readily agreed, but Emmie drew me aside.

"I thought we'd be going back to Croteau's after the show," she whispered.

"Then you were under a misapprehension. There is absolutely no way we're going back there at this time of night. When we were there last, the patrons were relatively few and on their best behavior. At this hour, their numbers will be far greater and they'll be far drunker. Just getting there would be dangerous. You may not have noticed, but that neighborhood is a little rough and the people who tend to congregate in rough neighborhoods at this time of the evening are not the type who make friends freely."

"Are you too frightened to go, Mr. Reese?"

"Most emphatically yes, Miss McGinnis. And another thing. If we keep walking into that saloon together, the other inhabitants will not assume we're trying to solve the mystery of your uncle's disappearance. Their first thought will be that I am a panderer."

"Which would make me a—"

"Let us use the term chippie."

"Chippie? I'm not familiar with that term."

"Well...."

"Oh, I get the meaning. I just hadn't heard it previously. Chippie. I rather like it. If I *were* a chippie, I would insist on being referred to as such."

Her seriousness left me nonplussed. But I quickly recovered. "You are a young lady of discernment, Miss McGinnis."

By now the procession had begun toward the Vendome, just a few blocks up Pearl Street. Emmie was still miffed at me for having nixed her plans, so I tried to amuse her along the way by pointing out several chippies—none as well costumed as her. It didn't work.

"I suppose I should be heading home, Mr. Reese. I told my mother I'd accompany her on a boat excursion in the morning."

"I'll walk you to the car." I'd seen Emmie in a bad mood, and it seemed like a good idea to help her on her way.

We cut over to Main Street to a stop at Lafayette Square. As we waited, a porter stepped out of the Tifft House, just a couple doors up the street, and whistled for a cab. As soon as one stopped, a woman came out carrying a small bag and got in. It was Sadie. The cab turned around and headed down Main Street in a big hurry.

"I wonder where she's off to? Did you recognize her, Miss McGinnis?"

"No, who was it?"

"Sadie Parker, your uncle's paramour."

"Why don't we ask at her hotel?"

"Aren't you anxious to get home?"

"No, not honestly. I was just annoyed at you for refusing to go back to Croteau's."

My friend wasn't manning the Tifft's desk, so I suggested Emmie make inquiries posing as Miss Parker's niece. She was dressed more like one of Sadie's associates from the parlor house, but I didn't think she could play that part convincingly.

She went over and spoke with the clerk for a minute or two. Then I followed her discreetly out of the hotel.

"She's gone to Rochester. The clerk believes she's gone to meet my father."

"Your father?"

"My fictional father. You see, as you suggested, I introduced myself as her niece and asked if Miss Parker was in. He said, 'She's gone off to Rochester. She received a postcard from her brother and has gone to meet him.' I thought I had to claim her brother as my father, since I was her niece, after all. So I said, 'Yes, I just came to tell her papa was in Rochester.' Though I suppose she could have more than one brother. Or I might have been her sister's child."

"Oh, I think your way made it more credible. No sense cluttering up the imaginary family."

"Does this mean Mason must be in Rochester?"

"Perhaps. Listen, go back inside and ask him as tactfully as possible if he happened to see the contents of the postcard."

She did so, and a few minutes later returned.

"He wasn't quite as talkative when I put the question to him directly, so I used my charm. It sounds like the card didn't really mention Rochester. It came in the late mail and when Miss Parker came in just after eleven o'clock he handed it to her. She read it, then immediately asked when the last train to Rochester left. He told her it was the mail train that left Exchange Street at 11:20. She told him to call a cab and then ran upstairs. A few minutes later she came down with her bag and got into the cab. Does it mean anything?"

"Well," I said, looking at my watch, "it means I won't be following her tonight. Besides, the late mail goes all the way to New York. She mentioned Rochester, but she might have been intentionally misleading. Look, here's your car."

"If it's all the same to you, Mr. Reese, I would like to accept your cousin's invitation."

We walked over and found the vaudevillians in the Vendome's taproom. Carlotta introduced us to some of the others from the show. Gertie Carlisle was there, but unrecognizable. On the stage, she plays a schoolgirl, with a silly wig of long braids and a rag doll outfit that hides her figure. In the flesh—I'm speaking metaphorically, of course—she was stunningly beautiful. Only in vaudeville would a young actress go to great lengths to hide her looks to help make the laughs come easier. When we were introduced, Gertie asked Emmie if she was on the stage. There were several similar queries in the course of the evening. I wasn't altogether sure if these were prompted by Emmie's innate good looks, or her arresting attire. But I could make a pretty good guess.

Tim Madden, Carlotta's rather unctuous partner, was there as well. I'd never really liked the fellow, though he was always pleasant enough. What their relationship was off the stage was a bit of a mystery—even to themselves, I think. Uncharacteristically, Madden offered to buy a round and went up to the bar to order. There I saw him speak to another fellow, who then turned and left through a side entrance. It was Jack Whitner.

"Do you know Jack Whitner?" I asked when he returned.

"Jack Whitner?"

"That fellow you were talking with at the bar."

"Oh, I never saw him before. He just asked if we were in the show."

Before long the Morton family showed up. From the attention he received, it was clear Sam Morton was the dean of the company. He was a genuinely funny fellow. Carlotta introduced me in a way she always found amusing.

"Sam, this is my cousin Harry. He's a Pinkerton, though he always denies it." Carlotta was having great fun. "Harry, Sam and his friends are forming a sort of vaudeville union. But please be a dear and don't crack any heads tonight."

This was Carlotta's little joke. I'd met her on the street a year or so earlier in the company of a Pinkerton man I was working on a case with. Since then she referred to me as a Pinkerton whenever she thought it might be embarrassing. Now, the problem with having someone accuse you of being a private detective for an agency that prides itself on discretion is that there is no way to credibly deny it. I would probably never see these people again, so offered only a mild correction.

"No, not Pinkerton, dear—I'm an insurance investigator. And we only rarely crack heads." I can't say it helped, but at least the conversation moved on to other subjects.

Then Emmie drew me aside.

"You really are a Pinkerton man, aren't you? That explains why you're looking for Robert Mason."

"No. I was never a Pinkerton man. And if Carlotta makes the same assertion again, I will feel at liberty to bring up her abbreviated college education."

"I'd rather you didn't do that, Mr. Reese."

"Then please don't mention the damn Pinkertons again."

I could tell my vehemence surprised her, but sometimes a man has to stand up for himself. Or at least allow himself to feel that he has. Carlotta came over and asked how we had met. I jumped right in.

"I knew her brother Tom at school. At least until the unfortunate accident."

"What unfortunate accident?" Carlotta asked.

"Well, you see, Tom couldn't stay away from the horse races. He'd spend all summer in Saratoga. In fact, he was a bit of a tout. Then one night, it seems Tom was trying to hobble a horse, but instead the horse hobbled him. It kicked him right through the stall and that woke up the trainers, and, well, the scandal just made returning to school impossible."

"I never knew you were familiar with touts, Harry."

"My dear Carlotta, I couldn't very well sully your reputation by introducing you to that sort."

"I'm sorry about your brother, Miss McGinnis."

"Oh, it all turned out for the good. He saw the light and now he's completely reformed. He's an evangelist."

"Oh, I *am* sorry," Carlotta smiled.

Not long afterward, I escorted Emmie back to her car stop.

"Do you plan on following Miss Parker tomorrow, Mr. Reese?"

"I'm not sure. I'm not even sure where she went. I just can't see Mason visiting Rochester, only two hours from Buffalo."

"If you do go, I'd like to come along."

"Seriously? Won't you be going with your mother tomorrow?"

"Oh, she won't mind if we put it off. If you do go after her, will you at least call the house and let me know?"

I told her I would and then put her on what was probably the last car of the night. I walked back to McLeod's ruminating on Sadie's departure. Maybe Elwell sent the card she had received that evening and it was him she was going to meet, not Mason. But it would be risky for them to meet before the insurance claim was settled. And it was hard to imagine that Elwell would have set up that close by, even with a new name.

As I was walking by the Iroquois, I decided to check

and see if Whitner was in for the night. He was. I took that to mean he was unaware Sadie was leaving town. Maybe the reason why Sadie left in such a hurry on the last train of the night was to make sure she couldn't be followed. In that case, the postcard may have just been a coincidence.

11

While I was dressing Saturday morning a messenger came by with a telegram from Dan Ratigan. He had sent it collect, but at least had made use of the night rate. He had traced the first two names, Osborne and Carbury, to Mason because they used addresses in Sodus, which happened to be Mason's home town. Mason had netted almost $30,000 between the two. The third, Matilda Crawley, had used an address in Montreal and made $6,000. The account of Frederick Pferd had realized a profit of $23,000, but Ratigan hadn't been able to trace it. The money was wired from one account to another, then another, until the trail seemed to die. I now recognized not only G. Osborne but also Matilda Crawley as characters from Thackeray.

I went up to the Tifft to see if my clerk was on duty and if he by chance had seen the postcard Sadie received. He was there, but it had come in the late mail and he hadn't seen it.

"Is it important to you to find out what was in it?" he asked.

"Yes—can you ask someone else?"

"Suppose I could get it for you, word for word. What would it be worth?"

"Two dollars, maybe."

"Make it five."

I did. He slipped it into his breast pocket and pulled out a folded paper.

"It reads: 'Becky, Will be at the Queen's Saturday.

Jos.' and it was mailed from Montreal, but the time stamp was smeared."

"I thought you hadn't seen it?"

"I didn't. But I made a deal with one of the night clerks to copy down anything arriving for Becky."

"I don't suppose you know what 'the Queen's' refers to?"

"Well, it was capitalized, so maybe it's a family name."

"So no apostrophe before the 's'?"

"Well, yes, there is."

I didn't want to take the time to give him a lesson in grammar, so I asked if I could have his copy.

"No, you can't. I may have further use for it."

"Has anyone else inquired about the postcards?"

"There may be others interested in Becky's comings and goings." He said this in a way that made it clear this window was open for business.

"How about I tell you?" I offered. "One is young Charlie Elwell. The other is the well-dressed fellow with a mustache who's been visiting Miss Parker." His annoyed look told me I had saved myself five dollars.

The postcard wasn't much help without knowing who or what "the Queen's" referred to. But it sounded as if Mason was leaving Montreal to get there. I still wasn't sure Sadie was going to meet Mason. There was also Elwell to think about. And Whitner. I went over to the Iroquois to see if he had gone out, but the clerk told me he had just gone in for breakfast.

It occurred to me that Sodus, where Mason might still have contacts, was northeast of Rochester. The quickest way there might be to take an express to Rochester and then catch a local to Sodus. I checked a railway guide at the desk and discovered that Sadie couldn't have gotten a local to Sodus until that morning. This was a longshot. It seemed unlikely I'd find Mason behind the counter at the family's dry goods store. But if I didn't check on it, it would nag at me.

I sent a wire to the chief of police in Sodus asking him if Mason had been seen in the area. I included a description of Sadie, her various names, and the fact she might be arriving on the 11:13 that morning. I also asked if there was a hotel or a family named Queen in town. I told the clerk to have the reply sent back to the Iroquois.

Then I telephoned the Elwell residence. Emmie had persuaded her Aunt Nell to go on the boat excursion in her place. I told her about the message Sadie had received.

"Could it be code, Mr. Reese?"

"Maybe, or maybe just their own shorthand." Emmie wanted badly to enter a dime novel. "'The Queen's' must refer to some place they're both familiar with. Maybe a town, or a hotel, or even some friend's. They've probably met there before. It could be in Montreal. Maybe Sadie caught the train east, but was never going to stop in Rochester."

Then I read out Ratigan's wire. She remembered the name Felix Carbury from another book in Mason's library, Trollope's *The Way We Live Now*.

"What was that fourth name, Mr. Reese?"

"Frederick Pferd—p, f, e, r, d, as in the German for horse."

"Oh. Are you bilingual, Mr. Reese?"

"Well, I can name certain farm animals, and give you the days of the week. And I remember one fascinating exchange about practicing my violin. But, no, I wouldn't claim to be bilingual."

"Do you play the violin?"

"Only in first-year German class," I confessed. "By the way, is Charlie at home?"

"Charlie? No, he went to the office this morning but rushed back and said he needed to go out of town. Some work for his law firm."

"Where was he going?"

"He didn't say. Why do you ask?"

"I just wanted to ask him about Mason, and where he might have traveled while he was living in Buffalo," I lied.

"Charlie wouldn't know that. He was away at school for much of that time. The General is probably the only person left who might know."

"Yes. Tell me, do you know of a photo of Mason anywhere about?"

"There's one taken of the original four officers in my uncle's study. Are you planning on following Miss Parker today? Remember, you said I could go along."

"I'm not sure, but if I do, I'll call you."

Just as I was about to hang up, Emmie jumped in again. "Could Frederick Pferd be Freddie, the pony?"

"Yes, I suppose it could."

"That would mean Uncle Charles was involved, wouldn't it?"

"Yes, it probably would. It's too bad we don't know where that payment ended up."

Next, I telephoned the General, as Emmie had suggested. First, I wasted fifteen cents calling his office just to learn he wasn't in. But he was at home, and he took my call. I apologized for imposing on him again, and then got to the point.

"General, I think one of the names your private detective identified as having profited from the stock manipulation was an alias used by Elwell."

"Why?"

"A 'Frederick Pferd' made $23,000. The Elwells once owned a pony named Freddie. It's the one name that doesn't seem to be linked to Mason."

"I see."

"Does it surprise you?"

"Not the lack of scruples, but I do feel betrayed. Elwell had assured me he wasn't involved. Was there anything in the detective's report that would help you locate Mason?"

"No, not really. But I think I've found someone who's been in contact with him. She wouldn't tell me anything, but I happen to know she recently received a message from him saying he would be at the Queen's on Saturday. Would you have any idea who, or what, 'the Queen's' would refer to?"

"The Queen's, like a proper name?"

"Yes, that's correct."

"No. But maybe a hotel? I think there's one across the border. But I can't remember where."

"Did Mason travel to Canada often?"

"Not that I recollect, but I doubt I would have known if he had."

"How about Elwell? Did he travel often?"

"Not more than the average commercial lawyer. But remember, we weren't in daily contact."

"Was there anywhere he did travel regularly?"

"He had clients in Niagara Falls. And he went to Albany from time to time."

"How about Rochester?"

"Almost certainly. But I thought you were looking for Mason?"

"Yes, but I think there may be some connection. Did Elwell travel much to Canada?"

"I wouldn't say often, but certainly he went there."

"Anywhere in particular?"

"Not that I recall. But I don't see the connection to finding Mason. Do you think they were meeting somewhere?"

"Perhaps, or maybe they planned to."

"I see. Well, I'm sorry I can't be more helpful."

I thanked him and apologized again for bothering him. Then I found a comfortable chair in the lobby and waited for Whitner to finish his breakfast. After twenty minutes, I checked the dining room and he wasn't there. I asked the desk clerk if he was in and was told he had left a while ago, but not with any luggage. I had let him slip by while I was on the phone. There was nothing to do now but wait for him to return, so I went back to my chair with a newspaper.

About noon Whitner finally returned. He spoke with the clerk and was handed a directory of some sort. He spent some time with this, then said something to the clerk again before going upstairs to his room. I approached and asked the clerk what Whitner had been inquiring about.

Unfortunately, this was the same clerk I'd spoken with twice already and he'd grown a little suspicious as to my motives. He suggested I ask Mr. Whitner myself and refused to be bribed. Or at least refused my offer. It could be the price for spying on guests was as elevated as the room rates at the Iroquois. But my ready cash was down to less than twenty-odd dollars, and if I was going to need to travel I would also need to be conservative in my bribing. A glance over the counter provided me with the knowledge that Whitner had been consulting a hotel directory.

I staked out another corner of the lobby and made sure the clerk didn't see me. I was worried he'd point me out to Whitner. When he came down, he was carrying a satchel and walked out the door without stopping at the desk. As I reached the door, I realized Whitey Schuler had come up beside me. We looked at each other stupidly for a few seconds.

"Well, I guess we might as well follow him," I suggested.

"I guess we might as well. But this time you follow close and I'll tail back. I think I let him see me last time."

The satchel Whitner was carrying made him easy to follow. I stayed back almost two blocks. He didn't waste time on this trip. He headed to the Terrace station and boarded a train going north to Niagara Falls. I was about to follow him on board when Whitey grabbed my arm and held me back. As the train pulled out, Whitner leaned out of a vestibule and waved to us.

"Come on, I'll buy you a beer," Whitey said.

He took me to a nearby saloon. It was dark and near empty. He got a couple of beers from the barman and we sat down at a table.

"Who's Whitner?" he asked.

"I thought you were going to tell me. All I know is that he calls himself Jack Whitner, says he was a friend of Charles Elwell's, and comes from New York."

"Then why follow him?"

"Well, I suspect he's got some kind of involvement with Elwell's disappearance. And I suspect that has something to do with Robert Mason's disappearance three years ago. I have a contract to find Robert Mason."

"I heard you were looking for opium smugglers."

"I think that was one of the projects Mason worked on while he was in Buffalo. I'm just trying to find a clue as to where he is now."

"Why would Elwell's drowning have anything to do with Mason's whereabouts?"

"What if Elwell didn't drown, but was killed? Say he knew where Mason was and was blackmailing him. Mason kills him, or has him killed. Maybe Whitner really is an old friend of Elwell's, and he knows where Mason is too. Now he wants to take up where Elwell left off." I had tried to come up with a story that would be plausible, and yet not look as if I were endangering the repayment of Boss Conners' loan. I'm not sure I succeeded with the plausibility part.

"What makes you think Elwell was killed?"

"Well, why else is Whitner here?" I was spreading it a little thick. But as long as I dished it out fast, Whitey wouldn't have too much time to think about it. "And why were you following him?"

"You mean the other night? I was following you. You were asking a lot of questions and it was upsetting certain people. I saw you in the Iroquois, and then saw you follow Whitner to the Tifft. I was waiting outside and he runs by me and then I see you come out. I figured if I followed Whitner, I wouldn't lose you. Then Whitner played his little joke and I figured you had spotted me by then."

"Then you went back and reported to your employer."

"Yeah. And now I have to go back and tell him all this nonsense. Hell, I can't even follow it myself."

"Maybe it would be better if I told it?"

"Maybe it would."

We left without paying for the beer. He led me back to the rear entrance of the Courier Building and then left me waiting in the lobby while he took an elevator up. Five minutes later he came back and we went up to the sixth floor. We entered a spacious office, then a smaller one off of that. A girl there pressed a button and told us to go in.

Conners was on the phone and didn't seem to notice us entering. His office was large and opulent. The woodwork and furniture were all ornately carved mahogany. Half of one wall was taken up by a marble fireplace. There were velvet curtains almost obliterating the windows and layers of oriental rugs below. Several paintings of nude women were on display. They had wings like angels, but they weren't acting particularly angelic. The shelves were packed with brightly colored china and a half-dozen sculptures were strewn about. Nor was there any shortage of palms and ferns. Put simply, the room looked as if it'd been decorated by someone who charged by the pound.

Conners himself was big and beefy with a square face. It was a lot easier picturing him on the dock knocking heads than behind a carved desk in an office like this—but there he was. Presently, he got off the phone and turned to look me over.

"So what the hell are you looking for?" he asked.

"I'm trying to find Robert Mason. I have some clients who would like to see him brought in."

"What clients?"

"Several insurance companies that have incurred losses in the past due to his various efforts. Do you mind if we sit down?"

"No, go ahead and sit down. What's the connection to Elwell?"

"Well, as I was telling Mr. Schuler here, I suspect that Elwell may have been killed, either by Mason or, more likely, someone working for him. So I was hoping if I could solve Elwell's murder, I'd be further along in finding Mason."

"And what about this fellow Whitey saw you following?"

"Jack Whitner. I think somehow he knows Elwell was murdered, but not who did it. Whitner figures it was either Elwell's mistress, Sadie Parker, or Elwell's wife and son. They all stood to benefit from insurance policies on Elwell's life."

"Wait a minute, that's not what you told me a little while ago," Whitey unhelpfully interjected.

This is precisely why I would never be good at working undercover. I never had a problem making up a story on-the-fly, it was just the remembering what it was I had made up. The solution was to make up a story so complicated no one else could remember the details either. I felt Whitey kind of let me down here.

"It doesn't matter what the hell he told you, Whitey. We already know he's looking for Elwell to prove he's alive."

"Oh, sure," Whitey confirmed.

"How would you know that?" I asked.

"I read your telegrams."

"How did you get copies of my telegrams?"

"How the hell do you think?"

"I thought the confidentiality of telegrams was sacrosanct."

"Then you're an idiot." He didn't say this in a mean

way, just as if he was letting me in on some small bit of news.

A waiter came in through another entrance and stood at attention. Conners raised three fingers and the waiter nodded and went back out.

"Come on, let's go eat and you can tell me the truth."

He led us through the door the waiter had used and into a dining room as lavish as the office. On the table was a spread sufficient for a large family—roasted chicken, cold beef, potatoes, carrots, beans, a loaf of dark bread, and what I suspected was smoked eel.

"Let's eat," Conners said by way of grace.

The three of us devoured the meal. I don't imagine it was pretty to watch, but the waiter didn't seem to mind. He refilled my wine goblet before I noticed it was empty. I couldn't say if Conners knew the proper use of each piece of silverware, but he managed to use every one of them. Once we had emptied most of the platters, Conners suggested I begin telling my story. I was glad we had eaten first, because I had a feeling he wasn't going to like it.

"Well, as you know, it seems Elwell's disappearance was a fraud."

"I don't know that. I just know you think that. Why?"

"I assume you know a fellow named Steuben came forward with a story that Elwell had approached him to help fake an accident. But then he says Elwell never showed up, so the police assume he drowned in the storm trying to get to the rendezvous."

"But you don't believe that. Why?"

"Why would Steuben come forward with this information unless it got him something? He lost his job over it. I don't think Elwell paid Steuben to help him disappear, but just to say that he had made those arrangements and then hadn't shown up. You see, Elwell *knew* everyone would think his disappearance was a fraud, so he set up a scheme where it would look like that was his intention, but then had had a *real* accident. Put simply, he faked faking the accident, then faked the accident again. Since everyone involved would be better off with him dead, they wouldn't be pestering the police to look for him alive. I guess he figured it was up to those getting the money to handle the insurance companies."

"I suppose you know why I'm interested?"

"The Elevator Company can't pay off the loan from your brewery unless they get the money for their policy on Elwell."

"That's right. Twenty thousand dollars. I let Elwell talk me into that."

"I wouldn't be surprised if some of that loan ended up feathering his nest wherever he is now. I suspect he built up a fair amount of assets there over the years. Including some real estate."

"Maybe so, but as soon as he's declared dead, I'll get my money without having to track him down and sue him. How does this Whitner fit in?"

"I think he came to the same conclusion about the accident and Steuben's story that I did, just a few weeks earlier. He came to town telling Elwell's family that he was an old friend of Elwell's who just happened to be here on business. I'm not sure what he's told Sadie Parker. He's figuring that either Elwell's wife or Sadie is in on the fraud. And after the insurance benefit is paid out, this helpmate will lead him to Elwell. But he won't be telling the insurance companies—he'll just milk Elwell for the rest of his life."

"And that's what you think, too?"

"Except I think he's wrong about Sadie or the wife being in on it. I think Elwell didn't trust either of them, and the policies are just to keep them content while he enjoys his new life."

"So you thought Whitner figured out where Elwell is and was going after him, that's why you wanted to follow him on the train?"

"Well, at this point I'm a little confused. You see, last night Sadie received a message and rushed out on the last train heading east, supposedly to Rochester. Then this morning Whitner gets ahold of the contents of that message and he immediately takes a train to Niagara Falls."

"He was going to the other Niagara, on the lake," Whitey corrected. "I heard him ask the clerk at the Iroquois."

"What was the message? Did you see it?" Conners asked.

"I was told its contents. It merely said that the sender would be at the Queen's on Saturday. It was addressed to Sadie, but the salutation was to Becky and it was signed Jos. It was a postcard, and Sadie's received a number addressed this way. I believe these came from Mason, who's using the alias Jos, or Joseph, Sedley. Sadie was his mistress before she was Elwell's."

"I know all about Sadie," Conners smiled.

"But Whitner probably *doesn't* know about Mason," I said. "He thinks the cards came from Elwell. And he's thinking Sadie's gone to meet Elwell. But I don't know why he went in the other direction. Maybe Sadie merely pretended to catch a train going east, but took one north when she got to the station."

"So you were following Whitner because you thought he'd lead you to Mason?"

"Yes. Before he left the Iroquois he was flipping through a directory of hotels. Maybe he knew there was a Queen's Hotel somewhere and was verifying it."

"So if I let you go now, you'll take a train north to follow Whitner?"

"Well, it's possible he only wanted us to think that's where he was going. He might have seen Whitey or me in the hotel lobby and just made sure we heard Niagara-on-the-Lake. He definitely knew we had followed him to the station. If Whitey hadn't stopped me, I could have kept following him wherever he went. But now I'd need to first figure out where he was going."

"And when you do, you'll go after him."

"Yes. I hope later today."

"Okay, you go find Mason. But when you do, you hand him over to whoever you need to and head right back here. And Whitey will go with you."

"Just so we're back for the races on Monday," Whitey said.

"All right, but like I said, I need to check some things first. I'll call you when I'm ready to leave."

"No, Whitey will stick with you. That way there won't be any mix up. But wait outside a minute—I have something I need to talk to Whitey about."

We shook hands and I went out and waited for Whitey.

12

Whitey and I left Conners' office and headed back to the Iroquois. The same clerk I'd annoyed earlier was on duty and I was reticent about renewing our acquaintance. But Keegan had told me there'd be a response from Montreal that afternoon so I went ahead and asked for it. He didn't have me thrown out.

"Oh, why didn't you say you were Mr. Reese? Mr. Keegan left a note for you this morning." He went and got it. "He also asked that we give you this wire when it came in."

In his note, Keegan said that his wife was leaving for Chicago, but he would be staying on until the case was completed. I wasn't sure which case he meant. The wire was more interesting. It was from the Pinkerton office in Montreal. There was a Joseph Sedley who'd been registered at the Hotel Balmoral in Montreal for three weeks. He had checked out Friday and left no forwarding address.

So we had guessed correctly about Becky and Jos, but it was too late to do me much good. However, I did learn that the Queen's must be within a day's travel of Montreal. Of course, that probably covered half of Canada and the whole Northeast down to Philadelphia.

Next I asked for the hotel directory Whitner had used. I wanted to use this particular one so I would see exactly what he saw. It billed itself as "a guide to the best hotels of the world," with the listings by city. There was a Queen's Royal Hotel in Niagara-on-the-Lake. I flipped through to see if there were others nearby. There was one listed in Toronto, one in Winnipeg, and a couple others elsewhere in Canada. Whitner seemed convinced it was the Queen's Royal. I had to assume he knew something I didn't. Maybe he'd seen something in Sadie's rooms? I handed the directory back to the clerk.

"Will you be in communication with Mr. Keegan today?" he asked.

"No, I don't think so. Why?"

"There was a mix up and one of Mrs. Keegan's bags missed the Chicago train. And then the porter mistakenly sent it on with Mr. Keegan's. He assumed they were going to the same destination."

"Were did he go?"

"Well, I don't know. He simply asked that his bags be sent to the station. But it occurred to me that if they were both going to Chicago, why wouldn't he travel with his wife? Why take a train an hour later? So I wonder if he didn't go somewhere else."

"Which train did she catch?"

"The morning Michigan Central. It left around 7:30."

I couldn't think of why Keegan would have misled me. Why would I care if he stayed in town or not?

I went over to the telegraph desk to see if the Sodus police had sent a reply. They had—collect. No one matching Sadie's description had come in on the morning train. As for Mason, I was told he was unlikely to show himself in Sodus. Apparently, even his own family was liable to shoot him on sight. He certainly knew how to burn his bridges.

We had about an hour before the next train to Niagara-on-the-Lake and I debated whether to call Emmie or not. I wasn't sure she wouldn't cause a complication if we found Elwell as well as Mason. And I didn't think she'd care to travel with Whitey along. But the matter most on my mind was money. I had been hoping to ask Keegan for a small loan, since I'd be hard pressed to do much traveling on the twenty-odd dollars I had left. Now, I would have to ask Emmie to bring along some ready cash, and that was always a little awkward. I flipped a coin and that decided it.

I told her about seeing Whitner off at the station and about the Queen's Royal Hotel. She was still keen on going along, even if it meant staying in a hotel some-where. Money wasn't a problem, nor did she seem at all bothered by having company. Of course, I didn't take the time to tell her who Whitey was or why he was coming. We agreed to meet at the station at 3:15 and she said she would bring the photograph of Mason.

Whitey and I swung by his apartment so he could pack a bag and then to McLeod's so I could. We still had some time left, so I offered to buy him a beer in the taproom there.

"Why did Conners want to send you along?" I asked.

"Because he thinks you're looking for Elwell, and I'm to make sure you don't find him. You are, aren't you?"

"No, right now I'm looking for Mason. It was the postcard from Jos Sedley that set everyone running around. And I have no doubt Jos is Mason."

"But why are you following Whitner and not Sadie?"

"Only because I think I know where Whitner's go-ing. There's no Queen's Hotel in Rochester, and I doubt Mason would come back across the border anyway," I answered. "Listen, Whitey, when we meet up with Miss

McGinnis, let's tell her I asked you to come along. I just don't want to frighten her."

"Sure. But don't try to lose me. I don't want to have to frighten you."

"No, I wouldn't like that either."

Emmie was waiting for us. I introduced Whitey to her as a friend coming along to help. Then we bought our tickets and joined the crowd waiting to board the train. Just as the doors to the track opened, a fight broke out blocking the way. Whitey reached over and thrust Emmie's small satchel up to her chest.

"Hold it in front of you, so no one can grab it," Whitey instructed.

Sure enough, a second later another woman was shouting, "My bag!"

The fight had ended as abruptly as it had started and the pugilists had disappeared. We boarded the train and found seats near the rear.

"How did you know that was going to happen, Mr. Schuler? Did you know the fighting was just a ruse?" Emmie asked.

"Well, I knew it wasn't for real, if that's what you mean. They were jamming up the breaks to make it easier for the gun."

"What gun, and what are the breaks?"

"A gun is a pickpocket. The breaks is any place people have to funnel through. Do you ever take one of the steamboats to the beach?"

"I have, yes."

"Well, most times there's a crowd of people waiting for the boat when it docks. As soon as they put the plank down, everyone moves in on it. Now they're all bumping into each other. Then some guy going up the plank drops something and stops to pick it up. The whole line stops and now everyone is leaning against someone else. A good claw might come up with two or three wallets before the line starts moving again."

"A claw is another term for a pickpocket?"

"Yeah. But this buzzard was an amateur. That lady probably caught him in her bag, so he just glommed it. He could have done that without the show and he wouldn't have to cut the two ginks in on it."

Emmie had taken out a small notebook and was writing everything down.

"Would a buzzard refer to any pickpocket, Mr. Schuler? Or just an amateur one?"

"Say a clumsy one. He goes after women because he's not good enough to get a wallet out of a man's coat."

"And glom?"

"Glom is the snatch. Like a guy who snatches a lady's purse and runs up an alley."

"I noticed you used it as both a noun and a verb."

"Yeah? Huh."

"And is a gink someone who creates the distraction for the claw?"

"Well, a gink's just a gink. Just some fellow who's not too smart."

"So, it doesn't denote a particular vocation."

"Ah, no. Not that."

"Do these men make much money?"

"Sure, the good ones. Say he got in that lady's bag without her seeing. She wouldn't notice until after she got on the train, or maybe not until she got wherever she's going. She wouldn't even remember him bumping into her. So now the crew can mope over to another station, or maybe the wharf. Then tomorrow they might go up to the Falls—lots of people lining up there. There might be a cop that sees them, but what can he do? Break up the fight and try to get the crowd moving. But if the chumps don't squawk, how can the cop spot the claw? In New York, you never have to leave town. Just move to a different precinct."

"Are you from New York, Mr. Schuler?"

He was. And he held Emmie's rapt attention for the next hour with the story of his life. And while it has to be said that Whitey had led a colorful life, Emmie's enthrallment seemed excessive. Frankly, it bordered on the schoolgirlish. Needless to say, there was no place for me in the conversation. A paving stone to the head isn't of the same rank as a sentence of six months on Blackwell's Island.

So I spent the time studying the photograph Emmie had brought along. It was of the four officers of the Elevator Company, taken in 1893. Mason was tall, trim, and clean-shaven. His hair and eyes were dark. Of course, he could be fat with graying hair and a full beard now. Elwell was medium height, maybe even short, and stout. His hair was already graying in the photo. Then there was General Osgood and the original treasurer. Emmie couldn't remember his name, but did know he had died soon after the photo was taken.

As we were passing through Niagara Falls, Whitey pulled out a deck of cards. He let Emmie shuffle them and then dealt out two hands: four kings and a queen to her, and four aces and a ten to himself. He then taught her how to palm them without being detected. She was a quick study. By the time we pulled into the little station at Niagara-on-the-Lake, she was well qualified to cheat her way through the local whist tournament.

We quickly found the Queen's Royal Hotel and there I inquired if a Mr. Sedley had arrived yet. He hadn't. Then I asked about Whitner and Sadie. I described them as well, saying they might have just stopped by. I couldn't very well tell the clerk they'd be using assumed names.

Meanwhile, Whitey was asking another clerk for a sheet on the races next week. Then he stepped out onto the porch to read it. Emmie followed him, probably for some lessons on playing the horses. With them both away I inquired about Charlie and Charles Senior, but with no more success than before. I could see the register clearly, but I wouldn't have recognized the scrawl of any of them. I asked when the next train would be arriving and was told there wouldn't be any more that day, but a boat from Lewiston would be arriving at six o'clock. Lewiston was just up the river, below the Falls. If Sadie's trip to Rochester was a ruse, she might take a train back west that would stop in Lewiston. Whitner might just be laying low until Mason showed up. The electric cars didn't make it this far, so the only other route running up from Niagara Falls was the road. Someone taking a train there could hire a carriage and show up at any time.

When I went out to confer with my confederates, Emmie was near the door and Whitey at the end of the veranda. I called over to Whitey and suggested we split up and canvass the town for Whitner. Emmie suggested she would go with Whitey since he was least familiar with Whitner. We agreed to meet back at the hotel just before the boat was due to dock.

It didn't take long to walk through the commercial district of Niagara-on-the-Lake. I took a seat on the patio of a small cafe and enjoyed a glass of beer—keeping an eye on the road from the south. There was an occasional farm wagon, and a carriage or two, but nobody I knew was on them.

At a quarter to six we were all at the hotel again, no one having seen anything of note.

"I don't think we should all be standing around waiting for the boat—it'd be too easy to spot us," Whitey pointed out.

"I suppose you're right. I'll go and try to find a discreet spot to watch from," I said.

"No, I'll go. I'm the one he doesn't know. Leave Emmie here and you go watch the road. That way I won't have to worry about you giving me the slip by hopping on the boat."

I agreed and we each went to our designated station. It wasn't until I was back at the cafe enjoying another glass of beer that I became conscious of Whitey having called Emmie Emmie. Things must have progressed some in the half hour we were apart.

From my vantage point, I couldn't see the dock. But I did see a stream of people going toward it and ten minutes later another stream coming away from it. Then I remembered Whitey's other comment, about me slipping away. If I wanted to go south, I wouldn't need to take the boat down to Lewiston, I could just hire a carriage. I had a vague feeling that I'd been had.

I walked down to the now-empty dock, and then back to the hotel. Emmie was practicing card tricks on a corner of the veranda.

"Has Whitey been back?" I asked.

"No, but a number of people did come up from the boat. I didn't see Mr. Whitner, and I'm fairly certain Miss Parker wasn't among them, but I've only seen her that once, last night."

"I'm afraid, Miss McGinnis, that he has given us the slip."

"Mr. Whitner?"

"Well, Mr. Whitner, too. But I was speaking of Mr. Schuler."

"I was afraid something like that might happen."

"You anticipated his departure?"

"No, not exactly. But he did receive a communication that he tried to hide from us. I assumed he had some other motive than merely helping you track down Robert Mason."

"What communication?"

"Would you mind if I tell you over supper, Mr. Reese? I'm rather hungry just now."

"Okay. Let me check something at the desk here. Then we can go up the street to eat."

We went inside and I inquired about the schedule of the boat that had just left. It was going to Toronto. I had thought it was just an excursion boat to the Falls and back. The clerk handed me a schedule for the Niagara Navigation Company. There would be another boat leaving at eight o'clock for Toronto. Where I knew there was a Queen's Hotel. There was also a schedule for the Richelieu & Ontario Navigation Company, which included a map of several steamship routes on Lake Ontario. One stood out rather prominently.

"Is there a faster way to Toronto than waiting for the next boat?" I asked the clerk.

"No, the boat would get you there around ten o'clock. You could take a carriage down to Niagara Falls and catch a train there, but you'd have to change trains in Hamilton or somewhere. The boat's a lot more pleasant, too."

I bought a map of Toronto at the hotel stationers while Emmie wired her mother. Then I led her back to the little cafe. We took my usual table.

"So, tell me about Whitey's secret message."

"While you were going through the descriptions with the clerk—and I have to say, Mr. Reese, I'm not sure that was the best way of handling that part of the affair—Whitey asked one of the clerks for a sheet on next week's horse races at Fort Erie. But he said something else to the clerk I didn't hear. The clerk handed him the racing sheet and also an envelope. Whitey quickly hid the envelope and went out on the porch, ostensibly to read his racing sheet. I tried to stay near the door and out of his sight. He read the message in the envelope, then burned it. But he used a pencil to write something on the racing sheet. That's why I wanted to stay with him when we went in different directions, so I would have a chance to see what he had written."

"And did you see it?"

"Oh, yes. Eventually."

"What did it say?"

"Well, he had just made some notation. Probably to help him remember something in the message. I wrote it down in my notebook as soon as I was alone."

She handed me the notebook, where she had written a sort of chart:

D 2 A
R 1 C
Y 2 E

"What do you think it means?" she asked.

"I have no idea. But he definitely took the boat to

Toronto. I guess it's something he's supposed to find, or do, there."

"Who was it who sent him the telegram?" she asked.

"It had to be his boss, Conners."

I then explained Whitey's connection to Conners and told her about the luncheon party earlier.

"Conners is worried that I'm looking for your uncle, and that the message to Sadie was from him. Whitey was sent along to make sure I didn't find him. Conners wants your uncle to remain dead until the Elevator Company collects from the insurance policy on him and pays off that loan. It may be that he somehow found out the message was referring to the Queen's Hotel in Toronto and he wired Whitey to go there and warn your uncle. Maybe that cryptograph you saw is just the room number and an alias."

"But you think Whitey's on the wrong track, because the postcards came from Mason."

"Yes, I think we can be sure the cards were from Mason. Sadie was receiving them before your uncle disappeared. Then there's the use of the names from Thackeray, which Mason had done before. And the connection to Montreal."

"But if the card was referring to the Queen's Hotel in Toronto, why did Sadie take the train east?"

"It suddenly dawned on me when I saw that map of the steamship routes at the hotel. There's a lake port just up from Rochester, called Charlotte. And there's a steamship that plies between there and Toronto. Sadie was just taking a roundabout way of getting to the Queen's Hotel in Toronto."

"So Miss Parker took the train to Rochester last night so she could catch a boat to Toronto. She hoped by taking that route we would mistake her intent. Mr. Whitner made you think his destination was here, but just passed through, taking the boat to Toronto. So presumably, Mason, Miss Parker, and Whitner are all converging at the Queen's Hotel in Toronto as we speak."

"That's it in a nutshell."

"So, we arrive at ten o'clock and surprise them. Unless Whitey unintentionally warns them off."

"Or intentionally. If Whitey sees Sadie, he'll assume she's there to meet Elwell and will tell her I'm on to her. Unless Whitner already has. All he's after is money. He too expects to find your uncle meeting Sadie. If he finds Mason there instead, he'll just work him. He doesn't want him caught as long as he can milk him."

"But would he know Mason?"

"I imagine he knows all about Mason's record, but perhaps wouldn't recognize him. He seems to know quite a bit about all of this. And I'd like to find out how he learned it."

13

The steamship *Chippewa* was crowded with people returning to Toronto after a day trip to the Falls. We found a spot on deck near the bow and away from the smoke. When we left the river for Lake Ontario, the wind picked up but it was still pleasant. Emmie suggested we pass the time with a few hands of nickel-ante poker.

"Miss McGinnis, are you planning to cheat?"

"You don't mind, do you, Mr. Reese?" She was now at her most artful.

"Me? No, I'm used to playing a cold deck."

"Well, don't worry, I won't trim you badly."

"And by all means, be careful. You must be aware of what happens to those caught cheating at cards on steamboats."

"Surely they are given some allowance during their apprenticeship."

"Have you apprenticed yourself to Mr. Schuler?"

"Could I have spied on him if I had?"

"Do apprentice card sharps have an ethical code?"

"Oh, I think they must. Are you afraid I'll betray you to Mr. Schuler?"

"Well, I do find the secret code a little romantic for Whitey. And there is the fact he referred to you by your first name."

"Why, are you suspicious or jealous, Mr. Reese?"

"Maybe a little of both."

"Well, let's dispel the latter right now. I thought you preferred the more formal address. You may call me

Emmie and I will call you Harry. Or is there another name your friends use?"

"No, just Harry. Don't you like it?"

"Frankly, not particularly. Do you?"

"No, not particularly. But it's short for Harrison, and I like that even less. And I guess I've grown accustomed to it. What name would you choose for me?"

"I'll need to think about that."

We watched the sunset from the deck and Emmie assured me the code was real and I assured her that I believed her. Now it was too dark to play cards, which was just as well as I had lost two dollars and ten cents. We had agreed that if I spotted Emmie cheating, it was my hand. If I unjustly accused her, it was hers. She quickly became as adroit at pretending to cheat as she was at cheating.

In making change for me, Emmie pulled a roll of bills from her purse. It caught my eye.

"How much money did you bring?" I asked. Financial necessity had trumped discretion.

"I started with just under one hundred dollars. I always keep that much at home."

"You don't trust banks?"

"Well, I have accounts in four banks and keep one hundred dollars in each. You see, my father once lost money in a bank failure and he taught me to always minimize my risk."

"Experience is a great teacher," I said. While it would be difficult to argue it had imparted any of its wisdom to me, I felt the situation called for a comforting platitude. "I don't mean to meddle, but do you think it's wise to be carrying that amount around in your bag?"

"I must admit, Whitey's pointing out those pickpockets did give me pause. What would you suggest?"

"Perhaps if you would allow me to hold some portion of it for you. That would reduce your risk of a total loss."

"All right. I guess I would feel easier."

She took out her stash and counted out fifty dollars and handed it to me. Given that my own fortune was quickly disappearing, the arrangement made me feel easier as well.

I suggested we go inside, where there was enough light to study the map I had bought earlier. But the cabin was too crowded to enter. There was a beer counter there and about half the passengers were in the queue. Some appeared to be getting back in line as soon as they were served. The citizens of Toronto were a thirsty bunch.

We found a bench on deck where there was just enough light to see the map. The Queen's Hotel was only a couple blocks from the wharf.

"The problem," I began, "is that if I'm right that Mason is meeting Sadie at the Queen's Hotel, then Whitner is also right. At least as far as Sadie goes. But he's expecting Elwell to show up and presumably knows what he looks like."

"Oh, yes, he's seen photos at the house."

"Well, he won't confront Sadie until Elwell shows up. Which won't happen. So he'll be staking out the lobby of the Queen's."

"What if Sadie has spotted Whitner?"

"We have to assume he's too smart to allow that to happen. I think he's an old hand at this type of thing."

"If Whitner is watching the Queen's Hotel he'll recognize us immediately."

"Yes, but what can he do about it?" I asked." If he

125

stays, we'll just watch him as well. But I doubt he'll stay. He'll assume that if we see your uncle we'll expose him—putting an end to Whitner's chances of blackmailing him. Of course, that still leaves Whitey."

"Perhaps he'll also make the mistake of waiting for my uncle to arrive?"

"We can hope so. He'll spot Whitner there because he expects to find him. I'm not sure what he'll do if he sees Mason."

"Would he recognize him?" she asked.

"I don't know if they would have crossed paths or not. He didn't show any interest in that photo you brought."

"How do you think Conners found out whatever information he sent to Whitey?"

"He could have wired someone in Toronto to monitor the hotels and that someone spotted Sadie and sent back the room number and the alias she was using."

"But why not just have the man in Toronto warn Sadie?" Emmie asked.

"Maybe it was someone he didn't trust with too much information, like a hired detective. And maybe he doesn't want Sadie warned *unless* she's meeting your uncle. He didn't seem at all upset about me bringing in Mason."

"If that's the case, maybe Whitey would turn him in before we get there?"

"Yes, I suppose that's possible. But since there's nothing for Whitey to gain by doing that, I think it's unlikely."

"So, we operate on the assumption Whitner and Whitey are still there, both waiting for my uncle. Then we arrive, just in time to apprehend Mason before either of them realizes what's happening. I don't think the odds are on our side, Harry."

"No, I guess not." Emmie certainly knew how to take the wind out of a man's sails. "Regardless, there's nothing else for us to do but go to the Queen's and hope for the best."

For the rest of the trip, we tried to think of names and rooms that could be created with the letters and numbers Whitey had recorded: D, R, Y, A, C, and E. Emmie expected to find a Mr. Darcey in Room 212, while I favored Mr. Cedray in Room 221.

The ship docked and as we waited our turn to disembark, a man on the plank before us stumbled and the passengers behind him closed in on each other. Emmie scanned the crowd for claws and buzzards and was disappointed when she didn't spot any. Lamentably, sometimes a stumble is just a stumble.

We soon arrived at the Queen's Hotel. We had agreed it would be better for Emmie to enter first, since Whitner wouldn't be expecting her. Then I would enter through a different door. We would both try to search the lobby quickly, then head to any saloon or restaurant opening off of it.

It was all over in a matter of seconds. We found Whitner seated in the saloon. He had hopped up when he saw me enter, but it was too late to hide himself.

"Good evening, Mr. Whitner."

"Good evening, Mr. Reese. I was wondering if you'd be making your way here. Ah, and Miss McGinnis."

"No sign of Becky yet?" I asked.

"No, no sign of Becky," he smiled.

"You know, it isn't Elwell she's planning to meet."

"No? Look, why don't we all sit down." He offered

Emmie a chair. "Tell me, Mr. Reese, who is she meeting?"

"A man named Mason." I was hoping to convince Whitner to give up and leave.

"I see. Why is Miss McGinnis here if it doesn't involve her uncle?"

"Curiosity, mainly," Emmie answered. "If you gentlemen don't mind, I think I'll go see what rooms are available for the night."

The waiter came by and I ordered a beer. Whitner laughed and suggested I try a lemonade. It seems the puritans of Toronto had instituted a particularly ruthless set of blue laws. No liquor could be sold from seven o'clock on Saturday evening until six o'clock Monday morning. That explained the thirst of the passengers on the *Chippewa*.

"Well, Mr. Reese, I think I've led you to the wrong Queen's Hotel, twice."

"Why do you think this is the wrong hotel?"

"For the simple reason that neither Sadie or Elwell has shown up. There are others, you know."

"Yes. Tell me, how is it you came to know so much about Elwell?"

"Oh, I have my sources. Not so different from yours." He was smiling.

"The other night, when you and I ran into Keegan, you recognized him, didn't you?"

"Of course, why wouldn't I?"

Just as the waiter brought us our lemonade, Emmie returned.

"They aren't here," she announced. "They must be at the Rossin."

This seemed to puzzle Whitner as much as it did me.

Before I could ask her to explain, two men entered and approached us. They had the unmistakable air of plain-clothes men.

"Are you the party who's been inquiring for Joseph Sedley?" a skinny cop asked Whitner.

"Why do you ask?"

"Never mind that. How do you know him?"

"He's a friend."

"Yeah? Well, then you'd better come along."

"He's a friend of mine as well," I announced.

"Yeah? Well, you better come, too."

As we were led out, I tried to signal Emmie to stay behind. But when we entered the lobby the clerk piped up.

"She just asked for Sedley, too! And she showed me a photograph."

"Yeah? Well, it will be a little crowded, but you better come, too. And I'll take the photograph. Which one's Sedley?"

"This is Robert Mason," Emmie said, pointing to the photo. "But we believe he's traveling as Joseph Sedley."

We all trooped out and into a carriage the cops had brought. A few minutes later we arrived at police head-quarters. The second plain-clothes man led us into the building while the skinny cop made off again in the carriage. The three of us were left to wait in a hallway with a patrolman. Twenty minutes later the skinny cop returned with an older cop whom he introduced as Colonel Livingston. They took Emmie into an office and five minutes later called me in.

"So the two of you came in by train this afternoon?" I hoped Colonel Livingston was just being sly. But there was always a chance Emmie had let her imagination get the better of her.

"By boat, this evening," I answered.

"Which boat?"

"The steamboat *Chippewa*, from Niagara-on-the-Lake. We got in at ten o'clock."

"All right, who's Joseph Sedley?"

"We believe it's an alias being used by a man named Robert Mason. Mason is on the run and I've been hired by several insurance companies to find him. But if you don't know who Sedley is, why are we here?"

"Because I know where he is."

"In Toronto?"

"Yes, in the morgue." Livingston watched me for a reaction, and he got one. Then he continued: "Sedley, or Mason, was shot and killed around nine o'clock."

"You're kidding me." My three-hundred-dollar fee for finding Mason had just evaporated.

"Why would I be kidding you? I'll need the name of someone to verify your story."

I gave him Keegan as a reference, and also suggested he contact Detective Donahy.

"How is it you're sure this fellow is the Joseph Sedley we're looking for?"

"For one thing, Detective Burton here checked him against your photograph. And for another, he had papers on him in the name of Joseph Sedley. Who's this fellow Whitner? Is he with you?"

"Whitner is a grafter from New York. He was hoping to shake down Sedley. Only he thought Sedley was some-one named Charles Elwell, who may also be on the run."

The explanation of all that required quite a bit of time.

"I don't suppose you'll be holding Whitner?" I asked.

"No. The people at the hotel say he was there all evening. But I will question him."

"You might want to put a man on him when he leaves."

"All right, I will," he agreed. "So who's Mike Schuler?"

He caught me off guard with that. I didn't see any way around telling him that whole story as well.

"Have you picked up Schuler?" I asked.

"He's the one who actually led the detectives to the body. But he denied having shot Sedley. Which seems likely, since he didn't have a gun and we couldn't find one. He showed some identification and said he came to pick up some papers from a Joseph Sedley at that address for a friend. But he insisted he had never seen Sedley before."

"Is he in custody?"

"No. He appeared to be a witness who voluntarily came forward, so our men weren't watching him as closely as they perhaps should have. I'm afraid he slipped away. I have people looking for him now. Did he know Mason?"

"I can't say for sure. It may be Schuler came to Buffalo after Mason left town."

Livingston pulled out his watch. "Well, I think that's enough for tonight. Let's save the rest for morning."

"One thing that shouldn't wait, Colonel. I believe Mason was meeting a woman who goes by the name of Sadie Parker. But she may be traveling as Becky, or Rebecca, Sharp, or possibly Sadie Collins. She received a message from him yesterday proposing a rendezvous, I believe at the Queen's Hotel here."

I gave him a thorough description of Sadie. Then he had a carriage take us back to the hotel.

"Emmie, remember when we were with Whitner earlier?" I asked as we went in. "What was that about the Rossin?"

"The Rossin House. I saw it on the map. I was trying to mislead Whitner."

"How so?"

"Well, remember our conversation on the boat about how the odds were against us catching Mason?"

"I'd put it out of my mind."

"I took the opposite tack—I formulated a plan. If we found Whitner waiting here, I would lead him to believe that I somehow found out Sadie and Mason were at another hotel. The Rossin House was on your map."

"I see. You are a woman of action."

Emmie had gotten us two rooms on the second floor and we sat down in mine to discuss the new developments.

"You don't think Whitey killed Mason, do you?" she asked.

"Well, it's a possibility. Maybe Boss Conners was involved in one of Mason's schemes and thought it was best if the matter were laid to rest. But I wouldn't think Whitey would allow himself to get caught with the body. Maybe he went to warn Mason I was on my way, and someone else had gotten there first."

"But who else would have wanted to kill Mason?"

"I'm not sure. Whitner probably didn't know who Mason was, but if he had, he would have been planning to milk him. It could be Sadie wasn't meeting Mason because she's still keen on him. Maybe Mason found out something about your uncle's disappearance and was planning to blackmail her for a share of the insurance. That leaves two other possibilities I'm aware of, but it could have been someone else entirely. There's no reason to think Mason had given up scheming since he left Buffalo, and I imagine he left a string of victims in his wake."

"What other two possibilities are you aware of? My uncle?"

"Yes, he's one. Assuming he isn't dead and marinating in the canal. Mason may have discovered his whereabouts and tried to milk him. Your uncle knew him well enough to realize Mason would see this as a lifetime annuity."

"And the other?"

"Your cousin Charlie. You see, he seems to have taken up with Sadie. Maybe he fell hard enough to be jealous of Mason."

"Is that true? That Charlie has been seeing Miss Parker?"

"Yes. But I don't know how seriously he takes it. I wouldn't have entertained him as a possibility, but you said he left in a hurry to catch a train earlier today. And I suspect he also was given the contents of that postcard Sadie received. The clerk at the Tifft more or less confirmed it."

"Still, I can't see Charlie killing someone over a woman. He just has never treated those things as very important."

"Then why was he interested in her mail?"

"I can't answer that," she conceded. "Why didn't you mention Charlie to the Colonel when you brought up Sadie?"

"I didn't want to impugn your family in front of a police detective. At least not before I can be sure there's something to it."

"There's something I haven't told you yet. The reason I took these rooms on the second floor."

"You don't like climbing stairs?"

"Don't be a gink. I saw the register and who do you think is in Room 212?"

"Let's see, was that Cedray?"

"No, nothing that absurd. A Robert Day."

"I see—R. Day. But what happened to the C and the E?"

"Maybe they're middle initials, or perhaps the abbreviation for an honorary title that follows the name."

"So, Mr. R. Day, E.C.?" I suggested. "At this point, Sherlock Holmes would instruct Doctor Watson to consult *Burke's Peerage* to determine the meaning of "E.C." Maybe if I ask at the desk they'll have one handy?"

"Don't play horse with me, Harrison."

I didn't like Emmie's expression. I thought to divert her by feeding her imagination. I told her all about Keegan and how he and Whitner seemed to recognize each other.

"I had assumed Keegan knew him from the rogues' gallery he keeps of insurance grafters," I said. "But I couldn't figure out why Whitner would recognize Keegan. Tonight, when we were alone in the barroom, I asked him about it and he said, 'Of course, why wouldn't I recognize him?'"

"That's very curious, isn't it? Does it mean Whitner could be working for Keegan?"

"Or maybe he did sometime in the past. That might be why he knows so much about your uncle, from seeing Keegan's files."

"But why wouldn't Keegan have just told you that?"

"Well, he has a lot of people working for him. If

Whitner was working as a clerk in the file room, Keegan might have seen him only rarely. But, of course, he would know Keegan. And a job in Keegan's file room would provide a lot of grist for someone with a penchant for blackmail."

"Yes, that would explain it, I suppose."

We said good night and Emmie went off to her room in a much improved mood.

14

When we came down the next morning, there was a message from the Colonel at the desk asking us to be at his office at ten o'clock. That left time for a leisurely breakfast in the dining room.

"Tell me, Harry, doesn't the fact that Mason is dead mean you'll be unable to collect on that reward?"

"Yes, I'm afraid it does."

"I'm sorry. But there's still the policy on my uncle."

"Yes, I'll need to concentrate on that now."

"But what if it turns out my uncle did die in an accident? Then you won't be able to collect on that either. Your whole trip will have been for nothing."

"You have a rather dispiriting way of putting things, Emmie."

"I'm sorry, Harry. Yes, we should hope for the best."

"Besides, I have reason to believe I'll succeed in the case of your uncle."

"Does that mean you think my theory of my uncle being killed for his involvement in the smuggling scheme is correct? Or maybe it was the stock scheme?"

"Well, not exactly. You see, I have reason to believe your uncle had been building assets elsewhere for the last several years."

This revelation necessitated my recounting the second burglarizing of her uncle's office and the results of my search. She didn't seem at all upset about the burglary. But she did grasp immediately that my success might make things awkward at home.

"So you expect to prove my uncle is alive and thereby collect the reward from the company's insurer. And render my aunt destitute."

"She must have some assets. There's the house. And Charlie must be doing well. I'm sure she'll be fine."

"Possibly, but it's unlikely she and Charlie will appreciate that when they learn that I've accompanied you on this effort. I'll need to move out of the house, certainly."

"Well, with your nest egg, you can set up on your own now."

"My nest egg?"

"The four hundred dollars in four different banks."

"Oh, yes," she acknowledged. "But don't forget the fifty dollars of mine you're carrying."

"No, I haven't forgotten about that."

We had a pleasant walk to the police station and Colonel Livingston was waiting for us.

"I have another name for your Robert Mason. It seems a Mrs. Redstone reported her husband missing late last night, but it was some time before our men made the connection. Mason has been living here as Lester Redstone."

"Are you sure?"

"His wife just identified the body."

"His wife?"

"That's right. He left a wife and two children."

"Did she know he was Mason?"

"She says she didn't, but who knows. You seem surprised. Didn't you expect something like this? You said he'd been on the run. And he used aliases."

"Yes. I just had a completely different picture of him. What about Mike Schuler?"

"We haven't turned him up, but it looks like his story is probably true—at least most of it. Mrs. Redstone told us someone matching Schuler's description stopped by the house last evening shortly after dinner and asked for her husband. She told him he had gone to meet someone about renting an office. He said he was that man, but had misplaced the address and hoped to catch him at home. She gave him the address and he went on his way. What's more, we have a witness who heard the shots and then saw Schuler go inside. And then there's the fact that he's the one who showed our men the body. If he murdered Redstone, he would have had to have been either angry to the point of insanity, or completely witless. He didn't strike our detectives as either."

"No, Mr. Schuler isn't a fool, and I doubt he had a personal stake in the matter," I agreed. "The shooting occurred at this office?"

"Yes, an office in a building Redstone, or Mason, owned. Are you sure Robert Mason was his real name?"

"Fairly sure. I saw his Princeton diploma," I said. "You mentioned shots fired just now. Was he shot more than once?"

"One hit, one miss. Do you want to see the place? It's right over on Queen Street."

"Yes, if it's all right."

"Maybe it was *on* Queen Street, and not at the Queen's," Emmie interjected.

"I beg your pardon?" Livingston replied.

"That message to Sadie Parker," Emmie explained. "Mr. Reese never saw it. He was told by one clerk what another clerk had transcribed. Perhaps the penmanship wasn't clear and what the clerk read as 'at the Queen's' was really something about this building on Queen Street."

"That makes sense," the Colonel agreed. "Information heard third-hand is almost always garbled. Does that sound plausible to you, Mr. Reese?"

"Yes. Mason may have still been carrying on with Sadie. From what I know about him, he didn't seem the type to be content as a simple landlord with a wife and children at home. Perhaps he asked her here to end their relationship. And if that's the case, Sadie Parker would be the chief suspect."

"I have men out looking for her," Colonel Livingston said. "The hotels have been checked and the station and steamship docks are covered. But so far, there's been no trace of her."

We walked the five or six blocks to a small commercial building with a grocer on the street and several offices above. The small office where Mason had been found was furnished, but otherwise empty.

"Redstone was sitting here," the Colonel said from behind the desk. "The bullet hit him in the chest and would seem to have been fired from the direction of the door. The doctor thought it either a 32- or 38-caliber pistol ball."

"And the shot that missed?"

"Right over here." The Colonel stepped over to a window sill about eight feet from the desk. "We tried to check the path on this, but the wood splintered. My guess is it also was fired from near the door. We have the bullet, and it also was a 32- or 38-caliber pistol ball."

"Kind of wide of the mark, isn't it?"

"Yes, and there's something else a little queer." He bent down and pointed to a patch of dark red on the floor in front of the window. "This looks like blood. I have someone testing it. But I don't see how Redstone's blood got over here. The coroner insists there was just one wound and that shot definitely hit him while he was seated."

"So maybe there was a third person here who was shot as well?"

"Possibly. Or maybe the blood has been there for six months. Or maybe it's paint the janitor spilled."

"That witness you have, who heard the shots and saw Schuler enter the building—did he see anyone leave after the shots were fired?"

"No, he came out onto the street from a shop next door after hearing the shots. He said it might have been a full minute before he got to the street. This building was empty at the time. The offices and the shop downstairs were closed as it was Saturday evening. A number of other people heard the noise, but they either didn't realize it was gunfire, or simply couldn't tell where it had come from. On our receiving a report of gunshots, a couple detectives were sent over. They were down on the street when Schuler came out and led them to the body."

"And no one saw anyone matching Sadie Parker's description?" I asked.

"Not seen entering or leaving this building, but that doesn't mean much. There's quite a parade of strollers out on Saturday evening. And someone of her description wouldn't stand out. I've sent to Buffalo to see if I can have a photograph sent here, but who knows how long that will take, or if there's even one available."

I suggested to Emmie that we should leave the Colonel to his work and head back to the hotel. She protested briefly, but it was clear this was the Colonel's preference as well, so we said good-bye and I wished him luck.

We started out toward the Queen's, but Emmie refused to be hurried.

"If we get back and pack quickly, we can check out by noon," I said.

"Check out?"

"Yes, we can catch an afternoon train and be back in Buffalo for dinner."

"I have no intention of leaving until the case is solved."

"The case is solved? Why do you care who killed Robert Mason?"

"I don't care who it is, exactly. But after investing so much time, I simply want to know who killed him and why."

"Do you realize it could be months before they solve this? Or, they might not solve it, ever."

"Not if we helped."

"You've been reading too many dime novels."

"*I* don't read dime novels. You may do as you wish, of course. But if you're leaving, please return my fifty dollars."

Well, that decided that. I could settle my bill at the hotel and buy a ticket back to Buffalo. Or I could return her fifty dollars. But I couldn't do both. I was hoping to get back to Buffalo and get a loan from Keegan before I needed to return Emmie's stash.

"All right," I generously conceded. "Suppose we agree to stay until tomorrow. If there's progress in the case, with or without our help, we may stay further. But if the Colonel is stymied, we head back."

"Only if both the Colonel and we ourselves are stymied."

I agreed, but I didn't like being driven deeper into

debt this way. It seemed a little selfish of Emmie not to consider my position. No man enjoys having to borrow from a woman. Though to be fair, she was unaware of her role as my banker.

"Given that the Colonel didn't seem to feel in need of our help, how do you propose we proceed?" I asked.

"We should check the other hotels, of course. Sadie could be registered under any name at all. And you're the only one certain to recognize her. Do you have your map?"

"I left it in my room."

"Then we should stop there for it."

"It will give us a chance to check on Mr. R. Day, E.C., as well."

That put an abrupt end to the conversation. Emmie was not someone who could share a laugh at her own expense. I brought the map down from my room and then suggested we have lunch.

"It's rather early, isn't it?" she correctly pointed out. "We shouldn't waste time."

"But we're paying for it, Emmie. This hotel operates on the American plan."

"Oh, for goodness sakes. Is it the fifty cents lunch would cost? They'll deduct it if we haven't eaten here."

"They'll deduct two bits, and we're likely to spend double that someplace else."

"You are a skinflint, Harry. All right, there's no sense wasting time arguing."

We had a fine, but hurried, luncheon. Emmie was anxious to resume investigations and she threatened to force-feed me whenever I paused. When we had finished we went to the lobby so Emmie could send another wire to her mother, but the desk clerk stopped her.

"Excuse me. Are you Miss McGinnis?"

"Yes. Is there a message?"

"This came for you a little while ago." He handed Emmie a large envelope. It contained the photograph she had given the police and a note from Livingston. It read:

Miss McGinnis,

I hope this arrives before you leave for home. We won't be needing it any longer, as we've made several copies.

Have a pleasant trip.
Col. Livingston

Emmie pulled out the photograph and stared at it for a few seconds, and then handed it to me. Someone had used a grease pencil to circle one of the four faces and had written the name "Mason" under it. It was the wrong face.

"It's Uncle Charles!" she cried. Her reaction was equal parts surprise and elation. No doubt that would strike many people as unbecoming in a niece who has just learned that her uncle had been shot through the heart. I took a more charitable view.

"Yes. Quite a mix up. Well, the Colonel will have to suffer our company again."

I used a phone in the lobby to call the Colonel's office. He had gone home for Sunday dinner so I telephoned him there.

"I'm sorry to interrupt your dinner, Colonel. But there seems to have been some confusion."

"About what, Mr. Reese?"

"In the photo you returned, one man's face is circled. Is that the man in the morgue?"

"Yes, Mason."

"That's not Mason. Your detective circled the wrong man. That's Charles Elwell."

"You're kidding me. Are you sure?"

"Yes, Miss McGinnis is certain it's her uncle."

Livingston had us meet him at the morgue, where Emmie confirmed it was Elwell who had taken the bullet. The skinny detective showed up and explained how he hadn't marked the photograph until after he had visited the morgue. By then he wasn't positive which figure Emmie had pointed to. But since the dead man matched one of them, he assumed that that had to be him.

We went back to the Colonel's office and explained who Elwell was, how he had disappeared, and what Emmie's and my connections to him were. But something seemed a little odd to the Colonel.

"If you'll pardon me for bringing it up, miss, you don't seem very upset at finding out your uncle has been murdered."

"Well, you see, I already suspected something along those lines. I was just a little early." Emmie wasn't making things any clearer. But at least she didn't bring up the fact that her family's coffers were greatly enriched by the murder.

"What she means, Colonel," I explained, "is that there was reason to believe the accident on the lake had been staged. Which meant it was staged either by Elwell, so he could take up his life elsewhere, or by someone who had killed him, in order to cover up the crime. Miss McGinnis favored the latter explanation. So, while she hadn't anticipated this particular scenario, she was fully prepared for this outcome."

I wasn't sure I had done any better than Emmie at

enlightening the Colonel. He sat open-mouthed for a minute or so. Then he ushered us out, saying he could think more clearly if we were someplace else. I could see his point. We headed outside and I felt sure Emmie would be chagrined about our banishment. I was wrong.

"This is probably for the best, Harry. I'm not sure the Colonel could be much help to us now."

"Couldn't he? What course do you recommend?"

"That we proceed in finding Sadie, naturally." She had taken the map from me back at the Queen's and was now setting a course for the nearest hotel. "You were right, Harry. Things did work out."

"Well, I guess they have for Aunt Nell. Your uncle's death is now confirmed."

"Yes, but for you, too. This means Robert Mason is still at large."

"Yes, that's true," I agreed. "But I have no idea where."

At the American House, I was elected to make the inquiry. There was no Miss Sharp, but there was a Mr. and Mrs. Sharp. This was good enough for Emmie. She took over.

"Yes, you forgot she married this spring, Harry...." Emmie caught her faux pas a few seconds too late. And she missed three others entirely.

The clerk looked perplexed. "Mrs. Sharp, along with her husband and their three children, is spending the day on Island Park."

As we left, I tried to console Emmie by pointing out the children may well have been from Mr. Sharp's prior marriage.

At the Rossin House, a noticeably grander hotel, it was Emmie's turn to venture forth. She asked the clerk if

either Joseph Sedley or Rebecca Sharp was in. Unfortunately, the clerk's literary tastes ran similar to Robert
Mason's.

"Sadly, the Nabob's party left for Belgium just an
hour ago," he said with a sardonic smile. "They've gone to
wish the Iron Duke every success on the field, and if all
goes well, they may be returning before the month is out.
Is there any message, Mrs. Osborne?"

Here was a man with a biting wit stuck in a position
that demanded tact bordering on obsequiousness. It was
probably the first time in months he'd been able to voice
his true thoughts and he made full use of the opportunity.

15

We left the Rossin House in silence and walked rather aimlessly for a while. When we came to a cafe, I suggested we take a rest and order something cool. Emmie looked like she could use some cheering up, so I tried a dose of the usual.

"There's one thing I neglected to tell you, Emmie. About Keegan."

"What?"

I told her about Keegan's note saying he would be in town and how the clerk said he had sent his bags to the station. She made a miraculous recovery.

"What do you make of it, Harry?"

"I have no idea."

"He wanted to lead you in the wrong direction."

"Or maybe he just changed his mind after writing the note," I said. "You know, Emmie, there is one aspect of all this that doesn't make any sense to me. Your uncle died carrying papers that identified him as Joseph Sedley. But we know Sedley had been sending postcards from Montreal, and elsewhere, long before your uncle disappeared. And if your uncle had created a second life here, why was he still corresponding with Sadie?"

"Uncle Charles did travel a great deal. And maybe he was still smitten with Sadie."

"Yes, I suppose that must be the case."

Our lemonade arrived. A cold beer would have been more appropriate. No doubt there were dozens of places around Toronto where liquor could be had on Sunday—if you knew who to ask. Emmie had taken her little note-book out and throughout my ruminations was alternately reading and making notations.

"You know, Harry, there is one explanation that would fit the facts nicely. Suppose Mason killed my uncle."

I pondered this for a bit. "And then switched identities with him?"

"Yes."

"Emmie, I think you have it. We need to go back to the Colonel's."

"Why?" Emmie asked. "Don't you think we can solve this ourselves?"

"Well, he does have a police force. That might come in handy."

Emmie finally agreed and we walked back over to the police station. The Colonel kept us waiting outside his office for quite a while.

"Aren't you glad now I forced you to stay, Harry? If I'm right, it means Mason was in Toronto after all. You wouldn't have known that if you'd left."

"Yes, Emmie, I'm in your debt," I granted. "But did you say 'forced' me to stay?"

"Well, let's say 'persuaded.'"

When the Colonel did finally call us in, he didn't seem altogether pleased to see us.

"I thought you'd be off to Buffalo by now," he said. "I hoped, anyway."

Emmie took no notice of his ill humor. "Colonel, I believe Mason shot my uncle and then switched identi-ties with him. It's the only way to explain why Uncle Charles was carrying Sedley's papers."

"How so?" he asked.

"You see," Emmie explained, "Sedley had been Mason's alias for several years, but he must have decided it had been compromised. He knew Mr. Reese was looking for him. He confronted my uncle and threatened to expose him unless he came through with some real money."

"Isn't that a reason for Elwell to have shot Mason, rather than vice versa?" the Colonel reasonably asked.

Emmie's pause was a little long, so I piped up: "Elwell knew Mason well enough to know he would never be left alone as long as Mason was alive. So perhaps he shot first, but only wounded him. That was the bullet you found in the sill, and the blood there *was* Mason's. Then Mason shot Elwell in defense. Unfortunately for Elwell, Mason was a better marksman. Then Mason must have left with both guns."

The Colonel stared at me for a while, and then said, "I suppose that would explain the second shot, and the multiple identities, but surely that's an awfully roundabout way of explaining it. I mean, one man traveling under an alias kills another man traveling under an alias, then switches aliases. It sounds like a... I don't know...."

"Dime novel?" Emmie suggested.

"Yes, exactly," he agreed.

"Mrs. Redstone should be able to confirm if her husband had been traveling to Montreal," I pointed out. "Sedley checked out of a hotel there just Friday morning. In the meantime, you might put out an alert on Robert Mason, traveling as Lester Redstone."

Emmie brought out the photo and we confirmed which was Mason. But the photo was old and neither of us had ever met Mason. Nonetheless, the Colonel sent out what information he had.

"What about Whitner, Colonel?" I asked.

"He caught a morning train to Montreal. I have a man on the train with him."

"Is there a Queen's Hotel in Montreal?"

"Yes, I believe there is."

"Can you have someone there check to see if Mason or Sadie Parker has been there yesterday or today?"

"Yes, but why?"

This required a recounting of the story of the postcards. Then I went over all the possible aliases Mason and Sadie might be using.

"My God," the Colonel stared at me again. "Do you know, the last murder I worked on was a man shooting his wife's lover. That was all there was to it."

After the Colonel made the inquiries to Montreal, we all went out again. This time to speak to Mrs. Redstone at her home, 212 D'Arcy Street. We now knew that Whitey's notation must have been the address. This was a more modest house than the Elwells' Buffalo home, and in a more modest neighborhood. Elwell must have decided to keep a low profile. Mrs. Redstone's parents were there and tried to prevent us from seeing their daughter, but the Colonel insisted. She was a thirty-year-old woman, with a face distorted by tears.

"Please tell me, Mrs. Redstone," the Colonel began, "about your husband's trip to Montreal last week."

"Last week? My husband was here all of last week."

"Did he travel to Montreal?"

"Up until this summer, my husband traveled frequently. Sometimes to Montreal. Sometimes to New York. He was often gone for weeks at a time. But he had recently retired from that work."

"I see. But this past week, you're sure he didn't go to Montreal? Even for a day?"

"We had all our meals together. I don't see how it would have been possible."

"Has your husband had any visitors recently?" I asked. "I mean, besides the man who came last evening about renting the office. Anyone you never met before?"

"Earlier yesterday evening a man called at the house. He asked if this was the Redstone residence. But he was looking for a tall, young man, whose first name he didn't know. I told him that it couldn't be my husband he was seeking. He apologized for bothering me and went away."

I asked Emmie for her photograph, and then showed it to Mrs. Redstone, making sure to obscure Elwell's face. I pointed to Mason and asked if that was the man who had come looking for a tall, young man. She took the photo from me, picked up a pair of eyeglasses, and went over to a window.

"Yes, I think that was the man, but I only saw him for a minute or two. Why is the word 'Mason' written under Lester?"

"That was our mistake, I'm afraid," the Colonel confessed.

"Who are these other men?"

"Former business associates of your husband's," I answered. She handed me back the photo.

"Was your husband home when this man stopped by?"

"No, he came home not long afterward. He'd gone in a carriage to pick up my parents for dinner. They arrived about seven. We had dinner and then shortly after Lester excused himself and said he needed to meet a man about renting an office."

"Did he leave in a carriage?"

"No, he had hired the carriage just for my parents. He walked over to Queen Street, as he normally did. Then, maybe ten or twenty minutes later, that other man stopped by and said he was to meet Lester about renting the office. So I gave him the address and directions there."

We offered Mrs. Redstone our condolences and then left without telling her the truth about her husband and his business trips. She'd have to find out from the newspapers like everyone else.

"So that first man to visit the house last evening was Mason?" the Colonel asked.

"Apparently," I said. "Mason would have arrived here on Friday. I assume he knew somehow that Elwell was living in Toronto but only had the surname Redstone. Perhaps Sadie Parker had given him that information."

"So he visited Mrs. Redstone and asked for a tall, young man," Emmie said. "Then when she told him her husband was neither tall nor young, he assumed it was Uncle Charles. Is that it?"

"Yes, something like that," I answered. "Then he could just wait out of sight until Elwell came home. But when Elwell returned in the carriage with his wife's parents, Mason had to wait until they left. Then he had a stroke of luck, when Elwell left to meet the man about renting an office. Mason either followed him to the office or approached him outside the house and they walked to the office together. They went up, talked some, probably argued, and then had their shootout."

"But what about the man who wanted to rent the office?" Emmie asked. "Wouldn't he have been there as well?"

"Maybe he never showed up," I suggested.

When we arrived back at the Colonel's office, he left us in the hall while he made some phone calls.

"Do you think Whitey was sent to warn Uncle Charles that you were looking for him?" Emmie asked.

"Yes, apparently Conners and your uncle were still in contact. Conners must have given Whitey instructions before we left Buffalo, but he didn't have an address. Somehow he found that out in the course of the afternoon and wired it to the Queen's Royal Hotel."

"What was the E for? If you make 212 D'Arcy out of the code, you still have an E."

"Maybe it was there to confuse prying eyes."

"Ha-ha. You don't think he could have been involved in the murder? The Colonel doesn't seem to think so."

"Not unless he shot it out with your uncle, left with the guns, hid them, and then returned to lead the police to the crime. I can't see Whitey coming up with something so convoluted. He'd have to count on no one seeing him the first time he entered the building, on his exit, or when he was hiding the guns."

"What if he just tossed the guns out the window and never left at all?"

"Then why was he seen entering after the shots? And there's also the papers in Sedley's name."

"Yes, I forgot that," she admitted. "That was my own feeling, too. I mean that Whitey wouldn't kill someone. I know he's a sort of tough guy, but I don't think he'd kill someone in cold blood."

"Well, I wouldn't be too quick with the testimonial. Maybe he would, and maybe he wouldn't. Men with his background tend to have a liberal definition of justifiable homicide. It might include the killing of someone causing him an inconvenience. Nonetheless, I don't think Whitey fired any shots."

"You know, the Colonel is right. This has gotten a little complex. Did you expect to find my uncle here in Toronto?"

"I was hoping that Mason and Sadie were meeting to confront your uncle. I felt sure your uncle had set something up in another city and I assumed it couldn't have been too far from Buffalo. And I seem to have been right. Imagine if I had been there before the shots were fired. I would have had them both."

"But you aren't armed, and they both were."

"That's a good point. I appreciate your concern for my well-being, Emmie."

"Well, if Uncle Charles had shot you, he probably would have been discovered. And where would that leave Aunt Nell?"

"Destitute. I see. But you would also feel some loss over my death?"

"Oh, I should think so." She paused, then added, "I might never see my fifty dollars again."

"What an odd sense of humor you have, Emmie."

Just then a detective came down the hall escorting Sadie Parker. She was directed to a seat opposite us and gave me a friendly smile.

"Good afternoon, Miss Parker," I said.

"Good afternoon, Mr. Reese."

"No talking, please," her escort cautioned.

A little while later, Sadie was led into the Colonel's office. And a little while after that, we were. We sat down and the Colonel looked over at me.

"Miss Parker says she came here to meet Elwell, as he was Joseph Sedley."

"Really? Why did she leave Buffalo Friday evening on an eastbound train?"

"I took the night train to Albany, and yesterday I traveled from there to Montreal. Then I caught the train this morning in Montreal," Sadie said.

"That's a pretty roundabout route," I said. "Where'd you spend last night?"

"At the Hotel Balmoral, in Montreal."

I hadn't expected her to answer that with such alacrity. "Can you check that, Colonel?"

"Yes. In what name did you register?" he asked.

"Oh, I don't even remember. I just made something up. Stevens, I think. Mrs. Stevens. Or maybe it was...."

"Sharp?" I offered.

"No, I don't think it was," Sadie answered.

"Where were you to meet Elwell?" I asked.

"At the Queen's Hotel."

"You had met him at the Queen's Hotel here before?"

"Yes, once or twice before."

"Did you know about his family here?"

"Yes. But you see, my relationship with Mr. Elwell was no longer...."

"You were no longer his mistress?"

"No longer as intimate as it once was. We were simply old friends."

"Old friends conspiring in an insurance fraud?"

"I don't think I should say any more. Am I under arrest, Colonel?"

"No, but you'll need to stay in town. Will you be registering at the Queen's?"

"Yes, you can find me there."

She left and the Colonel sent a man to watch her. I

suggested he also monitor any communications she might receive. Then the plain-clothes man who had brought Sadie in spoke up.

"You know, sir, I didn't so much spot her at the station as she spotted me."

"How do you mean, Rawlins?" the Colonel asked.

"Well, I was looking for someone leaving, not coming. So I was watching from a place everyone getting on the train would have to pass. She must have come off the train and passed me. Then she turns and looks straight at me for a second or two and asks me if I know where the Queen's Hotel is. But she just said she'd been there before."

"Do you think she realized you were a policeman?" I asked.

"You know how that is. There are some people who can spot a cop from two hundred yards. Of course, I don't know if this lady is that type of person."

"You can take it from me, she is that type of person," I said. "Colonel, we already know that Elwell wasn't Sedley from what Mrs. Redstone told us. I think Sadie Parker was meeting Mason. When things turned out badly in Elwell's office, Mason went to warn Sadie. Then, knowing you'd eventually figure out he had shot Elwell, he convinced Sadie to come here and confuse the matter. Meanwhile, he's headed off in some other direction."

"I don't suppose there's a simpler explanation," the Colonel said. "Well, I'm afraid I'll have to trust you've been telling me the truth with all of this. I haven't heard back from your Mr. Keegan, and Detective Donahy was a little equivocal, but I suppose that's all right."

A constable came in and handed the Colonel a message. After reading it himself, he decided to share it.

"There has been no Sedley, Mason, or Sharp registered at the Queen's Hotel in Montreal recently. There is a Mrs. Parker but she has been in residence there for several months and doesn't meet our Miss Parker's description."

Before he had finished, the constable came back to tell him there was a call from one of his detectives. He picked up his phone.

"Yes, Simpson. Where?... He got off there?... Well, where did you last see him?... Port Hope! What time was that?... Yes, Simpson.... No.... All right."

The Colonel put down the phone and shook his head. "That was Simpson, the man I had following Whitner. Whitner bought a ticket for Montreal and boarded the morning express, at nine o'clock. Sometime before eleven, Simpson saw him leave the coach and go to the cafe car and take a seat. But he thought it would be too conspicuous to do likewise, so he returned to the coach. After half an hour of waiting for Whitner to return to his seat, Simpson went looking for him. He wasn't in the cafe car. He searched the other coaches and found a man who had covered himself with a blanket and pulled down his hat, a derby, like Whitner's. Simpson recognized the satchel beside the man as Whitner's, convinced himself this was Whitner, and relaxed. The man just left the train somewhere before Montreal and Simpson finally realized his error. Whitner had given the man five dollars to pose as him. The last time Simpson saw Whitner was more than six hours ago, just before Port Hope."

"It's my fault, Colonel. I should have warned you Whitner had experience at this type of thing."

"Mr. Reese, I honestly wish it were your fault," the Colonel confided. "Why would he get off the train in Port Hope?"

"There's a Queen's Hotel in Port Hope," Detective Rawlins said.

"Yes, that's right," Livingston agreed. "Right on the water."

"Do steamships stop there?" I asked.

"Yes, there's a run from here twice a day," Rawlins answered. "But not on Sunday. And one to Charlotte on the American side."

"That's Rochester, isn't it?" I asked.

"Yes, Charlotte is, I mean," Rawlins confirmed. He left the office for a moment and then returned with a booklet of steamship schedules. "The boat leaves Charlotte about ten in the morning and arrives in Port Hope around three in the afternoon. Then it goes back to Charlotte and gets in around eight in the evening."

"I think we have it then," I said. "Mason arranges to meet Sadie at the Queen's Hotel in Port Hope Saturday evening. But first, he comes here on Friday to seek out and confront Elwell. That doesn't go as planned. With a corpse on his hands, he decides to make use of it and switches identities."

"Then he heads to Port Hope," Emmie chimed in. "And meanwhile, Sadie takes a train from Buffalo to Rochester and spends Friday night in a hotel there. Then she takes the boat to Port Hope and waits for Mason at the Queen's Hotel."

"Yes," I said. "They spend the night there and then today they split up. And Sadie comes here."

"Sacrificing herself to save him," Emmie said.

"Yes, very romantic. Now we just need to figure out where Mason went off to."

"He'd take the boat to Charlotte," Emmie interjected. "He knew that the police would be looking for him here. And why would Sadie go through all that to pretend to be coming from Montreal if Mason was going back there?"

"Yes, that makes sense. The police aren't actively looking for him in the U.S. now. Whereas here he's suspected of murder. Does that boat run on Sundays?"

Rawlins checked his book. "Yes, it does."

"Colonel," I said, "if you contact the Queen's Hotel in Port Hope, I think you'll find there was a Joseph Sedley, or Lester Redstone, registered there last night, and perhaps a Becky Sharp."

The Colonel had a telephone call put through to the hotel. He spoke with a clerk and gave him the various aliases used by Mason and Sadie. The clerk verified that a Joseph Sedley had registered the night before, as had a Rebecca Sharp. Then I asked to speak with the clerk.

"Has anyone else asked about Mr. Sedley?" I asked.

"Yes, a friend of his, right around lunch time. I told him Mr. Sedley had checked out but was in the dining room."

"Did they leave the hotel together?"

"I didn't see them leave."

"Did Mr. Sedley by any chance ask for a doctor?" I asked.

"A doctor? I wasn't working when he registered, but no doctor was called last night."

"Can you tell what time he registered?"

"He was the last one to register for the evening, so I would think it must have been after eleven. Why do you ask about the doctor?"

"It's possible he had been wounded earlier in the evening."

"The reason I ask is that there is a stain on the ledger below Mr. Sedley's name that necessitated we skip several lines when our first guest registered this morning. It's a dark red stain, and when I first saw it, I thought of blood."

I thanked him and hung up, then told the others what he had said.

"If we can wire the Rochester police, they may be able to find both Mason and Whitner among the passengers disembarking from the evening boat."

"An international cable? I suppose I have to."

The wire included all the details and aliases we had on Mason, mentioned the wound on his hand or arm, and explained that he was wanted in a murder investigation. The boat wouldn't dock for another two hours, so the Colonel sent us off and said he would await the reply at home.

16

We returned to the Queen's Hotel, where we went to our rooms to bathe and change for dinner. As I waited in the lobby for Emmie, I saw Sadie in a corner reading a magazine. I walked over and sat down near her. She looked up at me with a sort of expectant expression that seemed completely out of character.

"You're anxious to hear about Mason, I imagine," I said.

"I'm not sure what you mean."

"The police know you were in Port Hope last night."

"Do they?"

"And about your trip across the lake from Rochester yesterday."

"Is there a crime in taking a steamboat across the lake?"

Emmie joined us and I introduced her to Sadie.

"Miss McGinnis is Mr. Elwell's niece," I explained.

"Oh, I am sorry for your loss, Miss McGinnis." Sadie almost sounded sincere.

"Your loss as well, from what you said earlier," Emmie said.

"Yes. Your uncle was a good friend."

We said good-bye and went in to dinner.

"Does she know the police are after Mason?" Emmie asked.

"Yes, but I didn't mention they're looking in Rochester. I think she's waiting here in the hope that a message will arrive telling her he's arrived there safely."

"She must really care for him."

"Yes, I suppose she does."

"If Mason killed my uncle, could she collect on the life insurance policy?"

"Maybe. I guess it would depend on how much she knew about Mason's blackmail scheme. It would also depend on how good a lawyer she could afford."

When we'd finished our soup, I posed a question. "A minute ago you said *if* Mason killed your uncle. Are you doubting your own theory?"

"Well, it does seem a little odd. I mean, that they both had guns, and that my uncle resorted to trying to kill Mason. And then Mason taking both guns away."

"Your uncle was probably planning to meet Mason, so he might have taken a pistol as a matter of safety. Then Mason demanded a sum that would have meant impoverishing the Canadian branch of the family. Your uncle felt he had to risk shooting Mason and seeing if he could get away with it. Mason was a fugitive, after all."

"Yes, but even if he could avoid a murder charge, his identity would certainly be uncovered by the newspapers."

"Maybe," I said. "But who else could it have been? Whitey?"

"Maybe we were wrong to dismiss him so quickly. What if he went to silence my uncle, shot him, then shot Mason because he witnessed it?"

"Then let Mason go?"

"Maybe Mason pointed out that he was in no position to go to the police. Whitey allowed him to escape, if he agreed to take the pistol away with him. Then Whitey went out for a policeman, and by reporting it, removed suspicion from himself."

I pondered that for a bit. "There are two flaws with that account. If Whitey came here to kill your uncle, would he have walked up to his house and spoken with his wife just before doing the deed? Why not telephone?"

"Maybe they don't have a phone. What's the second flaw?"

"Why would Whitey have Mason switch identities with your uncle, or at least allow him to do so?"

"I'm not sure," Emmie admitted. "But if he wasn't helping Mason to get away, why didn't Whitey tell the police that it was Uncle Charles's body?"

"I can only guess that he thought it would make it easier to get away himself if he didn't complicate the story. He knew we'd be following him and your uncle would be identified soon. Then the insurance company would have to pay the claim, and the Elevator Company could repay his boss. By handling it the way he did, he both removed suspicion from himself and has gotten back to Buffalo for the horse races."

"Horse races?"

"Remember, the Grand Circuit trotters start running tomorrow. Whitey was keen on getting back in time."

After dinner, Emmie asked the clerk about Island Park. He told us it was a sort of resort island just off the harbor. The amusement park would be closed on a Sunday, but he highly recommended a visit.

The ferry left from a pier just below the railway station and we boarded with no gangplank incidents of note. It was full of young people who'd probably had to spend the day in church and now wanted some fun. Emmie decided she wanted some lemonade, so I headed over to a little concession stand not fifty feet away. But fifty feet was enough to get solicited by a young lady as I made my

163

way through the crowd. The soliciting was subtle—as was appropriate for the Sabbath—but clear nonetheless. When I returned with the drinks, I decided not to mention the episode to Emmie.

"Harry, in the brief time you were away, do you know I was twice approached by young men? One was just a boy. What friendly people."

"I'm not sure it can be attributed to mere friendliness. I'm afraid, once again, we have wandered into a place of assignation. Apparently, certain assumptions are made about unaccompanied young ladies on the evening ferry. And there seems to be some basis for this. I met a chippie just on the way to the lemonade stand."

Of course, Emmie wanted me to point her out so she could study her dress and manner. Out came the notebook.

Island Park was a sort of Coney Island, but a lot less noisy, at least on Sunday. The amusements were mostly closed, but there were hotels, picnic groves, and long sandy beaches. Hundreds of young men and women were strolling about—some in couples, some with friends, and some, apparently, looking for friends.

Emmie, feeling her study had been incomplete, wanted for us to split up and go about as if we, too, were looking for friends. Then she could record the number of times we were each approached and the methodologies used. I agreed, as long as we stayed in sight of each other.

"But do keep in mind, Emmie, if you are too suggestive, your potential suitor may feel a trifle let down when you give him the cold shoulder."

"I'll be careful," she promised.

We then each did a slow circle of the grove and ten minutes later reported back.

"I only had one hit," I said sheepishly. "But this girl made her intentions very clear."

Emmie recorded the terms I'd been offered and then made her own, rather boastful, report: she had been approached no less than five times. And several made unmistakable offers.

"Aren't there places like this in Massachusetts?"

"Nothing so brazen, and certainly not so commercial. At least, not where we live."

"Well, there are dozens of places in New York you should visit," I suggested. "For your researches, I mean."

"Oh, I'd love to. I wanted to move to New York with a friend from school, but mother was afraid I'd succumb to sin and vice. We compromised and I came to Buffalo to live with my aunt and uncle."

"The felonious bigamist?" I asked rhetorically. "What do you have in mind for all these notes you've been taking?"

"Well, you'll think it silly, but I fancy myself a writer."

"Isn't the subject matter a little sordid?"

"I wouldn't say sordid. Perhaps salacious," Emmie clarified. "You see, I thought I'd start out with dime novels and such. So the more salacious, the better."

"I thought you said you never read dime novels."

"I don't see what that has to do with it. Later, once I have an income, I can move on to more artistic work."

"In that case, you'll need to use a pseudonym for the salacious work."

"Oh, yes, definitely. But do you think it would be better to use a masculine name or a feminine one? I mean, which would sell better?"

"Well, that would depend. If you're writing detective

stories, I'd say a man's name. But if you were to special-ize in fallen women and their travails, I'd use a woman's name. It would give the appearance of a sympathetic author."

"That's sound advice. But I haven't settled on the exact nature of the books yet."

We left the island around nine in the hopes there would be news from the Colonel waiting for us at the hotel. Sadie was still in the lobby. The clerk handed me an envelope and we read it at the desk. It said:

Congratulations. Mason apprehended in Rochester using the name Redstone and with a bandaged wound on his right arm. I'll be leaving tomorrow on the 8:45 train to Buffalo. I would appreciate it if you would join me.

William Stark, Inspector of Detectives

"Who's William Stark?"

"Maybe Livingston's boss. His nameplate was on the desk."

"We should tell Sadie," Emmie said. "She's waiting for a message that won't be coming."

"The Inspector might not want us to pass on this in-formation."

"Well, he's not here." Emmie grabbed the message and carried it over to Sadie, who read it and gave it back. They spoke briefly and Emmie returned. Then we went into the hotel's saloon and Emmie ordered a bottle of champagne. The waiter pointed out it was Sunday. Then, sotto voce, he suggested he could have a bottle sent to her room. Emmie told him to send two bottles. I'm sure I needn't say at what cost.

Once we were upstairs and the champagne had arrived, Emmie offered some rare flattery.

"Harry, I wanted to tell you, your summation in the Colonel's office was excellent."

"Thank you, Emmie. I thought so too."

"Had you practiced it?"

"Practiced it? You mean solving cases like this?"

"No, I mean that particular speech."

"How in the world could I have practiced it?"

"Oh, it was just a thought."

The wine was excellent. But it required a large withdrawal from the bankroll Emmie had placed in my care.

17

By the next morning Emmie and I had what is commonly referred to as an understanding. The details of what had occurred shall be left unspoken. Suffice it to say the Rubicon had been crossed and the die was cast.

The conversation at the breakfast table was a little strained, at first. But before long, it had become exceedingly unpleasant. Emmie, rather belatedly, had decided to ascertain my financial condition. I provided a broad outline of my income over the last few years, which was nothing to sniff at, and evaded any talk of assets or current accounts. When she asked where we'd live, I offered a glowing description of my Brooklyn apartment. She showed no curiosity over whether or not the rent had been paid, so I made no mention of it. Then she asked me how much insurance I carried, whether there were payments on the furniture, and similar sundry details. But she always returned to the subject of hard assets. Not surprisingly, thirty minutes of crafting carefully worded evasions had left me exhausted and I was relieved when we finally needed to rush to the station.

Detective Rawlins was on the platform with a very serious-looking older fellow whom he introduced as Inspector Stark. Rawlins then left us and we boarded the train.

"It sounds like I missed quite a bit the last couple of days." Inspector Stark then went on to explain that he had been away on a family visit and so Livingston, who was a retired inspector, had filled in for him. "Livingston is a good man, but he dates from a time when things were simpler and not much was expected of the police. He was the colonel of a cavalry regiment."

"A cavalry regiment?" I asked.

"Yes, the national mythology has it he helped beat back the Fenians in '66."

"Why are you both looking at me?" Emmie asked.

"Well, Emmie, they were your people," I pointed out.

"I hope it isn't a sore point, Miss McGinnis," the Inspector smiled.

"No, not for my people. That would be the occupation and famine that incited the Fenians."

That effectively killed the conversation for a moment, but then the Inspector turned to less sensitive matters.

"Livingston and Rawlins have filled me in on the events of the last couple days, but I was hoping you two would go over with me all that you know."

We did that and it took most of an hour. Unlike Livingston, Stark took the rather complicated tale in stride, making careful notes throughout. Then he recapitulated it to us just to make sure he had it all straight.

I was developing a very positive opinion of Stark. But when I poked fun at his city's blue laws, he confessed he was all for them. In fact, he was an officer in a temperance league. I assumed this was a ruse of some sort. I knew for a fact that if liquor sales were ever eliminated in New York, the average cop's income would fall by half. Their informal system of taxation was as well known as it was lucrative and I found it hard to believe the police in Toronto hadn't taken it up too.

"Our train gets in to Buffalo at 11:40," Stark said.

"We should be able to catch the 11:50 to Rochester from the same station. I'm rather anxious to get there as soon as possible."

"To have first claim on Mason?"

"Yes, something like that. From what you've told me, he's wanted elsewhere in New York, but for nothing as serious as murder. I'm hoping I can convince the Rochester authorities that the simplest course would be for them to deport him back to Canada. Then I could have him in Toronto by tomorrow. I hope that won't interfere with your objective?"

"I guess not. I was to see that he was taken into custody. The only problem might be if he were acquitted in Toronto."

"Well, in that case he could be extradited back to New York."

"Yes, I suppose so. Was Whitner seen leaving the boat in Rochester?"

"No, no mention was made of him. Do you think he'll return to Buffalo?"

"No. If he was on the boat, he saw them take Mason and knows any opportunity for blackmail is gone. And by now, he'd know Elwell is dead. He'll probably head back to New York and look for some new game."

We arrived in Buffalo in time to catch the 11:50 local, but I convinced the Inspector it made more sense to take the one o'clock express and have a leisurely lunch in Buffalo. Emmie realized she had never wired her mother about staying away another night and rushed home.

The Inspector decided he'd rather spend the time looking in on Detective Donahy than at a restaurant, so I accompanied him to police headquarters and introduced him. Then I told Stark I'd meet him at the station at one and walked over to the Iroquois. I found Keegan in his room.

"How was your little trip?" I asked.

"My trip? Oh, fine, fine. I take it you have news?"

"Yes. They have Mason in Rochester."

"In Rochester? Why did he come back to the states? That wasn't very wise of him."

"Because he's wanted for murder in Canada."

"Murder? Who'd he shoot?"

"Charles Elwell. You remember him—he was the secretary of the Eastern Elevator Company who had disappeared. He was hiding out in Toronto, with a new name, a new wife, and two little girls."

"Yes. That was your other endeavor. I guess now those policies will be paying out."

"Yes, he's definitely dead now," I said. "The terms of our agreement on Mason were that he be in the hands of the authorities. Does it matter if he's sent back to Canada?"

"No, though Cowell might give you a hard time. That man hates to part with money, even if it isn't his own."

"Speaking of money, do you think I could get an advance on the $300?"

"I'm a little short right now, but meet me for dinner downstairs at eight and I'll have something for you then. Will you be heading back to New York tomorrow?"

"No, I don't think so. Why?"

"Just curious. I'll be staying on a few days as well."

I rushed back to McLeod's and made the mistake of checking at the desk for messages. Not having seen me for two days, the clerk asked that I make my account current—requiring a further dip into Emmie's cash reserves. After I paid him, he handed over a message from Carlotta saying she'd be in town until Thursday. I went up and put on a new shirt and collar and had just enough time to grab a bite at a lunch counter before heading to the station.

We all boarded the one o'clock express and the Inspector opened the conversation as soon as we were seated.

"There are some parts of your scenario that seem unresolved," he said. "For instance, the idea that Mason left carrying two pistols and then disposed of them. I had some men comb the neighborhood last evening and they found nothing. And I can't believe Mason would go very far carrying these guns, one of which was the murder weapon. I suppose it's possible he hid them nearby and we just haven't found them. Or someone else did find them and kept it to himself."

"That was just an explanation that fit the facts," I admitted. "I can't say I like it either, but you have a witness who says Whitey Schuler arrived after the shots. And Whitner was observed at the hotel during the shooting. Who else is there?"

"If you'd spent time as a policeman, Mr. Reese, you'd know not to put too much faith in witnesses. For instance, the bartender and the waiter at the Queen's had insisted that Whitner never left the hotel. Yet when I had them brought back in last evening, the waiter said he stepped outside at one point, just for a breath of air, and Whitner was outside apparently doing the same thing. But neither saw Whitner get up and leave. They saw Whitner at various times between six and ten and assumed he had never left."

"Does that make Whitner a suspect?" Emmie asked.

"Well, certainly not a likely one, but a possibility,"

he responded. "It's not that I have a good alternative to Mason. I just can't see a rational man acting in the way you describe. Think what you would do in that situation. You've just shot a man dead. You don't know how much time you have before someone comes to investigate the shots. Wouldn't you leave as quickly as possible?"

"But we know Mason didn't leave immediately because he took the time to switch identities," I reminded him.

"I know what I would have done," Emmie said. "I'd have taken the gun I had used to shoot my uncle—I mean the victim—and placed it in his hand. Then left with his gun."

"And then the simple-minded police would assume suicide?" the Inspector smiled.

"Why would it be so far-fetched?" Emmie asked. "What if he was being blackmailed and saw no way out?"

"For one thing, a shot fired like that would leave powder burns, and there were none," the Inspector explained. "For another, the first bullet hit the window sill on the other side of the room. But I grant you, it would make better sense than the murderer taking both guns out of the room."

"What were the other points that bothered you?" I asked.

"Well, one was that switching of identities you just brought up. Or rather, false identities. The only reason we linked this to Mason is because the papers of Joseph Sedley were found on Elwell. If he hadn't placed them there himself, what clue would we have that he had fired the shot?"

"But Mason must have realized that that alias had been compromised," I answered. "He needed a new identity, which is why he took Elwell's papers in the name of Lester Redstone. And by linking the Sedley name to Elwell, he might give himself some more time to get away while the police tried to figure out who exactly Elwell was. You see, he wouldn't have known I would be there."

"Yes, I suppose that's true," he conceded. "There is one other thing though. After the shooting, why did he risk going to Port Hope? How could he be sure Miss Parker hadn't been followed there? My natural inclination would be to go in some other direction entirely, like to Chicago."

"That's easy," Emmie chimed in. "They're in love. You should have seen her last evening at the hotel, hoping to hear from Mason."

"Yes," the Inspector agreed. "She did allow herself to be used in his escape. Though it didn't help him much."

We arrived in Rochester and took a car to police headquarters, where the Inspector met with the chief of detectives. Then we were all led to a room and Mason was brought in to be questioned.

"We can, of course, place you at the scene with Elwell," the Inspector started. "And we know you were shot there."

"Yes, but I didn't shoot Elwell," Mason insisted. "I've never carried a gun. And why would I shoot him?"

"For the very good reason he shot you first," the Inspector answered.

"Elwell didn't shoot me. What made you think that?"

"Who else was there?"

"I don't know who fired the shots."

"What time did you meet Elwell?"

"He'd told me to be at his building at half past eight. I was waiting outside by then and he arrived a little later.

He led me up to that office and lit a gas jet. It was still dark, so I went over and stood by the window, but we were just talking anyway. Then, all of a sudden, someone swung open the door and fired. The first shot was meant for me. I dropped to the floor and another shot went off. I just stayed on the floor for a time. When I rose, I was alone with Elwell, and he was dead."

"Did you see the killer?"

"All I saw was a flash, then I was on the floor. Then another shot. I waited a good bit before getting up."

"Then what happened?"

"Well, I went over to Elwell and saw he was dead. I started to leave, but then I got the idea to exchange wallets. I'd been traveling as Joseph Sedley—I imagine you know that."

"Yes, we were aware of that."

"That afternoon, I had seen a man asking about Joseph Sedley."

"Where?"

"The Queen's Hotel. There in Toronto. I was registered there under Carbury. I came in and asked at the desk for my key and here is this fellow asking if there's a Joseph Sedley registered there. I could see this guy wasn't a cop, he was dressed too well. And I imagine there are some real Joseph Sedleys out there. But this wasn't someone looking for a friend. He even slipped the clerk some cash, and then he describes this Joseph Sedley: a sixty-year-old heavyset man not more than five foot seven. That sounded just like Elwell. Then later it occurred to me that someone must've read the cards I'd sent Sadie and assumed they were from Elwell. So when I was standing there with Elwell's body, I thought I'd just play into that."

"How did you find out Elwell was in Toronto?" I asked.

"I had known that for a while. He'd been setting up there since before I left Buffalo."

"So you already knew he was using the name Lester Redstone?"

"Oh, yes. And that building he was killed in was bought years ago."

"Did you ever stop by his home in Toronto?"

"No, but I'd met him at that same building a few times over the years."

"Even before he staged his accident on the lake?"

"Yes. As I said, he'd been setting that up for quite a while. He traveled back and forth."

"Why did you visit him Saturday? Didn't you arrive in Toronto on Friday?"

"Yes, but Elwell insisted on Saturday. I sent him a letter earlier in the week asking to meet with him. I told him I'd be at the Queen's Friday registered as Carbury. When I arrived at the Queen's, there was a note from him telling me to meet him at his building Saturday evening."

"What were you meeting him about?"

"He wanted to borrow some money. He liked being a landlord and had found another building he wanted to buy."

"And you were going to lend it to him?"

"Yes. Not as much as he asked for, but a couple thousand."

"Where did you get the money from?"

"Oh, here and there."

"And when you switched wallets, you kept the money you had brought?"

"No, I left it in the wallet. I thought his widow, I

mean Mrs. Redstone, might be in a tough spot. Did she get the money?"

"He had only twelve dollars on him when we arrived," the Inspector said.

"Well, someone has that two thousand," Mason insisted. "Will you check into it, Inspector?"

"Yes, you can be certain I will," he replied.

We all got up to leave. But first Emmie leaned over and whispered something to Mason. He smiled and thanked her, then we left him.

"Do you mind my asking what you whispered, Miss McGinnis?" the Inspector asked.

"It was a personal message from Miss Parker." That was all Emmie would say about that, but she did offer that she thought Mason was telling the truth.

"There did seem to be some sincerity to his confession," the Inspector allowed. "But he's an admitted swindler. Those people can put sincerity on and take it off the way you or I change hats. That's how they make their living. And all that about leaving two thousand dollars on the dead man for the aid of his widow was really a bit much."

"You don't think that's true?" Emmie asked.

"No, I do not," he laughed. "But I will cable my men and have someone look into it, just to be sure."

"Do you think you'll have any luck having him deported?" I asked.

"No, unfortunately the warrants issued here will necessitate an extradition hearing. I'm staying on tonight to see if I can speed things along, but if he has a good lawyer, it could be weeks."

We said good-bye and asked the Inspector to keep us abreast of developments.

18

Emmie and I caught the 5:30 mail train to Buffalo. It was a hot afternoon and inside the coach the air was stifling. It's a situation where anyone with any sense simply succumbs to slumber. Emmie had other ideas.

"Do you think Mason was telling the truth?" she asked.

"I guess some of it was the truth. But as the Inspector pointed out, a man like Mason gets pretty accustomed to lying. For my purposes, it doesn't really matter. He's in the hands of the authorities, so I've earned three hundred dollars. And the Elevator Company will get their payment because your uncle is definitely dead and it had nothing to do with them."

"But after spending all this time on the case, don't you want to see it through?"

"Sure, I'm curious. But even assuming Mason is telling the truth, he can't identify the murderer. And he's the sole witness. The only way for Mason to convince the police he's innocent is to provide them with another killer."

"Let's assume Mason didn't kill Uncle Charles. Maybe we could identify the killer by reasoning it out. From what the Inspector said, Whitner may have had time to leave the Queen's, shoot my uncle and Mason, and get back without anyone realizing he'd left."

"I'll grant you that's a possibility, but it would mean Whitner must have come to Toronto with the purpose of killing your uncle. Remember, according to Mason, the killer fired without saying a word. Why would Whitner want to see your uncle dead?"

"Maybe he had some feud with Uncle Charles. Or maybe it was his intent to kill Mason, and he just shot my uncle as a witness."

"If it wasn't Mason, I think Whitey is a more likely suspect."

"Even though the witness saw him arrive after the shots?"

"Look how that waiter at the hotel changed his story about Whitner. With Whitey, at least there's a clear motive: Conners needed Elwell dead to collect on his loan."

"Yes, that's true. But what if it wasn't Whitner or Whitey?"

"Or Mason?"

"Yes, of course, or Mason."

"You might not want to speculate about that."

"You mean Charlie?"

"Sure. He left to take a train out of town Saturday morning. He could easily have been in Toronto. Maybe he knew your uncle was there all along. Now, with me poking around, he felt the secret would get out and his mother would never be able to collect on her policies."

"That's absurd. Charlie would never do anything like that. He was traveling on business."

"Okay, Charlie would never do that."

"What about the two thousand dollars Mason left in the wallet? If we could find that, we might have the murderer."

"Mason wasn't lending your uncle money. If I want to borrow two thousand dollars from a man, and he tells me to meet with him on Friday, I certainly don't insist that he make it Saturday. And he said he left the money on your uncle after the shots were fired and the killer fled. Where is it?"

"Whitey must have taken it."

"Well, I grant you Whitey would definitely have taken it if it was there to take. But the police must have searched him after finding him at the murder scene. There was no two thousand dollars."

"You aren't helping much."

"Look, the most likely scenario is Mason came to blackmail your uncle. Sadie and he may have been planning on leaving for Europe, or South America, using the money Sadie expected to collect from the policy on your uncle. But it looked like that might never happen without a body. Maybe Mason had already been blackmailing Elwell for a while. But if he and Sadie went off to parts unknown, this would be his last chance to bleed him. So this time he asked for a large sum. He over-played his hand. Elwell had been willing to pay the smaller amounts, but to meet Mason's new demand would mean selling the assets he had carefully amassed in Toronto. And he still couldn't be sure Mason wouldn't be back for more. He sets the meeting up for Saturday evening because he's planning to kill Mason and he wants the building empty of witnesses. He shoots, and Mason shoots back. Mason even explained why he switched identities: he thought Whitner was looking for Elwell posing as Joseph Sedley."

"But let's suppose Mason *is* a killer. He knew Uncle Charles was in Toronto. He could have killed him at any time. Then Sadie could have collected on her policy and they could have gone off."

"Yes, that's true enough," I admitted. "But there's a

difference between planning a cold-blooded murder and shooting a man in self-defense."

"And he didn't seem like a cold-blooded killer?"

"No, definitely not. You can tell by the eyes."

"He did have sincere eyes," Emmie agreed. But then she saw my smile. "You're playing horse with me again."

That put Emmie into a pet, but at least I was allowed to sleep for the rest of the trip. When we arrived, Emmie woke me with a rather unsettling request. She asked for the return of the fifty dollars she had entrusted to me. I wasn't up to explaining why there was only thirty-some remaining, so I lied.

"I'm afraid I left it at my hotel when I stopped off there earlier."

"You left it in a hotel room?"

"No, no. The manager put it in the safe for me. I'll bring it by the house this evening." If only I could lie as well as Mason, there wouldn't have been a problem. As it was, Emmie left for home with a look of consternation on her face. It was quite unbecoming.

I bought a newspaper and went over to McLeod's for a cool bath. The big news was that the muzzling of dogs was still required, though the public was assured that the recent rabies epidemic had ended. Further down the page was the headline "Man's Body Found in Cellar Hole." The story read:

Workers at a building site on Oakland Street were surprised this morning to find the body of a man lying at the base of the cellar hole they'd been preparing. It was quickly apparent the man had been dead for some time, and the police were summoned.

As no papers were found on the body, the man could

not at first be identified. Later, a photograph was taken at the morgue and shown at various hotels. The manager at the Iroquois identified him as John Whitner of New York. It is believed he lost his way in the dark, stumbled into the cellar, and hit his head on the masonry.

Why would Whitner have returned to Buffalo? I had assumed he would go straight to New York. But either way, he wasn't the type to drink himself into a stupor and tumble into a cellar hole. Jack Whitner had been murdered. The police might not have looked too closely at it, or, if they had suspected it was murder, decided it wasn't important. Most likely, they were right. Everyone who knew him in Buffalo would be glad to be rid of him. Any friends or relatives back in New York probably knew him under a different name. No one would be pestering the police demanding something be done. Certainly not me.

I dressed and then went off to the Iroquois. I found Keegan in the billiard room and we went in to dinner. He ordered us another exquisite meal, but there was still no smoked eel available. Apparently, Boss Conners had cornered the market.

"I was wondering about the advance on the Mason case?"

"I'm afraid I have some bad news there. And it's a little embarrassing," he confessed. "You see, the main reason I stayed on after Mrs. Keegan left was to spend a few days at the races in Fort Erie. The Grand Circuit is there this week. I never get a chance to visit the track at home. I stopped at the bank right after I spoke to you, but I'm afraid my luck went rather badly this afternoon. And, well...."

"I don't mean to sound mercenary, but I could really

use the money this evening. Even twenty dollars. Perhaps the cashier here would take your check?"

"I tried that, but it seems I've a rather large bill, and they really don't know me. But I'd be happy to write you a check. Or you can wait until I visit the bank first thing in the morning. They have my letter of credit."

I couldn't imagine explaining to Emmie why I was returning her money in the form of a check from a complete stranger, so I told him I'd meet him in the morning. I tried to extend the evening as long as possible in the hope that if I called Emmie late enough, she'd have to agree to put off the repayment until the next day.

"Did you see Jack Whitner was found dead this morning?" I asked.

"Jack Whitner?"

"Yes, that fellow I was with when I ran into you and the missus the other night."

"Was there an accident?"

"Well, he was found dead in the cellar hole of a house they're building somewhere. The police think it was an accident."

"Any reason not to think so?"

I recounted Whitner's part in the events of the last several days.

"Yes, a bit of a coincidence," was all Keegan said.

We lingered over our meal, had cigars and brandy, and then played several games of pool. Keegan won three dollars, but agreed to put it on account. It was long after ten when we went into the lobby. I told Keegan I needed to make a call and headed to the phone. As I passed the desk, I saw Detective Donahy speaking with the clerk. The clerk nodded at me and whispered something to Donahy.

Donahy cut me off before I got to the telephone. He

had a look of disgust on his face. At least, I took it as disgust. It may have been indigestion. Regardless, he didn't look in the best of moods.

"I guess we need to have a talk," he said. "Let's sit down."

"Is this about Jack Whitner?" I asked.

"Yeah. We got a call this evening from a Miss McGinnis. She insisted Whitner was murdered. So I got called away from home and had to listen to a long story of hers about following this Whitner to Canada, finding Charles Elwell dead, chasing that Mason guy, and what else I can't remember. She said you could tell me all about Whitner. You weren't at your hotel so I came here to see what they knew about him. The clerk just told me you'd been asking about Whitner."

I should have known Emmie wouldn't miss an opportunity to complicate things.

"Well, she exaggerated," I said. "I don't know much, really. But I suspect Whitner was a grafter who knew something about Elwell still being alive. He was from New York and there's probably something on him there. I think he assumed Elwell had set up an insurance fraud scheme with his wife or Sadie Parker, or perhaps both. So he was sticking around hoping to find out where Elwell was hiding. Then he'd blackmail him. But he mistook postcards sent to Sadie from Mason as coming from Elwell. He read one telling Sadie to go to a Queen's Hotel and ended up in Toronto expecting to find Elwell there. He was in the right city, but for the wrong reason. And he never saw Elwell. With Elwell's death, his set-up died, too. I have no idea why he came back here."

"This McGinnis girl says he must have known who killed Charles Elwell."

184

"Miss McGinnis has a restless imagination. The police in Toronto are willing to believe Robert Mason killed Elwell. Anyway, I thought your people determined Whitner's death was an accident?"

"Well, the boys kind of left it at that. There was a bash on the head, and plenty of stone to hit it on. But now there'll be an autopsy."

"Even if Whitner was murdered, I'd bet it was because of some other bunco he had going. He was in town for a few weeks, so he may have had several irons in the fire. Blackmail may have been a specialty. I'd see who else he met with here."

"Yeah. First I'll see what the autopsy finds. Maybe I won't have to bother," he said. "Where will you be tomorrow?"

"I'll be in town."

"Well, meet me in the office around eleven. By then I'll know what the doctor has to say about Whitner. And you can give me your version of what happened in Canada."

I agreed to do that, and then finally telephoned Emmie.

"I'm sorry for calling so late, Emmie."

"That's all right. Did you see Detective Donahy?"

"Yes." In fact, I was looking straight at him. He was over by the desk talking to Keegan. "Why'd you get involved in this, Emmie?"

"Well, doesn't it seem too much of a coincidence? Whitner goes to Toronto just in time for Uncle Charles's murder. Then comes back here the next day and is found dead just a block from the house."

"A block from your aunt's house?"

"Yes, didn't you realize that?"

"No. Donahy didn't mention it. I see what you mean now."

"I know what you're thinking."

"It doesn't matter what I'm thinking. It's what Donahy thinks. Did you find out where Charlie went on Saturday?"

"Lockport. He spent the night there."

"But he came back to town on Sunday?"

"No, not until this morning. He called Aunt Nell from the office. His business trip took longer than he had anticipated."

"Is he home now?"

"No, he told Aunt Nell he was going out with some friends after work."

"Isn't it kind of odd he hasn't been home since he and his mother learned about his father's death?"

"He was home for lunch. And it's not like Aunt Nell is in tears over Uncle Charles's death. I suppose it might strike someone else as odd. But Charlie didn't kill anyone. You need to make sure Detective Donahy understands that."

"Detective Donahy would be home in bed and have forgotten all about Whitner if you hadn't telephoned."

"I know. I should have waited until I'd spoken with Charlie. Maybe I could tell them it was a mistake."

"Too late. There'll be an autopsy tomorrow morning and it's a safe bet they'll determine it was murder. Are you going to the office tomorrow?"

"Yes, I suppose so."

"I'll meet you for lunch. By then I'll know the results of the autopsy."

She agreed. I felt bad for making her feel guilty. But at least the matter of her fifty dollars never came up.

I went over to the Vendome to see if Carlotta was in. It was late to be calling, but not for her crowd. She was in the taproom with a new cast of vaudevillians. These were the acts for the new week at Shea's. I got to regale them with the story of Elwell and Mason, and Sadie. I'd be able to buy drinks with this tale for years to come.

Madden wasn't there, so I drew Carlotta aside to ask about him.

"Our next show is three days in Cleveland, starting Thursday, so he went up to see his family, in Canada someplace."

"But you didn't go with him?"

"Why would I go with him? I stayed on to see you again, and for the horse races."

"You've been to the races today? How'd you do?"

"Don't ask. Another day like that and I'll be walking to Cleveland."

"I don't suppose you knew a fellow by the name of Jack Whitner in New York?"

"It doesn't sound familiar. Why?"

"Oh, I think he might have been a friend of Madden's. He was found dead this morning."

"Another murder?"

"Maybe."

Then I told her about my engagement to Emmie. She began to ask me about Emmie's family and just how much I knew about her. Which naturally made me laugh, given that Emmie's family had such an unflattering picture of Carlotta. I had to tell her all about her brief stay at college, and subsequent stumble into ill repute. She found it very funny. But when she was done laughing, and had had time to think about it, she asked if I was sure Emmie wasn't just a little queer in the head.

19

After breakfast the next morning I went directly to the Iroquois and camped out in the lobby until Keegan finally came down. I wasn't going to let him out of my sight until the banks opened and I had my advance. I sat through breakfast with him and tried to bring up Whitner again. But he kept changing the subject.

"I may have a job in Scranton for you," he said. "But you'd need to be there in the next day or so. Could you make that?"

"I don't know. You see, I've gotten myself engaged." I told him about Emmie and he congratulated me.

"So you're stuck in Buffalo making arrangements?"

"Yes."

"Then why don't you come to the races with me this afternoon?" he asked. "We can catch the 1:30 train."

"I'd like that. If I can make it, I'll meet you at the station."

Then we took a leisurely walk to the bank. He cashed a rather sizable check and handed me fifty dollars.

"There you are, Harry. That should tide you over until you receive the rest."

And of course it would have, except that the rest wouldn't come until the end of the month. Not only did I need to replenish Emmie's nest egg today, but I'd left Brooklyn without paying my rent.

I had an hour before I was to meet Detective Donahy, so I took a car uptown to have a look at Whitner's cellar hole. It wasn't hard to find. There were plenty of buildings going up in the neighborhood, and no shortage of cellar holes, but only one had a ring of spectators.

Now that it was a potential murder scene, the police had halted work at the site and a patrolman stood guard. He didn't need any encouragement to provide a run-down of the facts as he knew them. There wasn't much to see. If there had been any blood, some helpful soul must have washed it off the day before. The hole was deep enough that it was easy to imagine someone tripping in and receiving a fatal knock on the head. But the cellar was thirty-odd feet from the street and there was a street light not far away. And Whitner would have had to negotiate a path through various piles of building mate-rials just to get to the hole.

I took a car back downtown and headed to Donahy's office. He was just finishing a telephone call.

"That was the doctor. He said he can't be sure what caused them, but there were two blows to the back of the head. They occurred about the same time and it isn't clear which was the cause of death."

"Was there blood there when you found the body?"

"Yes—here's the report." He handed me a sheet of the most illegible scribble I'd ever seen.

"Can we get a translation?"

Donahy took it back and summarized it for me. "De-tective Sheppard was called to the scene at eight o'clock yesterday morning. The body was lying face down, as if the man had stumbled into the hole. There was blood on one stone and the back of his scalp. Sheppard went through the victim's pockets and found a wallet with a few Canadian dollars, but no identification. There was also a keychain, a pocket knife, and some coins. Then the ambulance came and took the body to the morgue. There it was photographed and Sheppard took the photo around to the hotels. Someone at the Iroquois identified it as Whitner and said he was from New York. Since he thought it was an accident, Sheppard sent what he had on to New York so they could find Whitner's family."

"How's it look to you now?"

"Well, if he was drunk enough, he could have stumbled into the hole and hit his head and been knocked out. Then he came to, climbed most of the way out, tripped, and then fell back in, hitting his head again."

"You'll leave it at that?"

"I would if it were up to me. But your friend Miss McGinnis wired that Toronto police inspector in Rochester."

"You're kidding."

"No, I'm not. He came in from Rochester this morning. He was at the morgue for the autopsy. And he's very interested. So if we close the case as an accident, and he says it looks like murder, it'll seem like we're covering something up."

Just then, a patrolman escorted Inspector Stark into the office.

"What did you make of the autopsy, Inspector?" Donahy asked.

"I'll speak frankly, Detective," he replied. "It could have been an odd accident, or it may have been murder. If I had a similar situation in Toronto—with some fellow from out of town, and no other evidence of murder—I'd probably call it an accident and leave well enough alone. Unfortunately, for the both of us I'm afraid, this man is tied to a murder in Toronto."

"But I thought you had your man in Rochester," Donahy said.

"Yes, that's what I thought. But there are some questions I can't answer. Mr. Reese is aware of some of these, but last night I received a cable from the man I left in charge and he said they had found a witness who saw a tall man leave the building after the shots were fired, then saw Mason leave a little while later. Whitner was a tall man. And he was in Toronto at the time."

"What would his motive have been?" Donahy asked.

"Well, I really don't know," the Inspector admitted. "But he was up to something, and whatever it was is still a mystery. Maybe he was a hired killer?"

"I've reason to believe that's not the case," Donahy said.

"Then you've learned something about him?" Stark asked.

"Yes, it seems he was employed by the same man who employs Mr. Reese here."

"How do you know that?" I asked.

"Your Mr. Keegan told me so himself. Last night."

"And he was working on something for Keegan here in Buffalo?"

"He said he didn't think so, but that his operatives worked on their own time and followed their own leads. He's sent to New York for his file on Whitner."

"His name really was Jack Whitner?" I asked.

"Keegan says it was as far as he knew. He didn't tell you about any of this?"

"No. He likes to keep things compartmentalized."

"Whitner may have simply been looking for Elwell for the same reason you were, Mr. Reese," Stark said.

"If he was, he sure was going about it in a bizarre fashion. I think it's more likely he learned about the Elwell case through work at Keegan's. When a man with

191

seventy thousand dollars of insurance on his life goes missing under suspicious circumstances, warning flags are raised. Perhaps Keegan's file room was consulted and Whitner learned about it. He saw it as an obvious fraud and thought he could profit from it. But instead of being satisfied with the five percent he would get from Keegan, he decided it would be more profitable to blackmail the parties involved. Then he could ask for fifty percent. Or more."

"Tell me, Detective, were you planning to let me know about this new information?" Stark asked.

"Only if I had to," Donahy grinned. "Do you have any ideas on where to go from here?"

"Remember I told you yesterday, a man from Buffalo named Michael Schuler discovered Elwell's body," Stark said. "You said you knew him."

"Sure. But I thought you said he wasn't a suspect."

"He was seen going in after the shots were fired. And it must have been after Mason had fled. I even had a man time his movements and his story seems to check out. So I dismissed the idea. But he could have been back in Buffalo by Sunday evening, well before Whitner's death."

"So you're thinking maybe Whitey—Schuler, I mean—did kill Elwell," Donahy said. "Then somehow Whitner found out. Whitner tries to blackmail Whitey and Whitey kills him."

"I doubt he shot Elwell, but he obviously has some connection with the affair. But whatever his involvement in the Elwell case, I think he has to be a suspect in Whitner's murder."

"But no one would call him tall," Donahy pointed out.

"Maybe not, but this witness was looking down from

the third floor and across the street. The man may have merely appeared tall from that angle."

"I've known Whitey Schuler for years and I can't see him shooting anyone. I doubt he even has a gun."

"Well, it may be that Whitner killed Elwell and Schuler was blackmailing him," Stark conjectured. "They argued, fought, and Whitner fell."

"I still don't see it. Schuler works for Boss Conners, who controls all sorts of legitimate rackets. He doesn't need to mix himself up in this kind of thing."

"But why did he flee Toronto?" Stark asked.

"That's easy," Donahy answered. "Because he didn't want to find out what the inside of a Toronto jail looked like. How would he know if you'd make him a suspect or not?"

"And there's the races," I added.

"Races?" Stark asked.

"Yes, I happen to know Whitey was anxious to get back for the horse races running over in Fort Erie."

"Of course," Stark interjected, "you'll admit that being involved in a murder might prove as sound a reason for fleeing as a fondness for the turf."

"That's true enough," I admitted. "I wonder if Whitey did go to the races yesterday?"

"Ah, I think I see what you're getting at," Stark said. "If he escaped from Canada on Sunday, would he cross back over the border to attend some horse races on Monday?"

"He could just as easily have placed his bets in a pool room here, right, Detective?" I asked.

"Well, it may be someone's running a wire," Donahy admitted. He could probably name a dozen places, but he wasn't going to make a confession in front of Stark. "I guess I need to go find Whitey Schuler. And it will be easier if I go alone."

"All right. Perhaps we can have lunch together, Mr. Reese?" Stark asked.

"I'm meeting Miss McGinnis, but you're welcome to come along."

"Since you brought up the girl," Donahy said, "I guess I should point out Whitner's body was found just around the corner from Elwell's house, where she's living."

"Are you suggesting she's involved in these murders?" Stark asked. "I'm afraid there's no chance of that. She was on a boat when Elwell was killed, and in Toronto Sunday night."

"You know that for sure?"

"Yes, I'm quite sure."

I thought it might be best to focus attention away from the Elwell homestead. "There is someone else I should mention. Friday night I was in the bar at the Vendome with some show people. One of them, a man named Tim Madden, spoke to Whitner at the bar, briefly. I asked Madden if he knew Whitner and he said he'd never seen him before. That's probably all there was to it. But last night, I heard that Madden had gone to Canada, where he supposedly has family."

I gave them a description of Madden and also had to tell them about Carlotta. Then Stark and I left Donahy and walked up to Lafayette Square and the Elevator Company office.

"Do you think he was serious about Miss McGinnis?" Stark asked.

"No, I think he was just being a little defensive on Whitey Schuler's behalf."

"Do you think Donahy can be trusted?"

"Well, I guess as much as any policeman who's had his territory invaded," I smiled. "He and Whitey are friendly, I've witnessed as much. But I have no idea if it goes beyond that. You didn't meet Schuler, but I'd say he isn't a thug. He's a smart guy, and he has a great set-up here. By the way, when he pointed the finger at Miss McGinnis, you said you were afraid there was no chance of that. *Afraid*, Inspector?"

"Did I really say that? Just a slip of the tongue. What about this Madden?"

"There's probably nothing to it. I just thought I should mention it. If you want, I can take you around to the Vendome after lunch and you can talk to Carlotta. What about your witness? Was there anything else to the description other than that the man was tall?"

"Yes, he was wearing a straw hat. Like most men in August. Is this Madden tall?"

"Yes, I guess he is. I have an errand to run with Miss McGinnis after lunch, but I can meet you at the Vendome at two." He agreed.

Emmie was surprised to see the Inspector, but recovered quickly. He left us to wash up, and she closed the office door.

"I forgot I had wired him," she confessed.

"Yes, you did. Anything else you forgot about?"

"No. How about you?"

"Me? This was your work."

"I was thinking of my fifty dollars." At least she was smiling.

I handed her a crisp fifty-dollar bill. Her stash had been in fives and tens. She looked at me quizzically, but then just smiled and put it away in a chatelaine bag that hung from her belt.

"To foil the dips?" I asked.

"Dips?"

"Pickpockets. I thought you were fly to the cant."

"I'm not completely fly yet," she admitted. She opened her chatelaine again and pulled out her little notebook, no doubt adding "dips" to the ever-expanding glossary.

"You know, Detective Donahy thought it mighty suspicious Whitner's body was found so close to your home. What with you having been in Toronto."

"He was thinking of me?" This idea seemed to please her. "What did he say about Charlie?"

Stark returned before I could answer. Which was too bad, as it would have saved Emmie some trouble.

At lunch, I asked Stark to tell Emmie about the new witness who saw a tall man leave the building after the shots were fired. She became visibly anxious and her thinking even more untethered than usual.

"There must be a large number of tall men in Toronto, Inspector," she began.

"Oh, yes," Stark agreed.

"And I don't think my cousin Charlie is especially tall."

"Isn't he?"

"No. Wouldn't you agree, Mr. Reese?"

"Well, he's rather taller than me."

"Yes, but surely most men are taller than you," Emmie pointed out.

"I suppose it's true they appear so," I conceded. "But other men tend to wear taller hats." The Inspector gave me a wink and I hoped that meant he hadn't taken Emmie's digression seriously. But Emmie wasn't satisfied that cousin Charlie was safe from suspicion. As a further precaution, she created a diversion.

"Inspector, did Mr. Reese tell you that his associate Mr. Keegan seemed to know Jack Whitner? And that Mr. Keegan lied about his whereabouts Saturday?"

"Indeed?" Stark addressed that to me.

Emmie's ploy necessitated me explaining about the encounter Whitner and I had had with the Keegans. And then about the note from Keegan and the comment the clerk had made. But none of us had any idea what to make of it.

After lunch the Inspector went to check in to a hotel and I walked Emmie back to her office.

"Harry, do they suspect Charlie or not?"

"Well, until you brought him up no one had mentioned him."

"Why didn't you say so?"

"I didn't have a chance. But if you're so sure he didn't do anything wrong, why are you afraid for the police to check on his story?"

"I don't know."

"Because you aren't sure. Sooner or later the police will be talking to Charlie and he better have a believable story. If he just went to Lockport, everything's fine. But I don't believe a business meeting went so late on Sunday he couldn't have taken a train home before morning. Lockport can't be more than an hour from here. I'll talk to Charlie later and we'll find out where the truth lies. Then, when the police come to talk to him, he'll have a convincing alibi."

"I suppose you're right. But you don't really think he had anything to do with his father's murder?"

"Of course not. He was probably with one of his colleagues' wives."

"Harry!"

"Just a joke, Emmie. I'll tell you what. Let's go to the horse races this afternoon. It will take our minds off all this. And you can meet Keegan and size him up for yourself."

The chance to interrogate Keegan piqued her interest. She agreed enthusiastically. Poor Keegan didn't know what he was in for. We closed up the office and she left a note on the door about a family emergency. She had begun adding a detailed description of the fictitious emergency when I pulled her away.

The little Grand Trunk station was crammed with people, but Keegan was looking out for me. He was delighted to have Emmie along. Even after she gave him a short lecture on the dangers of pickpockets in crowded railway stations. While she scanned the crowd for would-be dips, I whispered to Keegan a request that he escort Emmie to the races while I stayed behind. He was more than willing, and just as we got on the train, I jumped off with the excuse that I wanted to buy a newspaper.

20

Stark was waiting for me at the Vendome. We went up to Carlotta's room and she was coming out as we arrived.

"Hello, Harry. Come to escort me to the races?"

"Sorry, I can't today. Is that where you're off to?"

"Yes, I thought I'd try my luck again. I wanted to catch the two o'clock train."

"I think you've missed it." I held out my watch to her.

"Oh, well, there's another at 2:30. What did you come about?"

"Let's get a drink first," I suggested.

We all went downstairs to the taproom and I introduced Stark, who promptly ordered us three lemonades. I told Carlotta why we were there and told them both I needed to run another errand. I left before either could respond, my lemonade untouched.

I made my way over to Charlie's law firm and waited for him to finish a meeting. Then he came out and led me to his office.

"What can I do for you, Harry?"

"Have you spoken with the police today?"

"No, do you mean about father's death?"

"No, not directly. You know Jack Whitner was found dead yesterday morning?"

"Yes. I read it was an accident."

"Well, now the police aren't so sure. Did he visit your home Sunday evening?"

"No. I was out, but my mother and aunt were there. Perhaps he was on the way to our house when he fell?"

"Yes, maybe. Did you ever see him intoxicated?"

"No. He drank, but never to excess. And frankly, he didn't seem the type to get that drunk. I just assumed the police knew what they were talking about."

"Yes, we'd all like to think that. But in this case, they may have been a little hasty. You said you were out Sunday evening. With friends?"

"Yes. I met some people at the Bedell House. That's on Grand Island. I went there directly from Lockport."

"And when did you get home?"

"Well, I missed the last boat back—we'd gone off on a walk—so I spent the night there. In the morning, I had to come to work directly from the boat."

"Can I have the names of the friends?"

"Why? What's this to you, Harry?"

"Whitner was involved in what went on in Toronto. How, exactly, no one knows for sure yet. It's even possible he shot your father."

"I see."

"You don't seem surprised."

"Well, after you spoke with me about him, I was beginning to wonder what his game was."

"He's in Toronto on Saturday when your father's killed and then on Sunday evening he cracks his head and dies. Two blocks from your house."

"I see what you mean, I guess. The police are going to think there's some connection. Do they think Whitner was murdered?"

"Yes, almost certainly. So sooner or later they're going to come to you and ask where you were. If you were at a hotel in Lockport Saturday night, and with these friends on Sunday night, they'll be able to verify that and the police will move on. But if there's anything in that story that's not true, they'll dig a lot deeper."

"Saturday?"

"Yes, I understand you were out of town, on business."

"That's right, I had to meet with a client in Lockport. I took the eleven o'clock train and got there around noon. We had lunch and I was with him the rest of the day."

"But didn't return home?"

"No, it was late, so I put up in a hotel."

"You didn't go running after Sadie Parker?"

"Why would I do that?"

"Don't be coy, Charlie. I know you were reading the cards she received. I know she rushed out of town Friday night. And then Saturday you rushed off, probably after the clerk at the Tifft House read you the last card. It will be a lot easier for all of us if you tell me the truth now, rather than have the police dig it up later."

"All right. I did go to Lockport, and spent the afternoon with the client. I was intending to come right back, but while I was waiting for the train I remembered there was a Queen's Hotel in Montreal, where some of Sadie's cards were sent from. So, I went the other way, to Rochester. There's a night train from there to Montreal. I caught that and got to Montreal about ten the next morning. I spent the day at the Queen's Hotel, but saw nothing of Sadie. There weren't any trains back until evening, so I waited and took the night train back here. I had to come to the office directly from the train, after traveling to Montreal and back in the same suit of clothes."

"That's quite a story, Charlie. And kind of hard to verify."

"You don't think the police will believe me?"

"When they can prove it they will. But tell me, Charlie. Were you so beguiled by Sadie?"

"No, not at all. I was convinced she and my father were in touch and were planning something together."

"You thought the cards came from your father?"

"Didn't they?"

"No. Didn't you ever see them?"

"No, the clerk at the Tifft told me about them. He always read them before giving them to Sadie. And she must have destroyed them later. If they weren't from my father, who sent them?"

"Robert Mason. If you had found your father in Montreal, what did you plan to do?"

"I imagine you can guess that."

"Well, luckily you didn't find him. Did you have a gun?"

"Yes. I tossed it in the river yesterday."

"Well, when the police come by, tell them the whole story, including the gun. Otherwise, they might find out about it themselves and then use it against you."

"You do believe me, don't you?"

"Oh, I believe you. But I have to." That comment made it necessary to explain my current status with Emmie. Apparently Charlie hadn't heard and he was a little stunned. At first he didn't even believe me. But then his good manners took over and he congratulated me and invited me to dinner that evening.

"One more thing. If you spent two nights on trains and then came directly to work on Monday, how is it you were up for a late night that evening?"

"Oh, I sleep like a baby on a train. The secret is to have two drinks, but no more."

"I see. I'll have to remember that." I had a hard time believing anyone slept like a baby on a train. Babies certainly didn't.

I said good-bye and headed over to Donahy's office, where I found Stark waiting.

"How'd it go?" I asked.

"You were right when you said there probably wasn't anything in it. Madden was in a show here on Saturday night. And your cousin saw him off at the train station Sunday. And she knew he had family in Canada because she had visited them before." He gave me a hard look. "I hope you weren't just trying to keep me busy?"

"I didn't know anything beyond what I had told you. I was worried that if I didn't bring it up, it would look like I was trying to protect him because of my cousin."

Stark didn't seem altogether satisfied with my answer, so I changed the subject. I told him about Charlie and then recounted the revised version of his story.

"And you think that's the truth?" The Inspector seemed a little incredulous.

"I do, because first he told me a story that was even more feeble. He must not have given it much thought. A simple telephone call and it all would have fallen apart. If he had killed his father Saturday night, I think he would have come up with something a little sounder by today."

"So, because he was a bad liar the first time, you think he must be telling the truth now?"

"I wouldn't put it exactly like that, but that's the general idea."

"Doesn't it strike you as a little impulsive to be discussing contracts all afternoon and then jumping on an overnight train to Montreal with no change of clothes?"

"Well, he's young. And he's Miss McGinnis's cousin."

"Yes, I suppose that helps explain it. Is he tall?"

"Unfortunately, yes," I admitted. "Listen, Inspector. I want to check on Charlie's story myself. I'm hoping I can find a porter who remembers him. Would you mind not mentioning it to Donahy?"

"For how long?"

"I should have something by morning."

"Assuming he's telling the truth."

"Yes. If not, he'll still be in town."

He agreed to wait and not long after, Donahy returned. Stark told him about Madden and how he saw it as a dead end.

"I've got something else," Donahy said. "A voice from above told me to check on Elwell's son. Seems that he was out of town both Saturday and Sunday. And that he's been palling around with Sadie Parker."

I didn't have much choice now but to tell Donahy all about Charlie and his alibi. Each time I repeated it, it sounded more ridiculous.

"I should have been questioning him," Donahy said.

"Look, if you had questioned him you would have just gotten a lot of nonsense and then wasted a lot of time finding out it was nonsense."

"And you don't think what he told you is a lot of nonsense?"

"Well, it's somewhat less nonsensical than what he originally told me."

Donahy looked at me, then at Stark. Stark just shrugged, then asked, "Did you find Schuler?"

"Whitey Schuler was in Canada yesterday for the races," Donahy reported.

"You spoke with him?" Stark asked.

"No, but he was there. I talked with people who would know."

"Do you think he went back over for today's races?"

"I'd guess no. Now he's heard I'm looking for him and he might not be in the mood to take chances like that. But finding a guy like Whitey if he doesn't want to be found is a tall order."

"Still, I think I may venture over and see," Stark said.

"To arrest him?" Donahy asked.

"To hold him, anyway. Care to come along, Mr. Reese?"

"No, thanks, I have something here I need to attend to."

"I was hoping to have someone along who knows Schuler by sight."

Donahy obliged him by calling in an aged police doorman and asking him to accompany Stark. Having a sixty-year-old cop wearing his uniform and walking with a limp would be a great help to Stark. As soon as they left Donahy turned to me, smiling.

"If that guy can catch Whitey, I'll eat my hat," he said.

"You didn't make it any easier for him. He'll probably wait at the station over there to nab Whitey on his way back."

"Then he won't see him." Donahy's smile grew wider. "Conners will have taken his private car over."

"You might have pointed that out."

"Yeah, I might have," he chuckled. "By the way, our girl Sadie is back at the Tifft."

"Have you seen her?"

"No, but I heard. I'm going over there now if you want to tag along."

We walked over to the Tifft. Sadie was dressed and taking visitors. Donahy greeted her like the old friend he was.

"I'm surprised you didn't go over for the races, Sadie."

"I've had enough of Canada for a long while, Jimmy."

"Yeah, I can see why. What can you tell me about this Whitner bird?"

"Not much." Then she nodded at me. "Ask his traveling companion here."

"We traveled on separate boats," I smiled. "Why was Whitner hanging around here?"

"He might have stopped by a few times, but he wasn't hanging around."

"Come on, Sadie, just tell me what you know," Donahy pleaded. "What's it matter to you now?"

"Whitner knew Elwell was set up somewhere else," Sadie said. "But he didn't know where. He figured I was mixed up in it and that it was all about the insurance money. Nothing I was going to say would make him believe I wasn't, so I just let him think that."

"Was it something you said that sent him to the Queen's Royal in Niagara?" I asked.

"Well, I might have said something."

"You thought he might get ahold of a message from Mason. A message you were expecting?"

"Something like that. We always met at the Queen's in Port Hope. Bobby insisted on sending those damn cards. He always has to be cute."

"So when Whitner read about a meeting at the Queen's, he went off in the wrong direction?"

"Yes, and you and your girl, too."

"But then Whitner went on to Toronto, where Elwell really was living. Did you drop a hint about that?"

"Me? I didn't know it myself."

"You told the police in Toronto you did," I pointed out.

"Did I?"

"Regardless, Mason certainly knew."

"I guess he did, but he never told me. I figured Elwell was set up somewhere, just like everyone else with any sense. But he made sure everyone was better off if we all pretended he had drowned. I just did my share of the pretending. He was a smart guy."

"Are you assuming you'll be able to collect on the insurance?" I asked.

"If I find a lawyer who's keen enough."

She was probably right about that. "Why do you think Whitner came back here after Elwell had been shot?"

"I have no idea. But I'd bet there are lots of people who will be happy to hear he's dead."

"What was going on between you and Charlie Elwell?" Donahy asked.

"Oh, we were just friends."

"Were you stringing him along for a reason?"

"I don't know what you mean."

"Look, Sadie. Someone who matters told someone else who matters to tell me to look into what was going on between you and Elwell's kid. So I'm going to find out."

"He made believe he wanted to take his father's place with me. But I never bought it. I think he was hoping I could lead him to his father."

"And what do you think he'd do if he found him?"

"Well, not kiss and make up."

"Let's get back to Whitner," I said. "When did you first meet him?"

"He showed up in July sometime. He thought he had me figured, but I got more out of him than he did me."

"Money?" I asked.

"I let him buy me things. Why not?"

I couldn't think of a reason. We left Sadie and went outside into the heat.

"What do you think she'll do now?" I asked.

"Beats me, but she'll land on her feet. Maybe she'll find someone to marry. She's getting a little long in the tooth for all this playing around."

"What are you going to do next?"

"Work on Elwell's kid. But I better go alone."

"All right."

We parted and I took a car up to the Elwells'. If I was going to find someone on the train who remembered Charlie, I'd need a photograph. Aunt Nell answered the door. She came out and closed the door behind her.

"You better not come in, Mr. Reese. Your name is mud right now. Emmie's mother is sure you're leading her little girl to ruin."

"I am sorry, but I'm not sure I'm doing the leading. My family reputation notwithstanding."

"Where's Emmie now?"

"Honestly?"

"Yes, honestly."

"Over at the races in Fort Erie. But perhaps we could put off telling Mrs. McGinnis that."

"What have you done to our Emmie, Mr. Reese?" Aunt Nell laughed.

"Me? I was left here. But I assure you she's being escorted by a man of impeccable character."

"Well, I hope so. Charlie called and said he had invited you to dinner."

"Yes, but maybe we should postpone that," I suggested. "The reason I'm here is that I have a rather odd request to make."

"What is it?"

"Do you have a recent photo of Charlie I can borrow?"

"Charlie? Whatever for?"

I went ahead and told her what for and she took it very well. She went in and came out again with a photo and told me to be careful with it. I thanked her and went back downtown. On the way I walked the route to Whitner's cellar hole just to make sure I had the geography correct. There was no logical reason Whitner would be on Oakland Street, coming from or going to the Elwells'. But if someone had come out to talk to him, they might have strolled in that direction. It would definitely be more secluded.

I went back to the hotel to wash up and then consulted a railway guide. The train Charlie took from Rochester would leave Buffalo at eight o'clock. My best chance was to find the porter who had been on Charlie's car. I walked over to the train station to see if it would be possible to find the porters who worked on a particular train, perhaps while they were preparing for tonight's run. But I was told the cars would be brought in from the other side of town and that I wouldn't be allowed in the yards anyway. I would have to take the train, at least as far as Rochester, the first stop.

It was now after six o'clock, so I walked over to the

Iroquois to see if Keegan had returned from Fort Erie. He was up in his room.

"Here, you can look at this while I wash up." He handed me a thick file. "That just arrived from New York."

It was a file on Jack Whitner, aka Jonathan Whitman, aka Joseph Wellman. Apparently, he liked to be able to use the monogrammed handkerchiefs he got for Christmas. He had twice been convicted of insurance fraud and spent a short time in prison. Since then, he'd been working for Keegan.

"You hired someone convicted of insurance fraud?"

"You know what they say: set a thief to catch a thief."

"You weren't worried he'd use the information from your files for his own ends?"

"He didn't have access to the files. At least, he wasn't supposed to."

"Why didn't you mention this before?"

"Well, for the same reason I didn't tell him about you. He was working on something for me. I didn't see any connection to Buffalo, but as you know, one can never be sure where these things lead. With hindsight, I admit it was a mistake hiring him."

"I think you'll find he had a friend or two in the file room."

"Yes, I have people looking into that."

"I'll pass the file on to Donahy."

"All right," he agreed. "You know, we had a very good day at the races. I'm sorry you missed it."

"Good in what way?"

"Oh, we both did very well. Your Miss McGinnis seems to know a great deal about horses."

"Seriously?"

"Perhaps she was getting tips from her friend. A fellow named Whitey. Whitey Schuler. He said he knew you as well."

"Oh, yes, we're old friends."

"Did you know he travels in a private car?"

"I heard that."

"He asked me about my visit and I told him how much I enjoyed the lake sturgeon, but was disappointed in not finding any smoked eel. He said that was no problem, he'd have some sent to the hotel for me. And he doesn't even know me. I'll need to think of some way to thank him."

"Did Miss McGinnis go home from the station?"

"She did, yes. But I suggested she come back in for dinner. Of course you're invited as well."

"I'm afraid I need to catch an eight o'clock train."

"Where are you going?"

"No place. But I want to talk to a porter and the easiest way to find him will be to take the train to Rochester and hop one back."

"Well, we were planning on dining early. As soon as the eel arrives."

There was a knock at the door and a bellhop told us the smoked eel was in the kitchen. We went down and Emmie was waiting in the lobby.

"I hear you had a profitable afternoon," I said.

"Yes, in more ways than one." She was wearing a sly smile.

"Come on, you two," Keegan insisted. "You can talk over dinner."

The eel was brought out at once. And there was a lot of it.

"Your friend was most generous with us, Miss McGinnis."

"Yes, he was."

"Just how much did you win?" I asked Emmie.

"I made forty-five dollars. Can you believe it? That's more than the Elevator Company pays me in a month."

"You didn't need to hobble any horses, did you?"

"Oh, no. It was perfectly square."

"Was it?" I smiled. "And how did your friend Mr. Schuler do?"

"Equally well."

"You mean, he was content winning forty-five dollars?"

"No, I meant equally well on a percentage basis."

"I see. And how did you find the track?"

"It was a fast track today, wouldn't you say, Mr. Keegan?"

Keegan nodded. He had cleared the platter and now was going after the remains that Emmie had neglected from her own serving. "You don't mind, do you, Miss McGinnis?"

"No, certainly not. I think smoked eel must be an acquired taste."

After the eel, the rest of dinner was spartan by Keegan's standards. Which is to say there was barely enough to feed four ravenous teamsters. Emmie tried repeatedly to probe Keegan about Whitner, and his wife's visit, but he just gave her a series of elliptical answers. This routine must have gone on all afternoon, but it was obvious Keegan found it most amusing.

"When are you leaving for your train, Harry?" he asked.

"I guess soon." I hadn't wanted to bring it up in

front of Emmie, but now I had to tell her about Charlie's story and my plan to verify it.

"I'll come with you," she offered.

"There's no need," I told her. But the matter had been decided before I opened my mouth. We left Keegan to his brandy and cigar.

21

At the station, I bought a newspaper and two coach tickets for Rochester. Emmie had left her now bulging bankroll at home. As soon as the train got going, we made our way to the sleeping cars. I showed Charlie's photo to the porters of the two cars but neither remembered him. As we were leaving, the second man stopped me.

"Did you say he got on in Rochester?"

"Yes, Saturday evening."

"Then he might have been put on the sleeper they add there. You'll need to check with Johnson. He'll be working the same car tonight."

"What's the next stop after Rochester?" I asked.

"Syracuse. We arrive there at 11:40."

I thanked him and gave him a quarter. We went back to our car and sat down.

"If we're lucky, we'll get back to Buffalo in time for breakfast. What will your mother think then?"

"Poor mother. How is it Aunt Nell knew I'd gone to the race track?"

"I stopped by the house to ask for that picture of Charlie, and she asked me. Does your mother know you've followed your brother's path to perdition?"

"No. But what will I tell her tomorrow?"

"Oh, I'm sure you'll think of something. Perhaps you were kidnapped?"

"Ha-ha." She left me to my newspaper for a while, but not long enough to finish a story. "Mr. Keegan knows something he's not telling, Harry."

"Does he?"

"You heard how evasive he became whenever I mentioned Whitner."

"Do you think they conspired to kill your uncle?"

"Well, if they did, he'd have a reason to kill Whitner."

"To keep him quiet? Of course, neither of them had a motive to kill your uncle."

I then told Emmie all about Whitner having worked for Keegan. But she wasn't ready to let Keegan off.

"But maybe that gives Keegan a motive for killing Whitner. Did you find out where Keegan was on Saturday? Was he back by Sunday evening?"

"I don't know. Why don't I leave that to you to investigate?"

"All right, I will. There must be a receipt or something. Where does Keegan carry his wallet?"

"Emmie, given that Keegan provides me with the majority of my income, it might be in the best interests of our little family if you refrained from stealing the man's wallet."

"Oh, all right."

I went back to my newspaper and had read the better part of a paragraph when Emmie interrupted again.

"You must believe Charlie, or we wouldn't be making this trip."

"I'd *like* to believe him. But Charlie nearly made a muddle of things." I told her Charlie's original story and how easily the police would have seen through it.

"Do Donahy and Inspector Stark believe Charlie?"

"If they did, would I be on a train to Rochester?"

"They really think Charlie is a killer?"

"Let's just say they're reserving judgment."

This time I barely got through a sentence.

"Wait until Inspector Stark sees what I have to show him," Emmie crowed.

"What?"

"Remember I told you that the afternoon had been profitable in more ways than one?"

"Yes."

"Well, I wasn't referring to the smoked eel."

"You and Whitey grabbed a few wallets working the crowd?"

"We didn't need to. Remember, we were winning."

"Can we get to the crux of the matter?"

"I have the two thousand dollars Whitey stole from Uncle Charles."

"He gave it to you?"

"Well, it took some persuasion. But it seems he used that as his stake over the last two days and won a lot of money. Several thousand. He didn't know anyone else knew about the money. Now that they do, he wanted to make amends."

"He said that he wanted to make amends?"

"Well, I suggested he should."

"And he found this money in the wallet?"

"No. I think Mason made that up. Whitey searched the office before going for the police."

"He was probably looking for anything that could incriminate Boss Conners. Where'd he find the money?"

"Taped behind a drawer."

"A very thorough search."

"He said that was an obvious place."

"So, Mason was blackmailing your uncle for two thousand dollars and he had the money to pay him off. Otherwise, how would Mason know the amount? He probably looked for it, but couldn't find it quickly enough."

"But why make up a story about deliberately leaving the money there?"

"I guess just to confuse things. If the police found the two thousand they'd assume it was to pay Mason. So he offered another story. Where is it now?"

"Safe at home." Her half-smile left the distinct impression she meant safe from me.

When we arrived in Rochester, I suggested that if we hurried, maybe we could talk to the porter and make it off before the train left the station. No go. By the time we were able to speak to him, we were on our way—next stop: Syracuse.

He did recognize the photograph, however, and immediately started laughing.

"Sure, I remember him. He came on with a ticket for the sleeper. But he thought this car went to Montreal. I told him he'd have to change trains in Utica. He said that was all right and climbs into upper number one. He could have had a lower in the middle of the car, but he said he should stick close to my room so I could wake him in Utica. I said, that means I have to stay awake. So he gave me a dollar. At Utica, he was dead to the world, but I got him up and wrote him a slip so he could get a berth on the Montreal train, assuming one was left to be had."

"What time is Utica?"

"One a.m."

I took down his name and address and gave him a dollar. Then we went back to our coach.

"Are you planning to catch the train for Montreal, too?" Emmie asked.

"No, we've established Charlie was on the train Saturday night, not in Toronto. He obviously wasn't involved in your uncle's murder and I think we can assume the rest of his story is true. Or at least something like the truth."

"Do you think Detective Donahy will think so?"

"That I don't know. And of course it doesn't let your family off completely."

"What do you mean by that?"

"Aunt Nell knew Whitner. Maybe she *was* working an insurance fraud with your uncle, just as he suspected. Only the plan wasn't to meet up with him later, but to live their separate lives. Whitner may have discovered something about it and was trying to blackmail her. He came by Sunday and she led him away from the house so your mother wouldn't overhear. They argued, and, well...."

"And Aunt Nell overpowered him?"

"Maybe she hit him from behind while he was admiring the cellar hole."

"I know you're just playing horse again, Harry, but stop it. And after Aunt Nell said such nice things about you."

"Did she? Well, then, I take it all back."

By the time we reached Syracuse I was reading the want ads out loud just to keep Emmie awake. We arrived at 11:45 and I immediately went to the ticket counter and asked about the next train back to Buffalo.

"Well," the man at the window said, "there's the Lake Shore Limited that stops here in about an hour. It goes to Buffalo. But you can't take it."

"Why not?"

"It only carries passengers to points west of Buffalo.

You can get on in Buffalo, but you can't get off in Buffalo."

I was beginning to understand why these men were protected by bars over the window.

"What would be the next train to Buffalo that would allow us to both get on and get off?"

"That would be the Western Express. Leaves here at two a.m."

I bought the tickets, stopped at the newsstand, and went back to Emmie.

"We have two hours to wait. What do you say we look for a saloon and try out Charlie's technique for sleeping on a train?"

"What's that?"

"Two stiff drinks. No more. No less."

"I guess it would be better than listening to you recite the to-let ads."

"No need for that. If the drinks don't work I bought you this." I handed her the latest Nick Carter. "Not quite Thackeray, but the pinnacle of dime detectives."

Emmie seemed genuinely touched by my gift. It turned out she had truly never read any dime novels, which seemed a little odd given that she intended to make her fortune through them. It didn't take long to find a saloon, but Emmie was being selective. She chose the seediest, of course. I ordered our drinks and we sat down at a table. Emmie immersed herself in Nick Carter, so I went to the bar for some conversation. A while later she joined me.

"You know, Harry, this is quite awful. And it isn't the least bit sordid. Is it really the pinnacle?"

"That, of course, is a matter of opinion. Let's just say there are far worse."

"Honestly?"

"Oh, yes."

"Any more sordid?"

"You mean salacious, don't you?" I smiled. "There are some romances in which the subject of sex comes up now and again, but usually just the merest allusion. Unfortunately, the reputation of dime novels for being corrupting is not well deserved. Are you reassessing your plans?"

"It would certainly be easy to do better."

"You're assuming better is what the readership wants."

"How much do you think they pay the writers for these?"

"As it happens, I know a fellow who writes them. He does pretty well, but only because he can do one in a few days."

"Write a book in a few days?"

"Only if you define the word book rather loosely."

"Mrs. Rohlfs told me she rarely finishes more than one book a year."

"Mrs. Rohlfs?"

"You know her, she writes as Anna Katharine Green—Detective Gryce and Amelia Butterworth. She's a friend of Aunt Nell's and I've spoken to her several times about writing."

"Well, compared with the average dime novelist, she's Charlotte Brontë. Of course, her books aren't particularly corrupting either. I mean, you aren't going to find old man Gryce and Amelia having a tumble out in the garden."

"No. It's true her books lack a certain liveliness."

We had a second round and Emmie spent the rest of

our stay exchanging card tricks with the bartender. Meanwhile, I had a scintillating conversation with some drummer about the cost of collars and the advantages of a collared shirt. We caught the two o'clock train and Emmie promptly fell into a deep sleep. I dozed some, but when the train arrived in Buffalo at six a.m. I was in need of a good night's rest and went straight to my hotel. Emmie went home to explain to her mother where she had spent the night.

22

I made it to Donahy's office by eleven Wednesday morning. I was told he was out with Stark, so I sat down to wait. Half an hour later I was woken by a sharp kick to the shin.

"Cut out that damn racket." A large detective seemed to be of the opinion that I snored too stridently. Luckily, the intense pain he had engendered prevented a relapse into slumber, the likely result of which would be a matching bruise on my other, still healthy, shin. Donahy and Stark showed up soon afterwards.

"Looks like you had a busy night," Donahy began.

"You heard about our little trek?"

"Yeah, we've been talking to the future Mrs. Reese." Donahy was visibly amused. "We were invited to the wedding supper."

"Wedding supper?"

"Yes," Stark joined in. "This evening. You seem surprised."

"Oh, no. It just slipped my mind. What else did she tell you?"

"We have the name of the porter," Donahy said. "But I'll need to check that out for myself. And it doesn't mean he wasn't in Buffalo Sunday night."

"Yes, Detective," Stark said. "But if young Elwell didn't kill his father, it eliminates the motive for killing Whitner."

"One motive, maybe," Donahy conceded.

"Did she tell you anything else?"

"Well, she produced the two thousand dollars taken from Elwell's office," Stark said. "I must say, though, the explanation seems a little difficult to believe."

"What was her explanation?"

"She told us Schuler took it from Elwell's wallet in order to give it to her aunt, Elwell's real widow. And that yesterday afternoon Schuler had entrusted it to her to deliver. But she thought it better to turn it in. You know Schuler, Detective. Does that sound believable?"

"It sounds as believable as anything else involving the Elwell family."

"It also jibes with Mason's story," I helpfully added.

"Yes," Stark agreed. "A story Miss McGinnis was privy to." Then he added quickly, "Not that I doubt her veracity, Mr. Reese."

"Oh, certainly not, I'm sure," I said.

I thought it a good time to consult my future wife and see if I might be let in on the wedding plans. I said good-bye and found a telephone to call the Elwell residence. Aunt Nell congratulated me and then gave the phone to Emmie.

"Everything's set for one o'clock this afternoon, Harry."

"Is it? Seems kind of sudden."

"I'm afraid mother insisted."

"I see. She believes I'm leading her little girl astray, and so she insists we be married."

"Well, led astray. I told her everything."

"Everything? Why in the world did you do that?"

"In hindsight, it wasn't the best strategy. But I wanted to assure her your intentions were honorable."

"Were they?" The chances that Emmie had been outmaneuvered by her mother were nil. But I was hardly in a position to argue the case. "Where's the ceremony?"

"We've found a judge to perform the ceremony at the courthouse—well, General Osgood did. You're to meet Charlie at his office at half past twelve. He has a suit you can wear. In the meantime, why don't you invite Carlotta to the supper this evening?"

"All right. Where did we decide to hold it?"

"Charlie offered to host it at the Iroquois. Tell her seven o'clock."

"Who else did we invite?"

"Just the family and a few friends—Mrs. Rohlfs, General Osgood and his daughter, and several people you don't know. And Inspector Stark and Detective Donahy, of course. Oh, and be sure to invite Mr. Keegan as well."

"All right. You know, Charlie seems to be taking a big interest in getting you married off."

"I suppose he sees himself as the patriarch now."

"Or maybe he wants you out of the house?"

"You better get going."

I did so. Carlotta was off somewhere but I left a note for her. Over at the Iroquois, I found Keegan in the billiard room. He was keen on attending the supper, but begged off the ceremony.

"But why don't you bring the wedding party to the track this afternoon? I'll stand for that."

"That's very generous," I lied. It would set him back all of ten dollars. I'd have hoped for something a little more substantial. Then I told him all about Emmie's suspicions. Luckily, he was amused by it all.

I told Keegan we'd see him at the station in time for the two o'clock train, provided the others were game, and then went to meet Charlie. He thanked me for helping to clear him and then tried to get me into one of his best suits, but it wasn't meant to be. Emmie, her mother, and Aunt Nell were waiting for us at the courthouse, where the judge first had us sign for a wedding license and then performed a sort of express wedding service. We used Emmie's mother's ring, on the understanding it was temporary. By quarter past it was all over. My new mother-in-law suggested we all go back to the house for a light lunch, so I jumped in with Keegan's offer. Mother needed some convincing, but Charlie and Emmie soon talked her into it.

We all walked over to the station and found Keegan waiting. The trip to Fort Erie was a short one, and as we were leaving the station we ran into General Osgood and his daughter. Charlie confirmed they'd be coming to supper, but there seemed to be some awkwardness. As we walked to the stands Charlie pulled me aside.

"The old man seemed a little cold, didn't he?"

"Yes, there did seem to be something eating him."

"You see, I'm all but engaged to his daughter, Catherine. I suppose, in his eyes, we are. But I've never said anything definite."

"So no chance of a breach of promise case?"

"No," he laughed. "It's not that I want to end it. I just don't want to make a mistake by rushing into anything."

"Oh, yes," I agreed. "Marriage isn't something that should be hurried. But how does she feel about it?"

"Well, that's where I really put my foot in it. She called me at work Monday morning, asking where I'd been all day Sunday. And I told her that tale about staying Saturday night in Lockport and then at the Bedell House Sunday. Well, naturally, it sounded pretty suspicious to her that I'd gone on this outing without mentioning it. Then I stumbled in telling her who I was with, because of course they would all be people she knew. So I'm sure she assumes the worst."

"I see. I thought you had invented that story for my benefit."

As we were making our way to join the others, I ran into Carlotta. She was seated with a couple fellows I'd never met. She congratulated me and said she would be coming to our supper. I reminded Carlotta about Emmie's construction of her past and suggested it would be great fun if she could play the part at supper. And it would relieve Emmie of having to explain her contorted tale was a fabrication. She agreed it was a great idea.

"There is one thing, Harry. How did Emmie know you had a cousin Carlotta?"

"Well, I had to supply the name, of course. Your name just came readily to mind."

"Did it? Well, never mind, Harry. I'll see you at seven."

I was delighted with my little scheme. The only fly in the ointment was that I forgot to tell Emmie about it.

I went and found the others busily going over the horses in the first race. It's always amazed me how those in attendance at horse races seem to honestly think the record of a given horse on similar courses, or how dry the track is, has the least bit to do with which will win. I've always assumed the winners are decided the evening before in a smoke-filled room someplace.

Once the races started, Keegan and Charlie made frequent trips to the bookies both for themselves and for Emmie. Whitey stopped by and Emmie invited him to our supper. He said he'd try to make it, then left us—without offering any tips.

But Emmie had no need for them. She had another profitable day. This worried me. Nothing stokes the gambling bug quite like early success. The day before, her winnings could be attributed to Whitey's expertise. But today she would see it as her own knack for the thing. If luck was involved, then she knew herself to be blessed with it. I saw danger ahead.

On the train back, Charlie and I were seated apart from the others and he took the opportunity to ask for the details of what had happened in Toronto. I asked him if he was surprised by it all.

"I was surprised that he had this other family, but not the rest. I began to suspect he was up to something about a year ago, when I came home after law school. For the last few years, the story had been that money was a little tight. My mother cut back on things so I could stay in school. He made a show of cutting back, too. He even sold his boat. That one he used for his accident was a recent purchase.

"But then I started working at the firm, and meeting other lawyers here. They all spoke of my father as having one of the most successful practices in town. I'd hear about lucrative deals he'd been in on and things like that. At first, I suspected maybe he was gambling. Then I found out about Sadie and I assumed that was where the money went. What was Mrs. Redstone like?"

"Well, she was pretty upset when we met her."

"She must have known there was more to his story. She couldn't be that naïve."

"People can be pretty naïve when they want to be."

"Another thing that isn't clear is how they misidentified father after the shooting. Emmie said she gave them a photograph."

"It was a group photograph, of all the officers of the Elevator Company. We were focusing on Mason. But to the cop who took it, they were just four men. When the body looked like one of them, he just assumed it was the man we were looking for. We told them we thought Mason was traveling as Joseph Sedley, and that's whose wallet was on the body."

"Who do you think killed him?"

Before I could answer, the train jolted to a stop and a stout woman fell into my lap. We eventually disentangled ourselves, to the great amusement of all around. I met the others on the platform.

"In front of my mother, Harry," Emmie sighed. "And on our wedding day...."

"It's okay, Emmie. I threw her back."

Our party went its separate ways and Emmie insisted she and I go shopping for rings before the stores closed. I told her it wasn't a good time financially, but she was willing to dip into the day's winnings. We got a respectable pair for less than thirty dollars. Then she went home and I went to McLeod's to bathe for supper.

23

At the Iroquois, Emmie, her mother, Aunt Nell, and I greeted our guests in the lobby and Charlie escorted them to the private room he had reserved. When all but Whitey had arrived, we followed them in. The table was set as a buffet and the guests were grouped about.

Carlotta went over to Emmie's family and began speaking of her and Emmie's time at school together. She even got misty-eyed when recounting how she had to leave her little child with her mother while she eked out a living on the road. Emmie, her mother, and Aunt Nell all stood open-mouthed and speechless. Carlottta drew me aside.

"Not a very sympathetic family you're signing up with."

"It does seem an odd reaction, but they'll come around."

"I thought of renting a kid to bring along, but I figured you wouldn't want a brat getting underfoot."

"Yes, a wise decision."

Emmie came over and explained that, on the way here, she confessed to her family that she had made up the story about Carlotta. Then she turned to me and said rather crossly, "This wouldn't have happened if you hadn't used Carlotta's name."

"Now, now," Carlotta said. "Not on your wedding day. Cousin Carlotta will take care of it."

She went over and explained things to Emmie's mother and Aunt Nell. Emmie's aunt laughed, but her poor mother seemed more confused than ever. Then the pianist arrived and started in on something Baroque.

Charlie was with the Osgoods, apparently trying to get back in their good graces. Whitey showed up, with another supply of smoked eel as a wedding gift. Keegan told him how thoughtful he was, and then pumped him for tips on the next day's races. Mrs. Rohlfs stopped by briefly and gave Emmie a copy of *The Circular Study*, her latest chronicle of the sexless Gryce and Butterworth.

I persuaded Whitey to go over and give Stark his story. I didn't listen in, but I'm sure it was a tale worthy of the name. Meanwhile, Emmie cornered Donahy and inquired after the etymology of "the Hooks." He shrugged. After that, the detectives stayed off to one side. It had been a little awkward introducing them to the other guests, what with Charlie still being something of a suspect. I wasn't entirely sure why Emmie had invited them. But I'd find out soon enough.

There was a bit of a lull in the proceedings as the champagne was being handed out, but Emmie livened things up by upsetting a tray onto the General. Whitey made an attempt to catch it, but tripped over Keegan instead. This caused Donahy to laugh uproariously, which in turn led Stark, still standing next to him, to blush with embarrassment.

The General was none too happy either. Charlie and his daughter rushed to his aid and Emmie went over to help Whitey off the floor. Then she and Catherine left the room, Catherine carrying her father's soiled coat. The piano player, who'd progressed to Chopin a little before, jumped into a cake walk. It was then that I recognized him from Croteau's saloon.

Everyone recovered their good humor pretty quickly. I guess a bride can get away with a lot on her wedding day. Whitey was now standing near the door and I went over to him.

"Nicely done, Whitey."

"You think so? I think he knew I took it. But he didn't say anything. Is Emmie fooling with me?"

"I wouldn't venture to say. She has a rather playful nature, but she means well."

"Yeah, maybe. All I can say is, better you than me."

"That's an odd way of offering your congratulations, Whitey."

"Oh, I just meant you seem to take it in stride. She'd drive me crazy."

Emmie arrived back and I went to join her.

"What'd you find?" I asked.

"Find where?"

"In Keegan's wallet."

"You knew?"

"Well, only because you told me last evening."

"Did you tell him?"

"I may have hinted at it."

"That explains it."

"Explains what?"

"The only thing in the wallet is a check for five thousand dollars, made out to Mr. and Mrs. Harrison Reese."

"I don't believe it."

"It's true."

I made Emmie give me the wallet and sure enough, the only thing in it was the check, just as she described. I was dumbfounded.

"I guess you had better return it."

"Yes. But maybe it would be better if you returned it?"

"No, I don't think it would."

Emmie took the wallet over and gave it to Keegan with some completely ridiculous story of how it must have fallen into the folds of her skirt. Keegan made a show of believing her, but gradually lost himself to laughter. Then he pulled the check out of the wallet.

"You didn't want this, my dear?"

"I beg your pardon?" Emmie tried.

"Your wedding present!"

"Oh, what is it?"

Keegan handed her the check. Emmie told him how generous he was and I walked over and thanked him and pretended I was seeing the check for the first time. And, in a way, I was. Though it was a real bank draft, it had one deficiency. In place of his signature, Keegan had written the word "Void."

Then Charlie offered a toast and I made a little speech that ended with me saying I was sorry Emmie's father wasn't there, but I hoped to be meeting him soon. It was then that Charlie informed me Emmie's father had died a few years before. Next we handed out little tea cakes and the hotel photographer showed up and we posed for a couple photographs. I had a hard time convincing the man I was the groom and not Charlie, but he eventually accepted that I was just an extremely shabby dresser.

The piano player was now providing a vocal accompaniment to himself. Fortunately, he confined himself to tunes which, while they may not have been less risqué than those he had performed the previous Friday, made more artful use of allusion. Now Emmie recognized him, too. She asked if I had arranged for him to be there, presumably for sentimental reasons. I simply smiled.

A porter came in carrying the General's coat and

brought it over to Catherine. She handed it to her father, who immediately noticed his wallet was missing. He went out after the porter. Then Whitey helpfully pointed out it may have just fallen on the floor. We all began looking for it and, lo and behold, it was found under a table by Charlie, who handed it over to Catherine. She, unfortunately, dropped it. It quickly became apparent that the General was one of those men who use their wallet as a sort of portable filing cabinet. The floor was littered with bits of paper, and soon we were all on our knees helping to gather them up. When we were done, Catherine did her best to cram them all in and then went off in search of her father.

While it was true we set a meager table, and served third-rate wine, there was no denying we kept our guests amused.

"Take a look at this, Harry."

Emmie had drawn me aside and was showing me a receipt. It was from the American House in Toronto and was dated August 5th, the Sunday before.

"Why was the General in Toronto Sunday night?" she asked.

"You mean Saturday night. He would have paid when he left Sunday."

"That's even better."

"I guess he could have been there on business."

"You don't believe that, do you?"

"No, not really," I admitted. "Well, now you have something to show Donahy and Stark, after all. Congratulations, Emmie."

"Thank you, Harry."

We went over to the far corner where Donahy and Stark were hiding.

"Gentlemen, I believe I can solve both murders," Emmie began. "General Osgood killed my uncle and then killed Whitner because he tried to blackmail him."

The policemen both looked at her quizzically. It was a response I had come to realize Emmie elicited rather frequently.

"Osgood? Why would he kill Elwell?" Donahy asked.

"Who exactly is General Osgood?" Stark asked.

As the piano player broke into a lively rendition of *Henrietta, Have You Met Her?*, Emmie answered them.

"General Osgood is the president of the Eastern Elevator Company, where Robert Mason had been superintendent and my uncle, Charles Elwell, secretary. He was counting on a life insurance policy the company had on Uncle Charles to pay off a loan the company had taken from Boss Conners. Somehow, he must have known that my uncle was alive and living in Canada. But he kept it to himself. Not to do my uncle any favors, but because if he gave that information to the police, the policy would never pay off. So, like everyone else involved, he went along with the drowning story.

"Then Harry started looking into the Elevator Company and asking about Uncle Charles. It was just Saturday morning that he revealed to the General that my uncle had been involved in the stock scheme. So the General decided to seal the thing before Harry could expose Uncle Charles. He went up to Toronto, where he knew my uncle had set himself up, and shot him."

"But that's all conjecture, Miss McGinnis," Stark pointed out.

Emmie handed Stark the receipt.

"What's this?" he asked.

"It's a receipt from the American House in Toronto dated Sunday," Emmie answered.

"And where did you get it?"

"General Osgood's wallet. He must have spent Saturday night in Toronto."

"Why would Osgood go to a hotel if he had just shot Elwell?" Donahy asked. "Why not take a train back Saturday night?"

"I've encountered this myself," Stark said. "The only way to get to Buffalo after seven is to catch a local that leaves just before midnight. You are required to change trains twice and won't get in here until eight in the morning. Nonetheless, the man could have had an innocent reason for being in Toronto."

"There might be another piece of real evidence, Inspector," I said. "Remember I told you how I had showed Mrs. Redstone the photo and she said she thought she recognized the man who had stopped by Saturday afternoon?"

"Yes—Mason."

"But when you interviewed Mason in Rochester, he admitted he knew not only that Elwell was in Toronto, but also about the building he was killed in," I pointed out. "He had no reason to visit the Redstone residence. I'm afraid I made the same mistake we'd made earlier by not making it clear who it was in the photograph I was referring to. When she said she thought she recognized the man in the photo, she must have been referring to Osgood. It was Osgood who went to D'Arcy Street, spoke with Mrs. Redstone, and then followed Elwell. He must have hoped Elwell would lead him someplace less conspicuous. Unfortunately, Elwell obliged him. He saw Elwell meet Mason and the two of them go upstairs. He entered the building and followed the sound of their voices to the office where Mason and Elwell were having their talk."

"But wouldn't he be afraid of killing Elwell in front of a witness?" Stark asked. "Why not just wait for Mason to leave?"

"Because he hated Mason as much as he hated my uncle," Emmie answered. "It was Mason's schemes that drove the Elevator Company close to bankruptcy. So he opened the door on them and shot twice. He most likely thought he had killed Mason as well as my uncle."

"And Whitner saw him leave the building?" Stark asked.

"Yes, he must have slipped away from the Queen's," Emmie answered. "And then got back before he was missed."

"I just don't see how that makes sense," Stark interjected. "Whitner is waiting at the Queen's Hotel all evening and then happens to sneak away and be near the murder scene at the exact time Osgood shoots Elwell, then he returns to the Queen's Hotel and waits. The next day, he goes off to another Queen's Hotel. No, I don't think Whitner had any idea what had happened Saturday night."

"Of course," I added, "Whitner would have known who Osgood was from his studying up on Elwell. He may have just seen him in Toronto, maybe Saturday, or maybe Sunday morning when they both took trains out of town. When he got to Port Hope and saw Sadie with Mason, he realized I had told him the truth. He knew Mason was on the run, so while they were on the boat over from Port Hope, Whitner confronted him, offering his silence in return for money. Mason would have agreed to anything, since there would be no escaping if Whitner wanted to turn him in. He tells Whitner what happened in Toronto, and that it was Elwell who had been killed by some third party. When the boat lands in Charlotte, Whitner sees the police nab Mason and realizes he needs to find a new game. He remembers seeing Osgood in Toronto. He has no idea if Osgood killed Elwell, but it seems too much of a coincidence. And now he's desperate to find some way to make his investment in time and money pay off. So Sunday evening he takes a train back to Buffalo and confronts Osgood. If the General had an innocent reason for having been in Toronto, he would have just told Whitner to get lost. Whitner risked nothing by trying."

"Nothing outside of having his skull cracked open," Donahy pointed out.

"A slight miscalculation," I conceded. "You see, that cellar hole is around the corner from the Elwells', but just a block or two further from the General's own home."

"Maybe there is something to this," Donahy said. "It was Osgood who called the chief and told him about Elwell's kid being away on Saturday and Sunday. He said he just wanted to keep his daughter from being involved in any trouble. It seemed reasonable at the time, but maybe he was trying send us in the wrong direction."

"Well, it's an interesting theory," Stark said. "But the receipt doesn't prove anything beyond that he was in Toronto Saturday night. And your only other evidence is that Mrs. Redstone *might* have been identifying Osgood rather than Mason in the photo. We'll need to wait until I can have someone show her the photograph again."

"There's one way to find out this evening," I said.

"What's that?" Stark asked.

"Whitner's technique: bluff him. If you go over, Inspector, and tell the General that Mrs. Redstone pointed him out in the photo, we'll know one way or the other. He and his daughter have just returned."

"All right." And Stark did so. We didn't get a dramatic confession, but Osgood refused to talk further without his lawyer. Then he led his daughter out without another word.

Donahy followed them. Then Stark left to wire his people to take a copy of the photo to Mrs. Redstone.

Charlie came over with a puzzled look on his face.

"What was that all about?" he asked.

"I'm afraid Emmie may have put you in badly with Miss Osgood, Charlie."

By then the guests were beginning to say their goodbyes and making as if to leave. But Emmie would have none of that. She had everyone sit down again and recounted the whole story. More quizzical looks ensued. Your average wedding guest just isn't expecting the bride to finger one of the other guests for murder after serving the cake.

Keegan came up and congratulated us. Emmie insisted he tell us where he had gone on Saturday.

"To Saratoga, for the races," he told her.

"But why did you tell Harry you'd be in town?"

"Well, my wife was standing over my shoulder when I wrote the note. She doesn't approve of gambling. I had told her I'd be stuck in Buffalo for several days. This way I was able to spend an afternoon in Saratoga, and this week go across the river for the trotters. And I'll still get home before her. It was too good to pass up."

"I see," Emmie said. "I'm glad it was nothing untoward."

People bitten by the bug are very forgiving of each other's deceits, provided they're directed at nonmembers of the fellowship.

"Harry," he said, "if you're done here, there's that little job in Scranton that needs to be looked at. But you'd need to leave tomorrow."

"A honeymoon in Scranton?" I said. "We thought we'd stay in town a few days. You see, now I'm in line to net the three hundred for that policy on Elwell. I'm guessing the Elevator Company can't collect when it was the president of the company who pulled the trigger."

"Yes, I imagine you're right," Keegan agreed. "Well, then, we can go back to the races tomorrow."

I didn't like that idea any better, but it was Whitey who cinched it by pointing out that his boss wouldn't be pleased to hear we had gummed up the repayment of his loan. He advised us to go to Scranton first thing in the morning.

Emmie went home and packed what she would need until the rest could be sent on and I went to McLeod's for the last time. That night, we had a room at the Iroquois booked.

24

We caught the Lackawanna Limited at 9:30 the next morning. I expected some tears at the station, given the suddenness of our marriage and departure. But Aunt Nell and Charlie, and even Emmie's mother, seemed rather happy to see us leave. I can't say I blame them, really. But wouldn't you think an occasion like this calls for the show of some emotion besides relief?

Later, as the train made its way toward Scranton, I asked Emmie about her part in the breathless summation of the case against the General.

"It really was well done, wasn't it, Harry. My only regret is Mrs. Rohlfs wasn't there to hear it."

"It was a virtuoso performance, Emmie. But I thought you had fingered Keegan, at least for Whitner's murder."

"Well, I don't know if I should tell you."

"Tell me what? We can't very well start out our marriage by misleading each other." Though I had to admit it had worked well enough during the engagement.

"All right. I'll confess," she smiled. "You see, Harry, I was sure I could solve it, even if you weren't willing to help. I knew it would end this way. Ever since last Friday, the night we went to Croteau's."

"You knew the General had done it—that is, was going to do it?"

"No. I mean, I knew it would end with me telling the police who did it."

"I see. Sort of an Amelia Butterworth act?"

"Well, yes, something like that. Of course, at that time, I wasn't sure who killed my uncle."

"Of course, at the time, he was still alive."

"Yes, but I never believed that. I had worked out cases against all the people who might have killed him, or had him killed. The General, Boss Conners, Mason, and one or two others I eliminated later. Then, after what went on in Toronto, and the death of Whitner, I had to revise everything Monday night."

"And add Keegan to the list."

"Yes. Here, you can read them if you like."

She handed me her notebook. There were indeed similar summations making a case against each of the central characters. All had been written in a small script and had been repeatedly revised, so they were a little hard to read. But in addition to the version naming the General, there was one where Conners had Whitey shoot Elwell and then bludgeon Whitner, one where Whitner killed Elwell and then Keegan killed Whitner, and, lastly, one that had Mason killing Elwell and Donahy killing Whitner.

"Donahy?"

"That was a good one, wasn't it?"

"Well, creative. But you had the General first?"

"Yes. Remember how I told you it seemed like he kept me in that job because he felt sympathy for me?"

"Yes."

"Well, it occurred to me that maybe it wasn't sympathy at all, but guilt."

"I see. So you solved the case based on the mistaken belief that your uncle had already been murdered."

"Well, not mistaken. Premature, perhaps. But I missed the part about Mrs. Redstone and the photo. That helped a lot, Harry."

"I'm happy to have lent a hand, Emmie. But I have to admit I hadn't really suspected the General myself until you found that receipt."

"Honestly? You came up with all that about the photo, and Whitner guessing the General shot my uncle, only after I showed you the receipt?"

"Well, parts of it had been in my mind, but just as a jumble of facts. For instance, Mason telling us he knew all along where Elwell's building was. I thought maybe the man who spoke to Mrs. Redstone just happened to look like Mason. But it kind of stuck in my mind. Then when you found the receipt, it all fell into place. I take it you had Whitey steal the General's wallet as well as Keegan's?"

"No, Whitey must have done that out of habit or something."

"Seems a little odd to have lapsed during our wedding supper. But maybe when you told him to snatch Keegan's, he figured it was open season."

"You don't think Whitey knew something and was just making it easier for us to find some evidence?"

"No, I think Whitey's altruistic streak is a figment of your active imagination." I handed her back the notebook. "I noticed several pages have been ripped out. Charlie?"

"Yes, but don't ever tell him. He might not understand."

"No, no. Mum's the word," I agreed. "Didn't it seem possible someone else, someone we never knew existed, might have killed your uncle?"

"No, of course not. Not in this genre."

Since Emmie had confided her secret, I thought it was a good time to confide my own. I came clean about my precarious finances.

"I suspected that was the case," she said.

"Was it that obvious?"

"Oh, yes. For one thing, there was the way you hung on to my fifty dollars. And for another, you broke into a sweat every time the subject of money came up. I brought it up Monday morning just to watch you squirm. It was very amusing."

"How charming. I hope you won't expect that sort of entertainment at the breakfast table every morning. I might develop a permanent tic."

Then Emmie made another trip to the confessional. She hadn't saved five hundred dollars. In reality, it was less than a hundred. And she had paid for the private room and supper at the Iroquois, not Charlie. The truth was, we had about sixty dollars between us. If we were frugal, and the job in Scranton took no more than a couple days, we'd have just enough left when we got to Brooklyn to pay the back-due rent.

Of course, I pointed out, there were two three-hundred-dollar checks coming to me by the end of the month, with any luck. Emmie didn't like my wording.

"I think you mean *we* have two checks coming to *us*, don't you? I'm the one who made the arrangement with the Provident Life Insurance Company, and the one who solved the case first."

I could have pointed out that if I had been allowed to make the arrangement with the Provident Life Insurance Company, I'd be waiting on a check for a thousand dollars or more. But I had seen Emmie sulk and it wasn't something I wanted to relive.

"Of course, Emmie. I merely meant they'd be in my name."

"I forgive you, Harry. It's just that you ridiculed my idea that Uncle Charles was killed because of his association with the Elevator Company. And it turns out I was right all along."

A little later, we had a relatively reasonably priced lunch in the dining car. It took me the entire meal to persuade Emmie to tell me what it was Sadie had asked her to relay to Robert Mason.

"You have to promise not to reveal it to anyone, Harry."

"Of course, I promise."

"Well, I think Sadie was crying when she said it, so it wasn't altogether clear. But I believe she said, 'Tell the sap to buy some envelopes next time.'"

"Sage advice."

On our way back to the coach we passed some fellows playing poker. I sat down, but Emmie went back and tried to talk her way into the game. They kind of resisted the idea at first, probably because they felt uneasy about cheating a lady. But she pestered them until they relented. Then, once they realized Emmie was cheating, they paid her back in kind. I was sitting some distance away, so I can't say exactly what brought the game to a conclusion. But while there were some raised voices, there were no fisticuffs. Emmie sat down beside me with a look of defeat.

"Those men cheated me, Harry. I lost eight dollars."

As she was speaking, the three fellows she'd been playing with went by and tipped their hats. It was only then that I recognized them—the three drummers I'd plucked on the train into Buffalo. They were up four dollars on us.

I said nothing to Emmie about that, but promised I'd write the president of the railway as soon as we reached Brooklyn. Then I tactfully suggested it might be better to avoid games of chance until we'd paid the rent.

Thankfully, she agreed. For the rest of the trip, she contented herself with reading Aunt Nell's wedding present: *How to Cook Husbands*.

The case in Scranton involved a common accident insurance bunco. Some sort of accident occurs, maybe a train wreck, or a boat sinking, and an enterprising insurance agent goes and sells the injured victims accident policies with a date of issuance a week or two before the accident. If he's smart, he makes sure each policy is with a different company. Then he takes half of each payout and moves on to another town with a new name.

In Scranton, a gas explosion had destroyed two buildings and injured more than a dozen people. Four new policies showed up at four different companies, all within a few days of the accident. There was a time when the agent might have gotten away with this. But Keegan's file room made it a lot harder to put over such a scheme. That's what did in the agent in Scranton.

By three o'clock the next afternoon, I had signed statements from the four injured parties. They hadn't received any payout, and they probably wouldn't even get their premiums back. What happened to the agent wasn't my affair. That night we arrived in Brooklyn to an empty larder and an apartment that desperately needed airing. But Emmie was clearly excited to be in New York.

A couple days later, there was another elevator fire in Buffalo, just as Ed Ketchum had predicted. The Dakota, not far from where the Eastern had stood, likewise burnt to the ground. No one asked me to go to Buffalo this time. Instead, I was sent to Glens Falls, where yet another fire had occurred. Unfortunately, Glens Falls was also the next stop of the Grand Circuit trotters. I felt a chill in the air, and it was too early for autumn.

Humbug on the Hudson

Or, Bunk for Two

For a crib sheet with maps, characters and a short glossary, please visit:

streetcarmysteries.com/humbug

Taking Chances

I'd only been back in Brooklyn a few days when I was called across the river to Keegan's office on William Street. That was Tuesday morning, the fourteenth of August. Samuel Keegan was president and sole proprietor of the Gotham Insurance Bureau. It was here an insurer could find out if someone applying for an accident policy had already taken out similar policies with three other companies. Or if someone made a habit of suffering losses by fire. In a nutshell, Keegan made his money by uncovering fraud. Over the last few years I had worked for him on a number of cases. But this case wasn't like any of those.

I took out a notebook and Keegan laid out the facts. The previous Sunday morning there had been a large fire in Glens Falls, a village of lumber mills on the upper Hudson River. A number of buildings had been completely destroyed and the estimated losses were well over a hundred thousand dollars, most of it insured.

Several of the insurance companies involved had hired a fire expert named Ed Ketchum to go up and look things over. Ed was a sort of arson bloodhound. If there was an innocent explanation for the fire, he'd report back quickly. But if he found something indicating it had been set intentionally, he'd keep at it until he found the evidence necessary to deny the claim and usually convict the arsonist. He was so good he commanded a fee of twenty dollars a day, plus expenses.

Ed had come across something suspicious up in

ROBERT BRUCE STEWART

Glens Falls. The fire had started in an idle shirt factory. But Ed heard that the place had been set up as a betting parlor and then found something to substantiate the rumor.

Normally, I was hired to detect fraud. I made six dollars a day and expenses. If I could provide cause for an insurance company to avoid paying a claim, I would receive a bonus of around five percent of what I had saved it. This time the assignment was more unorthodox.

"Put away your notebook, Harry," Keegan directed. "What I'm going to tell you now can't go any further. I'm depending on your discretion to keep this completely to yourself. Don't mention it to anyone, not even your wife." Then he changed his tone completely and added, "By the way, how is Emmie finding Brooklyn?"

"Oh, she likes Brooklyn well enough," I said. "She's trying to set up housekeeping with the little money we have left." My mention of our strained finances was meant as a prod: Keegan, and some others, owed me for some work I had completed the week before in Buffalo. But from his wounded look, Keegan must have thought it was a reference to the trick he played on Emmie on our wedding day, pretending to give us a check for five thousand dollars. To be fair, that was merely his response to Emmie's having had his pocket picked at the wedding supper. But that tale has already been told elsewhere.

"Back to the matter in Glens Falls, Harry," Keegan began. "Remember the Grand Circuit races last week outside of Buffalo?"

"All too well."

He looked puzzled, but went on. "Well, those same horses are running at Glens Falls this week. It's the big event of the year for the track there, and it means a lot to the town to make a success of it." Then he paused a bit. "Well, it can be difficult to draw people to a small town like that, what with all the other races running this week—Newburgh just up the river here, and Saratoga just down the road from Glens Falls." There was another little pause. "So, people there decided they needed to provide a way for their guests to play these other races. Well, they set up a betting parlor on the unused floor of the shirt factory."

"Which people?"

"Oh, all the best people. The promoters of the races, the owners of the hotels and horse farms, and so on. Now, strictly speaking, it was illegal."

"Strictly speaking," I smiled.

"Yes, but we all know these places are everywhere. Why, there's one not far from this very office."

I didn't doubt that, and Keegan was probably their best customer. "So Ed Ketchum is onto something?"

"Well, yes, in that there was this set up. But it had nothing to do with the fire. The fire marshal has determined it wasn't at all suspicious."

"The fire marshal whose salary is paid by all the best people?"

"Now that's not fair, Harry. I know some of these men."

I could guess which ones. "What would be my job?"

"Well, you know Ketchum. There's no way we can approach him. But perhaps you can sort of divert his attention."

"So, I'd be going not to solve the case, but to keep Ketchum from solving it?"

"Oh, there is no case, at least as far as we're concerned."

"No case means no chance of a bonus."

"No, but how about ten dollars a day, and all expenses?"

"How about twelve?"

The speed with which he agreed suggested I could have gotten fifteen. We shook hands on it and he gave me a three-day advance. I consulted the railway guide in the outer office and headed back to Brooklyn.

Emmie was out when I got home. We'd only been married six days and outside of a night in Scranton, we'd had no honeymoon. I had told her she could come along on my next trip, but there was no way I was bringing her to the next stop on the Grand Circuit. Of course, I didn't like leaving her alone in Brooklyn either. New York was completely new to her and there were dangers around every corner. While I hoped she could content herself with buying drapery and such on account, there was always a chance she'd come across a ladies-only pool-room, or some open-minded fellows shooting craps. But these were risks I had to take.

I was packing when she came in. She wasn't at all upset about being left behind, especially after I described Glens Falls as a muddy little lumber town with mosquitoes the size of sparrows.

"You'll have to leave me some money, Harry."

"I'm afraid Keegan barely gave me enough to travel on, Emmie," I lied. "The grocer and the butcher both know you now. Here's five dollars for whatever else you need."

I gave her a kiss good-bye and reminded her of her promise to avoid games of chance. She asked how she could gamble when I had barely left her enough to live on. During the three and a half hours between New York and Albany, I thought of about two dozen ways she could manage it. None of them pleasant.

Women and Economics

In Albany, I caught the Delaware and Hudson to Lake George and arrived in Glens Falls just before seven that evening. Ed was waiting at the station for me. He was a tall fellow, too tall, really. At a certain height, a man seems commanding. Add a few more inches and he just looks improbable. Ed was about an inch into improbable.

"I'm glad you came, Harry. There's something queer going on here, but I'm not sure where to go with it. Let's grab your things and I'll take you to the boarding house."

"Boarding house?"

"Yes, I'm afraid you'll be bunking with me. The hotels were already full because of the horse races, then two of them were destroyed in the fire. I was lucky to find a room at all."

We hired a carriage and I asked Ed what he had found so queer. Then he basically told me what Keegan had already. Right after he got in to town, on Monday afternoon, he was surveying the fire scene when a man walked up and told him about the betting parlor. So Ed went and spoke with the police chief. But before Ed had even finished telling him what the man had said, he told Ed there was no truth in it. Not that it was unlikely, but absolutely untrue. So, of course, Ed knew it must be true. Whenever some official denies vice is taking place, it's a safe bet he's in on the game.

We passed by the fire scene and shortly arrived at the Park Street Cottage. The exterior of the house was unassuming, but the inside was decidedly Victorian. There seemed to be drapery hanging everywhere.

"This is Harry Reese, Mrs. Butler," Ed said to the woman who greeted us.

"You're most welcome, Mr. Reese," she said, then quickly got down to terms. I would be charged three dollars a night for half a room and board. About the price of a nice room in one of the finest hotels in New York. Mrs. Butler was making the best of the situation and I couldn't fault her for it. She explained that her house was normally reserved for young women, but she was making a couple rooms available during the shortage "for the good of the community."

Mrs. Butler was about forty, reasonably good-looking, and unusually vivacious for the matron of a boarding house. After we put my things away, I was introduced to Mr. Holt, a middle-aged man and another temporary guest. Then Ed led me off to inspect the ruins while there was still some light. We went around the corner and part way down Glen Street, the main thoroughfare of Glens Falls.

"This was the Rugge building, where the fire started." Ed was pointing at a large cellar hole.

"Not much evidence left one way or the other," I said.

"No, we aren't going to find a bucket of gasoline here. The third floor, where the fire started, was used by the shirt maker, Heffron & Linehan. Their main building is a few blocks away. As I mentioned, the machinery here hadn't been used in several months."

"But it was insured."

"Oh, yes. For ten thousand dollars. The two floors

below were used by A.S. Rugge as a laundry for shirts and collars."

Next we looked over the ruins of the Glens Falls Gas & Electric Light Company's generating plant, just to the north. Then, above that, a hotel, the Central House. And around the corner of Park Street, the Park Hotel, and in back of that, a carriage shop.

"The hotels stand to gain the most, Harry. They were both old, wooden-frame buildings, but they're within a fire district now. That requires masonry construction. To modernize them the owners would have had to pay to have them torn down, then pay for the new construction. Now, most of the tearing down's been done for them, and they have the insurance money to put towards rebuilding."

Ed tried to bring up the betting parlor again, but I pointed out we'd need to hurry to be back at Mrs. Butler's in time for dinner.

Mr. Holt had traveled the world as an agent for a street car manufacturer and entertained the table with colorful stories of his adventures. The other boarders, three young women, were all dressed for an evening out. There was a very friendly blonde, named Phoebe, a somewhat reserved dark-haired beauty named Estelle, and a caustic-tongued redhead named Louisa.

I was told the young women worked in the nearby factories and said that I hoped the fire hadn't put any of them out of work.

"Oh, no. We've never been busier," the blonde one giggled.

"It has been a hardship, Mr. Reese," the landlady interjected. "But luckily, all my girls have found employment."

Then Louisa made a cryptic toast to the plungers of the Grand Circuit.

Ed had taken on the role of gentleman of the house and was constantly getting up and holding chairs for the women. He was particularly solicitous of Estelle and it was soon obvious Ed was smitten.

After dinner the girls left us. For work, we were told. But still dressed to the nines. Mrs. Butler offered us drinks in the parlor (just twenty cents each, I was discreetly informed). I suggested Ed and I go out for the evening and he told me of a poolroom just down the block. Ed went upstairs to fetch his hat and just then Estelle came running back into the house in tears. She and Mrs. Butler hurried into the kitchen to confer about something. Mr. Holt and I just looked at each other, and then he smiled.

"I must say, I had no idea accommodations in Glens Falls would be so... well, accommodating." He gave me a wink.

It was then I noticed the parlor's well-stocked bar and, tucked in a corner of the room, a faro bank—furnishings not normally found in a small-town boarding house.

Well, that clinched it. Ed had booked us a room in a brothel. And Ed being Ed, he was too guileless to have noticed. I wasn't sure how to remedy the situation, but I was certainly glad I had left Emmie back in Brooklyn. Ed came down and we bid Mr. Holt good evening. Just up the block, there was a deserted factory building, and as we passed Ed noticed something inside.

"That's him, Harry!" And with that, Ed charged to the entrance of the building. The street was dark, since the fire had knocked out the electric generating plant, but

I saw the fellow head out another door of the building just as Ed entered. I assumed this was the fellow who had told Ed about the betting parlor, so I was content to have him escape. Ed came out and confirmed it was the man in question and suggested we pursue him. But I convinced him there was no way we were going to catch a man with the streets dark, and him knowing the lay of the land. So we headed on to the poolroom.

Ed, of course, wanted to talk about his mysterious informer and the betting parlor. But I made him forget all about that by telling him the true nature of Mrs. Butler's enterprise. It took two rounds of beer for Ed to see the light, and a third before he conceded the possibility that the girls weren't off sewing shirts on the night shift. Most likely, I explained, they were making the rounds of the hotels, picking up what business they could.

Ed took this news with great equanimity. He wasn't the least bit constrained by middle-class puritanism. He explained, in detail, why he thought Estelle may well have made her choice of career for the soundest of reasons.

Three rounds were the limit for Ed so he led me over to the pool tables. He soon got into a game and proceeded to run the table. Ed was a bit of a pool sharp. I believe it was due to the fact he had such a logical mind—and always stopped at three beers. The game of many players improves with the first beer or two, maybe three. But the average fellow in a poolroom doesn't stop at three, especially if he's winning.

By now, the local boys were interested and they brought out the house sharps. Ed beat them all. Finally, a tall, gaunt-looking fellow came over from the bar. He looked more like a man in need of a good meal than a pool sharp, but one can never tell. Most of the other tables went quiet now. All eyes were on the combatants.

What followed was the sloppiest game of fifteen ball in all of history. Now, to those of us watching—all of us attentive readers of the *Police Gazette*—the explanation was clear. Each of the sharps was trying to deceive his opponent, provide him with false comfort and thereby run up the odds. The atrocious spectacle of the first game merely confirmed we were in the presence of masters. Ultimately, Ed was the victor, and when it was over, he gave me a wink. I took that as confirmation that he had things well in hand and put five dollars down on the next game.

It was in the pause between games that I realized this was a battle between equals. The skeletal local sharp drank nothing but lemonade. He was an Achilles without a heel. My faith wavered. The second game went to the skeleton.

Then he made a fatal error. He quickly downed three tall glasses of lemonade. During the third game he faltered. Minerva may have been watching over him, but his own attention was firmly on his bladder. In no time at all Ed had prevailed.

It was raining when we walked back to the cottage. As we crossed the street, we saw Mr. Holt leaving a buggy off at Griffing's stable, which was between the ruins of the Park Hotel and the abandoned factory. We caught up to him and startled him rather badly, having come up from behind. He explained that he and Mrs. Butler had gone out for a ride. When the three of us went in, Mrs. Butler was drying her hair with a towel. Then Estelle rushed up to Mr. Holt and gave him a kiss on the cheek.

Not at all professionally, but rather sort of daughterly.

Up in our room, I laid awake for quite a while, thinking of another dozen or so ways Emmie could manage to betray her pledge.

Hawk-eye Returns

When we got up the next morning, no one else had risen and so we went to the kitchen and made a simple breakfast. Ed was focused on the betting parlor again and insisted we pursue that. I told him I thought it was probably just the tall talk of a drunk. But it was no go. Ed was determined to get to the bottom of it. So I agreed to look into it with him. "All the best people" should have had plenty of time to cover their tracks by then.

"I think I know how to prove it, Harry."

"How, Ed?"

"What's the one thing anyone taking bets on horse races has to have? The one thing that requires a work order?" When I didn't answer with sufficient alacrity, he did for me. "A telegraph wire."

Well, he was right, of course. Everyone knew Western Union made a pretty penny running wires to poolrooms and gambling houses. And a company that size can't order a bottle of ink without a form and a duplicate.

So, we walked over to the little Western Union office on Glen Street. A young kid was at the desk and Ed asked him if there had been any work ordered over in the Rugge building recently. He said he thought there had, and that a crew had been over there on Saturday. Then he went in the back to look for a work order. But he didn't return, an older fellow did. And he said the kid was mistaken, the crew had been repairing a line across the river.

Now Ed was convinced there was something to it, and with good reason. If "all the best people" were going to enter into conspiracies, they had better bone up on the subject. There was nothing for it now but to tell Ed the truth. We went for a walk and I told him everything. He was pretty annoyed at being taken for a patsy, but then gave me a surprise.

"Harry, I'll be honest. There really wasn't much in this pointing to arson. I just wanted to stretch out the job some."

That was so unlike the efficient Ed of lore that I stopped dead for a second or two. Then it dawned on me why Ed wanted to linger: dear Estelle. Ed offered a deal: he'd forget about the betting parlor nonsense if I agreed to play along and keep the case open as long as possible. I was apprehensive about leaving Emmie alone in Brooklyn for much longer. On the other hand, I could use the twelve dollars a day, so I agreed.

"I have just the thing, too, Harry."

"Thing for what?"

"Well, we need a pretext. I was keeping this in reserve, in case the betting parlor story turned out to go nowhere." Then he stopped walking and smiled at me. "It seems a young boy saw a sort of projectile hit the building where the fire started."

"What sort of projectile?"

"You'll think I'm joking. A flaming arrow."

It would have sounded like a joke coming from anyone else. But Ed had never told a joke in his life. And I'd wager it was only on rare occasions that he even understood a joke. "Are there Indians nearby?"

"The police don't believe it either."

"Do you?"

"Well, I'm willing to keep an open mind," Ed said. "Why don't we go over and see George?"

Ed led me back to Park Street. Then, just after the empty factory, and just before Mrs. Butler's, we headed down a side street called Park Place. There was only one house on the block. Mrs. Phelps, George's mother, let us in and then called her son.

George was eager to repeat his story and the three of us went up to his bedroom. The house was on a sort of hill and the window beside George's bed had a clear view of the rear of all the destroyed buildings. He explained how he often was awake at night reading. That he was an avid reader was attested to by a long shelf of the classic works of Diamond Dick, Buffalo Bill, and the Old Sleuth. On the night in question, he had just gotten up to turn out the lamp when he saw what he was sure was a flaming arrow hit the Rugge building. He said he watched the fire for a while before it occurred to him to go pull an alarm. By then the bells were already sounding, so he just sat and watched. We thanked him and left him in the able hands of *Cad Metti, Female Detective Strategist*.

"What do you think, Harry?"

"I think young George reads too many dime novels. But I guess we have to have something to spend our time on."

Ed had something else he wanted to spend his time on. We went back to Mrs. Butler's, where in lieu of luncheon we shared the girls' breakfast. Then we all spent the afternoon exploring the rock islands of the river. This included a visit to the cave that featured prominently in *The Last of the Mohicans*—a book the denizens of Glens Falls took to be historical record. The girls spent much time teasing Holt, dubbing him their Hawk-eye. Frankly, I didn't see the resemblance.

Later at dinner, Holt was given the head of the table. I had assumed the attention he was receiving might be due to his lucrative trade, but the fraying sleeves and the shiny patches on the elbows of his jacket seemed to belie his prosperity. After dinner Ed and I wandered back to the poolroom and returned to the subject of the flaming arrow.

"Pardon me for asking, Ed, but why would an arsonist think of using a flaming arrow?"

"Well, maybe the person who wanted the building burned down merely hired the archer because he knew of his skill. This way, no one could be seen entering or leaving the building. And if it failed, the only evidence, the arrow itself, would surely have incinerated. The doors would still all be secured, and people would just dismiss it as a small trash fire."

"But if it succeeded, as it did, it could destroy half a dozen buildings. Who would take that kind of risk? What if someone had been killed?"

"I've been thinking about that. Most of the losses were to fairly prominent businesses in town. And they all suffered real losses. None of them will come out ahead. Except the owners of the two hotels."

"Didn't the hotels have guests?" I asked.

"Oh, they were both pretty full, because of the races. But you see, by setting the fire down the block, there was plenty of time for all the guests to be evacuated before the hotels caught fire."

"But how could they count on the fire going in that direction?"

"I haven't figured that out yet. Of course, it may be the arrow missed its intended target."

We were interrupted by a man who politely, but assertively, invited Ed to share a game. Ed obliged and was promptly trounced. Then trounced again. And again. It seemed clear that this fellow had been summoned to defend the honor of Glens Falls, and he did so ably.

When Ed had had enough, we went back to the house and played whist with Mrs. Butler and Mr. Holt, who both cheated unashamedly. Then I went up to bed and dreamt of Emmie playing fan-tan in a Pell Street opium den.

When I got up the next morning I was alone in the room. I found Ed in the kitchen making our breakfast and in an unusually good mood. I assumed he had finally won the attention of dear Estelle—how he won it was none of my concern.

"I had a thought as I was dressing, Ed. Remember how you mentioned that the arsonist may have missed?"

"Yes. It makes sense a shot going any distance might miss its mark. Unless, of course, we're dealing with an expert archer."

"Either an Apache or one of King Arthur's longbowmen?" I smiled. "Well, assuming your theory about the hotels was correct, the obvious target was that carriage shop beside the Park Hotel."

Ed pondered that for a few moments. "I see what you mean. The fire would be detected in time to warn the guests and empty the hotel, especially if the owner were watching for the fire. But since the shop was so close to the hotel, it wouldn't be in time to save the building itself."

"And maybe the owner of the carriage shop was in it as well. Was it insured?"

"Yes, but for just five hundred."

"Well, five hundred might be a lot for a carriage shop."

"You may be right, Harry. I guess we should check on the owners of the shop and the Park Hotel."

"And maybe look for an archer," I added.

"Then you do believe it?"

"For the lack of anything else. Frankly, I'd be willing to drag this out just for my day rate. My accounts are a little low, and I got married back in Buffalo."

"I'd heard, Harry. I'm sorry I forgot to congratulate you." Ed gave me his hand and patted my back and whatnot.

"By the way, Harry, there is something the girls here told me that I dismissed but might be important—if the shop was the target. On the night of the fire, they went out to watch and as they passed that stable down the street, they heard the horses inside. The fire was getting nearer, so they took it upon themselves to lead the horses out of the building."

"Very commendable. But why's that important?" I asked.

"Well, it seems the horses were in their stalls facing outward. Which made it much easier to lead them out. But who leaves horses in the stalls facing out? And that stable is just this side of the carriage shop."

"So someone wanted the horses to be saved?"

"Yes, someone who knew there'd be a fire," Ed pointed out.

We agreed that Ed would look into the owners of the buildings while I delved into the mysterious orientation of the horses.

A Day in Ten Bar-Rooms

The stable was open, but no one answered my call. There were a dozen stalls and half a dozen horses. All facing frontwards. I saw bales of straw being sent down from the loft and climbed up to surprise a man with a claw in his hand. I explained who I was and then repeated what the girls had told Ed.

"I wouldn't know anything about that. We close up by ten o'clock. But it'd be easy enough for someone to break in. Maybe some boys did it on a whim."

"Had it happened before?"

"Not that I recall, but you might ask Mr. Griffing."

He gave me Griffing's address and told me he was at home working on something. Then I gave him his laugh of the day.

"Would you know anyone proficient at archery? I mean really good at it."

"You mean bow and arrow?"

"Yes, that's the idea. More specifically, a flaming arrow."

He studied me for a few seconds. "Are you making fun, mister?"

"No, I'm very serious."

I left him snickering to himself and walked the ten blocks up to Griffing's. It looked like it might turn into a pleasant day and I decided the odds would improve if I showed more prudence in introducing the topic of archers and flaming arrows. Griffing was in the carriage house behind his home mending a harness. I asked him about the direction of the horses and he told me the girls must have been having some fun at my expense.

"So that type of thing never happened before?"

"Never happened ever."

I came to the conclusion I would get nowhere with this fellow, so I thanked him and headed back downtown. Along the way, I spotted Ed and we walked back together.

"I think we may be wrong about the Park Hotel, Harry," Ed began. "It's owned by a couple fellows who are both well-off and have nothing to do with running the place. One doesn't even live near here anymore."

"What about the owner of the carriage shop?"

"That's who I was just seeing. The fellow seemed pretty upset about losing his tools and his clients' goods. It sounded like the insurance wasn't going to come close to covering his losses. What about the stable?"

"I spoke with the owner and his hand, and they both claim to know nothing about the arrangement of the horses that night."

"Any luck finding an archer?" he asked.

"I have to think about how to go about that. It's a little hard to ask someone you just met whether he knows anyone who can shoot a flaming arrow."

"Yeah, I tried it myself."

By now we were down along Glen Street, where most of the shops were situated. It was outside B.B. Fowler's dry goods store that I had my little surprise. There was Emmie, in the company of two other young women.

"Oh, hello, Harry." Emmie spoke as if the occasion was little deserving of note. She introduced me to her companions. And I introduced them to Ed. Then I drew her aside.

"I thought you agreed to stay put in Brooklyn, Emmie."

"That was my intention, Harry. But your Mr. Keegan contacted me and suggested I accompany him here. He thought a young couple shouldn't be separated so soon after the wedding."

"And then you simply forgot to look me up when you arrived in town?"

"Well, we didn't get in until last evening, and it would have been rude to our hosts to rush off."

"Your hosts?"

"We're staying at the Spiers'. Mr. Spier is an old friend of Mr. Keegan," she explained. "But I am glad we ran into each other."

"Are you? Do you have any plans for the afternoon?" I knew damn well she did.

"Well, the Spiers have asked us to accompany them to the races. Mr. Spier raises horses."

"Does he? You do remember our agreement, don't you?"

"Of course, Harry. Besides, I have no money of my own." She smiled. "Well, I must be off now. Where are you staying?"

"It might be better if I find you. I'll visit the Spiers' this evening."

She gave me the address and we parted.

"Harry, you sure seemed surprised your wife was here."

"Yes, I didn't realize she could be this cunning."

"She really came with Keegan?"

"Oh, I'm sure of that."

"I am sorry, Harry. She's a very attractive girl." Ed got thoughtful for a while. "It's hard to imagine her with Keegan. The man must weigh in at three hundred pounds."

"Damn, Ed. She's not carrying on with him. They just have the same disease."

"Same disease?"

"An addiction to the turf. Keegan just wanted someone along to share the fun."

"Oh. Yes, I knew he liked playing the horses."

"But he can afford to. We barely have enough set aside for next month's rent. Let's go get a drink."

Ed insisted we partake of the second breakfast at Mrs. Butler's before visiting any saloons. The young ladies were just sitting down and everyone was in high spirits. I gathered it had been a lucrative evening, but was careful not to show the poor taste of alluding to it. It took some doing to draw Ed away from the house. Intentionally or not, young Estelle had her claws in deep. I hoped she wasn't overly mercenary, else Ed was in big trouble.

"Where to now, Harry?" he asked as we left.

"I have a plan, Ed. Suppose we act like a couple of big-mouth out-of-towners. I tell people how you're the finest archer in the whole country, and there isn't a man alive who can shoot as well as you."

"Well, I certainly wouldn't say that, Harry."

"It's a bar-room boast, Ed. But if we say it often enough, in every saloon in town, sooner or later the locals are going to find someone to put up against you."

"And that fellow will be our man. That's a great idea, Harry."

It was a completely absurd idea, of course. But I had just managed to convince Ed Ketchum to go on a bender with me. Something no man had done before. I was angry enough at Emmie to go on my own bender, but a bender is always more interesting with company.

We began at Fitzgerald's, just up Glen Street. And

then went next door, to Dolan's. Then McAuliff's, and on the next block McSweeney's, Murphy's, and Mellen's. Our outing had quickly developed a Gaelic theme.

I had done the boasting, and most of the drinking, but Ed had held up his end. His critical interest in the enterprise seemed to increase with each drink, and he soon determined that we needed the proper accoutrements. I found a bow in a shop across the street, but Ed was unimpressed.

"That's a toy, Harry. I'm not going to challenge a man with a toy. He'd laugh at me."

They'd been laughing at us for most of the afternoon, but apparently it had escaped Ed's notice. What troubled me was that by encouraging Ed to go beyond his three-beer limit, I had changed his very nature. He was now running the show and there was no arguing the point. We were directed to a store on Warren Street and there found a bow that met with his approval, and a set of arrows he pronounced only tolerable.

Ed strutted down the sidewalk, carrying his bow with comical authority. It was undeniable now: I had created a Frankenstein.

He led me into the bar-room of the Globe Hotel. We'd lost some momentum and it took a few drinks before I could work up the proper enthusiasm. But I offered my best performance yet, and we finally got a response. One of the bartenders promised us a dollar if Ed would shoot apples off my head out in front of the hotel. He even offered to provide the apples. I declined and hustled Ed out before he lost control. Monster men didn't take well to being taunted.

We next went around the corner to Mr. Sullivan's establishment on Glen Street, just across from the scene of the fire. By now, the game was a little long in the tooth, and my effort was lacking in spirit—and clarity. Luckily, the patrons of Sullivan's were well practiced at interpreting the slurred speech of their fellows. We soon learned there had been a man living in Glens Falls who, years before, had performed in one of the Wild West shows. Some fellow insisted he'd witnessed an exhibition of this archer's prowess with a bow. No mention was made of flaming arrows, but when I asked why he was spoken of only in the past tense, we were given another curious detail. This man had been found dead the previous morning, floating in what they called the feeder canal.

His name was McGee and the bar-room seemed unanimous in the opinion he was difficult to get along with, though they used a colorful colloquial phrase instead. I never expected my excuse for a bender to hit pay dirt and I just stood there kind of stupefied. Ed took over, and inquired about McGee's home. We were told McGee had worked for William Spier at a horse farm Spier owned at the far end of town, and had boarded there as well. Then someone said he had seen him Saturday night in Moynihan's saloon, on South Street. That was the night of the fire.

The shock of the news and the walk up to Moynihan's sobered us up a little. Ed more than me. He asked the fellow behind the bar if he remembered seeing McGee on Saturday.

"Yeah, he was in here. Until we had to kick him out, around ten."

"Why'd you kick him out?"

"The same as always. He comes in, buys a few beers, cadges a few more, starts getting ornery, we boot him."

"Do you think he could have made it home?"

"He wasn't going home. Probably to one of the rougher places, like Foley's down on Canal."

"Did he speak with anyone while he was here?"

"Well, he kind of makes the rounds. Ask Mr. Breen, there," he nodded toward a well-dressed gent at the end of the bar. "McGee was over with him and Mr. Chambers for a while."

Scott Breen was a lawyer, and remembered seeing McGee.

"McGee made an art form of sponging a beer," Breen told us. "He'd listen intently to what you were saying, laugh if you told a joke, show sympathy when prompted, and take umbrage on your behalf at the least provocation. I was here speaking with Dwight Chambers, about nothing in particular. We bought McGee a beer or two, just to get him to move on. He did, and not long after got into an argument with some fellow, and then was shown the door. He could be downright obsequious one moment, insanely quarrelsome the next."

"You don't remember who he got into an argument with?" Ed asked.

"No, but there aren't many people in town who hadn't gotten into an argument with McGee at one time or another."

He gave us the address of Chambers, who ran a real estate office, and we thanked him. Then Ed asked the bartender who McGee argued with.

"Me! He said I served him flat beer, so I should give him another. A beer he hadn't even paid for."

"Had you seen him since then?"

"No, the last time he was in here was Saturday."

Then a fellow standing at the bar spoke up. "I saw you with him after that, mister."

"Me?" Ed asked.

"Yes, it must have been Monday. Right by where Rugge's had been."

"The fellow with long blond hair?"

"Yeah, that was McGee."

We left and Ed explained the man identified as McGee was the one who told him of the betting parlor. He was hot on the scent now and led me down to Canal Street at double pace. Foley's was difficult to find because there was no sign and few windows. This was the type of place where all the regulars stare at you when you enter. And not because they're anxious for your company. We had a couple rounds to brace us up, and then made a few tentative inquiries. But no one would even admit having heard of McGee.

By now it was obvious we were in no condition to investigate anything. So we headed back to Mrs. Butler's and slept until just before dinner was served.

The Tyranny of Tears

The nap brought Ed back to his normal self and I was much relieved. Frankenstein Ed had grown rather tiresome. I, on the other hand, awoke in that sorrowful state where one is suffering the after-effects and, at the same, still half drunk. And not the good half.

At dinner Mr. Holt was again being fawned over by the females. Ed tried some to compete, but it wasn't until he began telling about our adventures of that afternoon that he got much notice. At first, the story was met with some polite chuckles, though there were incipient signs of unease. Then when Ed got to the part where the archer was revealed to have been McGee, the girls all looked at each other nervously and Mrs. Butler asked Ed to help her carry something into the kitchen. Estelle quickly followed and the other two started clearing the table.

Holt made some vague comment about being thirsty and led me into the parlor. He made himself a drink and asked what I would have. When I begged off, he properly diagnosed my affliction and recommended a treatment. He sent to the kitchen for some eggs and concocted a lively beverage that did indeed give me hope. I asked for another, and he complied. Then, merely as an attempt to open a friendly conversation, he brought up the horse races.

"I heard they got a late start today, but they should be over now."

I'd forgotten all about the damn horses, and Emmie. Now it all came back like a bullet to the head. I bolted out of the room, packed my bag, paid my bill, and trooped off to retrieve my wife.

The Spiers had a big house not too long a ways up Glen Street. I told the girl who answered the door to fetch Emmie immediately. Apparently my state had given her some apprehension and she instead fetched the master of the house. Mr. Spier, on learning who I was, led me into a small parlor and soon Emmie appeared. She was in tears.

I showed no mercy. I told her to pack her bags at once and be down promptly. She managed only a meek "All right, Harry" in reply. Then I went out and found a carriage to hire. By the time I returned she was ready. The driver loaded her bags and I gave instructions to take us to the station.

"The station? What for?" he asked.

"To catch a train, of course."

"You won't be catching any train before morning."

This was a key piece of information that I had been lacking when I formulated my strategy. But I gave no indication I was put out by the news. I told him to take us to the Park Street Cottage. Only I said it as if it were the Astor Hotel.

"The Park Street Cottage? You mean Mrs. Butler's place?"

"Yes. Take us there at once."

He did. But he wouldn't cease his looking over his shoulder and chuckling to himself. So I gave him nothing as a tip. Perhaps the story of taking a girl from the grand Spier house to Mrs. Butler's was tip enough.

When we arrived I made arrangements with Ed and Mrs. Butler to allow us use of the room. Then I brought Emmie upstairs to break the news about our accommodations. We hadn't spoken a word since leaving the Spiers' and tears still periodically streamed down her face. I assumed she was upset that I had embarrassed her in front of her hosts, but that wasn't it.

"Emmie, I have something to tell you."

"I have something to tell, too. Harry, I made a big mistake."

"Well, I'm glad you're willing to admit it."

"Oh, it's worse than you know, Harry. I lost at the races today."

"How much did you lose?"

"A hundred and twenty dollars."

"A hundred and twenty dollars!"

"Yes, I borrowed it from the three hundred you were due for finding Robert Mason."

The trouble was there wasn't three hundred coming. I had also borrowed against it, some of which was known to Emmie, but some wasn't. Then the sobbing came in earnest.

I tried to be hard, but I'd never seen that kind of bawling. Soon I was comforting her. The absurdity of it was readily apparent. Here I was, consoling her because she had made a worse mess of things than I had suspected. But as soon as I tried to make that point, Niagara was set off all over again.

The scene brought to mind an English comedy I had seen the year before. The plot involved a woman who manipulates her husband in all sorts of ways by breaking into tears at the right moment. At the time, the idea struck me as beyond ridiculous. But here I was, soothing Emmie in much the same way. It wasn't enough to change my opinion of the play. *The Tyranny of Tears* was so insipid it would be charitable to call it drivel. But I did develop a certain sympathy for the woman's husband.

I decided it was time to broach the subject of our lodging. You might be thinking this would only be adding fuel to the fire. But that would be because you were unfamiliar with Emmie. The news we were staying in a brothel prompted a near-total recovery. Though I used the phrase "chippie boarding house" out of modesty, she got the message. There was a short pang of worry that I may have availed myself of the wares, but as soon as I assured her otherwise, out came her little notebook. We all have a weakness for the sordid. But for Emmie it was ambrosia and nectar combined. She wanted every detail and was disappointed that most of the action seemed to be happening elsewhere while we were guests.

Emmie insisted on going downstairs but I warned her not to confront Mrs. Butler about the matter. She agreed and restricted herself to cataloguing the furnishings. Then she found the faro bank. She asked how it was used and Ed explained the game. He mentioned that the dealing box was probably rigged and they examined it carefully. Then they shared a discussion on the probabilities of outcomes and to what degree the rigged box adjusted the odds in the house's favor. Emmie's aptitude for the subject was as surprising as it was troubling.

We went back to our room and in a little while Emmie became contrite all over again. At the first sign of a tear I gave her another dose of the only remedy necessary. I told her about the flaming arrow and our adventure of the afternoon. This worked for a time, but then the "I'm so sorry" started up again. I gave her the final cure-all. I told her all about the betting parlor and McGee's body being found in the canal. Emmie has a weakness for bodies found in canals. There were no more tears on that trip.

A Mad Betrothal

We were late rising the next morning and found Ed in the kitchen eating a large breakfast prepared by Estelle, who, we were informed, had reverted to her given name of Annie. Certain machinations had occurred during the night and it appeared Annie would be accompanying Ed back to West Orange.

"Harry, do you think we can arrange to be married today?" Ed inquired.

"Ask Emmie," I suggested. "She's an old hand at arranging express marriages."

"Oh, yes. I have several under my belt," she smiled. Then she was thoughtful for a moment. "I would think you might be able to use the information you have about the betting parlor to gain some cooperation in the matter."

"You mean, blackmail the town clerk?" Ed asked.

"Oh, certainly not blackmail," Emmie corrected. "A discreet hint that the only thing keeping you in town is the want of a marriage certificate should provide the proper incentive. And perhaps net Annie something for her trousseau from the local merchants."

After breakfast Emmie and Ed went off to make arrangements, while Annie packed and I went out for a walk. There was much activity at the abandoned factory. A man in a suit was supervising things and I walked up and asked what was happening. It seems the Rugge laundry had taken the building as a new home, but it required a great deal of refurbishing.

"A lucky break for the owner of the building," I said.

"Yes, it's sat empty since '93."

"Who owns it?"

"Mr. Chambers owned it until yesterday."

That news seemed to necessitate a visit to Chambers's office, where I found him reading the morning paper. He remembered seeing McGee the night of the fire.

"What did you talk about?"

"Well, I was speaking with Scott Breen, the lawyer. McGee was just hanging about."

"Did the subject of your building on Park Street come up by any chance?"

"It may have."

"Perhaps in a conversation that also touched on fires?"

"Yes, all right. I made some offhand remark that my only misstep in business had been buying that damn factory building. And that if it would just catch fire, I might get some of my money out of it. But I never said it as a serious proposition. We were all laughing about it. Hell, it was only insured for $1,500. And if I were going to torch it, I certainly wouldn't have involved McGee.

"Then the next morning I heard about the fire and I must admit it crossed my mind that that fool McGee might have taken me seriously. But when I saw that the fire had started down at the Rugge building, I assumed it was just a coincidence."

"But you do come out ahead?"

"Well, some. But you can't really think I hatched a plan whereby I'd hire an arsonist to burn down a block of buildings just to increase the odds of selling that wreck?"

I had to admit, that seemed rather unlikely.

I went back to Mrs. Butler's, where Emmie informed me the wedding was on for half past one. Ed and Annie had gone off to do some shopping. The plan was to try to catch the 2:10 directly after the ceremony. Emmie and I went up to get our things packed and I told her about my conversation with Chambers.

"So," I concluded, "McGee, thinking Chambers wanted him to torch the old factory, went and got the horses in the stable arranged for a quick exit, then performed his flaming arrow act, missing his target by an incredible 500 yards."

"I suppose that explains it, Harry. But are you really going to write that up?"

"There's no point. And who'd believe it anyway?"

"Do you think Chambers killed McGee?" Emmie asked.

"Why would he bother? No, the fact that McGee was killed two days after starting the fire was just a coincidence."

"Well, I guess it doesn't matter much who killed him," she said.

That kind of took my breath away. I'd only known Emmie for a fortnight, and there was much about her I had yet to discover. But the one thing I was certain of was that her interest in unsolved murders bordered on the obsessive.

"Is your lack of interest in poor McGee due to his connection to your erstwhile host, Mr. Spier?"

"What connection did he have to Mr. Spier?"

"Well, he worked at Spier's horse farm. And he was killed not long after telling Ed about the betting parlor."

"What does that have to do with Mr. Spier?"

"Spier was almost certainly in on it. Keegan had been contacted by an old friend to help in covering it up. One of 'the best people.' Now Keegan is at his house as a guest. Spier must have called him after Ed came asking questions. But as the questions kept coming, 'all the best people' were becoming increasingly nervous. And then... McGee's body is found floating in a canal." I laid special emphasis on those last four words. But she wouldn't bite.

"It must have been a coincidence," she said.

"This case has already had its requisite coincidence. Another would create a coincidence of coincidences. We can't expect anyone to swallow that."

"Well, I can say without qualification that Mr. Spier wasn't involved in the murder of McGee. That will have to suffice for now."

Ed had just come up to fetch us. We got to the village hall by half past one and the procedure was completed before two. Then we all hurried to the station in time for the train.

Annie went through a sort of transformation during the trip. By Albany, her speech pattern seemed a little different, and any reference to Mrs. Butler, or even Glens Falls, was quickly batted down. Later, when we all went to the dining car, she and Ed contrived to sit well away from us.

That was just as well, because I would have been expected to buy the wedding party dinner and Emmie and I between us barely had enough for a light meal and car fare back to Brooklyn. It also gave me an opportunity to needle Emmie into revealing what she knew. It didn't take long.

"It's really kind of funny, Harry."

"How so?"

"Well, you were the only one actively trying to find out who killed McGee, and by the end, you were the only one in the dark." She paused for dramatic effect, then added, "Mr. Holt killed McGee."

"Mr. Holt?"

"Yes, but only because he had to. You see, a few years ago, Annie fell in love with McGee, and agreed to elope with him. They were both living in a place called Sandy Hill then. Annie soon learned of his rather mercurial nature and called it off. But McGee refused to leave her alone. Then her father died and she felt defenseless. She ran away and wound up at Mrs. Butler's. McGee found out where she was a year or so ago and followed her. He hovered about Mrs. Butler's and generally terrorized the poor girl. He came by Tuesday night, in his usual inebriated state, and Mr. Holt told him to leave and stay away. When he wouldn't, Mr. Holt grabbed a poker from the fireplace. Well...," she paused. "At Mrs. Butler's suggestion, Mr. Holt hired a buggy and they took McGee to the canal and dumped him there."

"I suppose that's why all the ladies treated Mr. Holt like he was their white knight," I commented. "Who told you the story?"

"Ed, when we went off this morning. He wanted me to make sure you would drop the matter."

I was glad Emmie seemed back to normal. But I couldn't help thinking that the loss of her insatiable hunger for homicides might have made for a more serene home life.

Madame Butterfly

When we returned to the coach, Annie's progression into middle-class respectability sped onward. By Pough-keepsie she was a prude, and by Scarborough a scold. By the time the train pulled into Grand Central, it was clear she would rather not be seen with the type of people who would spend a night in the Park Street Cottage. The metamorphosis was complete.

The hard lesson of Glens Falls—that Emmie could lose money a lot faster than I could earn it—weighed on us both. Though Emmie seemed to bear the weight a little too easily.

One morning, she announced she'd be bringing in some money soon, so I shouldn't worry so much. But she was a little vague on the source of her anticipated earnings, and frankly, that worried me a great deal more than any lack of money.

It will come as no surprise that Ed and Annie settled down to a happy home life. With time, Annie even felt secure enough to shed some of her out-sized propriety. When she resigns her membership in the W.C.T.U., perhaps we'll invite them to dinner.